PRAISE FOR

THE UNVEILING OF POLLY FORREST

"Full of unexpected twists, *The Unveiling of Polly Forest* is a mystery that keeps the reader guessing. Whitney brings history to life with authentic details of Depression era farm life, and characters who show their complicated humanity. A rich and satisfying read."
–Rae Meadows, author of *Motherland* and *I Will Send Rain*

"Charlotte Whitney delivers another exceptional historical fiction novel set in the farm country of Middle America during the Great Depression. Thoroughly researched and brilliantly written, *The Unveiling of Polly Forrest* is a riveting mystery that will keep you guessing with each chapter until the end."
–Todd Holmes, PhD, Historian, Oral History Center, The Bancroft Library, University of California, Berkeley

"As danger mounts, the veils of deception, deprivation, jealousy, and impulsivity finally lift, and Polly recognizes the power of family, generosity, community, genuine love, and an ethical way of life. Though set in the isolation of two small farms, this story encompasses the dilemmas, forgiveness, life lessons and resilience of a much larger world. An engaging read with lasting impact."
–Barbara Stark-Nemon, author of *Hard Cider* and *Even in Darkness*

"Charlotte Whitney's new novel, *The Unveiling of Polly Forrest* is an atmospheric mystery set in the rural Midwest during the Great Depression. Whitney does a masterful job immersing the reader inside the lives of family members dealing with a tragic

death. Even better, she provides a shocking twist to the murder of Polly's abusive husband, an ending no one will see coming."
  —Nicole Bokat, author of *What Matters Most* and *The Happiness Thief*

"The Unveiling of Polly Forrest is full of twists and turns. It kept me guessing from the first to the last!"
  —Addison Armstrong, author of *The Light of Luna Park* and *The War Librarian*

"As in her absorbing previous novel, *Threads*, Charlotte Whitney brilliantly evokes life on a small farm in Michigan during the Depression. When a death occurs, suspicions brew: Was it a convenient accident or brutal murder? I was swept away by this compulsively readable, suspensefully plotted page-turner."
  —Pat Roessle Materka, author of *Twenty for Breakfast*

"A vivid portrayal of the myriad challenges and dangers of life on a Michigan farm during the Depression for a family with a variety of secrets."
  —Ames Sheldon, author of *Eleanor's Wars*

"A well-constructed novel built upon layers of secrets that keep the reader guessing."
  —Jerry Maples, author of *The Divine Discovery*

"Charlotte Whitney's third novel has something for everyone. Suspense, historical content, strong relatable characters and a well-told story that keeps you guessing."
  —Connie Wesala, author of *The House on 4th Street, We'll Find a Way,* and *A Far Away Star*

"A highly engaging mystery set in Depression era America featuring twists you won't see coming."

–Risha Henrique, journalist and author

"This vividly-crafted, pastoral coming-of-age drew me in from the turn of the first page. I remained spellbound watching young Polly spiral into a dark and tangled web of lies as she courageously battles for the truth while her self-worth and freedom hang in the balance."

–Suzanne Simonetti, author of The Sound of Wings

Also by Charlotte Whitney

Fiction

Threads: A Depression Era Tale

I Dream in White

Nonfiction

How to Win at Upwords

Win Win Negotiations for Couples

The Unveiling of Polly Forrest

A Mystery

By Charlotte Whitney

Lake William Press

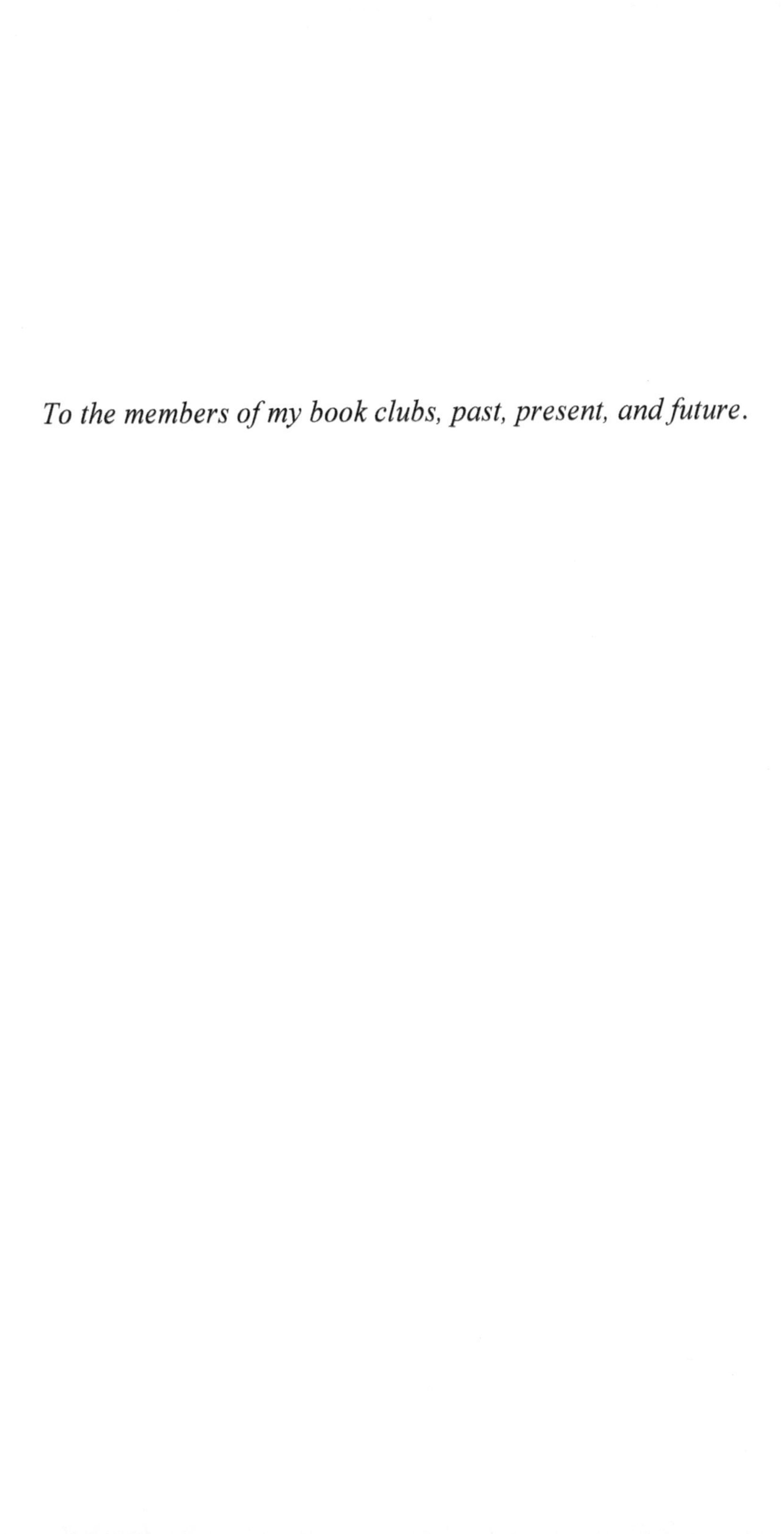

To the members of my book clubs, past, present, and future.

Part 1

Marshall Evening Chronicle

Marshall, Michigan
Saturday, February 10, 1934

Local Man Killed in Farm Accident

Mr. Samuel R. Forrest, age 41, of Cornfield Road, Marshall Township, was killed in an unfortunate farm accident on Thursday, February 8. He was born on January 16, 1893 to Olive and James Forrest of Rutland, Vermont. He is survived by his wife Polly Wolcott Forrest; a brother Mitchell Forrest, who resides in Wyoming; and a sister-in-law Sarah Wolcott Johnson; her husband Reverend J. Wesley Johnson; and their three children. He was predeceased by his parents and his first wife, Johanna Polk Forrest.

Services for Mr. Forrest will be held at the Convis Union Methodist Church on Monday, February 12 at 11:30 a.m. His brother-in-law, Reverend J. Wesley Johnson will be officiating, and the deceased will be interred in the church cemetery. There will be a reception following at the Forrest farm.

Circumstances of the accident are under investigation.

Samuel Forrest Farm

Marshall Township, Calhoun County, Michigan
Wednesday, February 7, 1934

Dear Mother,
Can you please come visit? Samuel won't let me travel to Connecticut to see you and I'm feeling so unsettled. This winter has been so frigid; I long for spring. Come in May and avoid all the snow and ice that's been relentless since November. Last week's blizzard was horrendous. We had ten-foot drifts in front of the toolshed and the snow was higher than my knees in the rest of the yard. Wesley canceled church since no one, and I mean no one, could get out.

Sam wants me to stay at home every day in case the cattle break out of the barnyard fence. So far they never have gotten out, but I'm worried if that happened, I'd have trouble herding them back to the barn. Also, there's Black Devil, the bull. He goes into rages and runs across the barnyard as if he's on the attack. Samuel, of course, worries about thieves. If we lost our cattle, we'd lose the farm and that would mean the end of us. We would have to join all those poor homeless people, leaving for Detroit to live in tent cities and stand all day in bread lines. I know Samuel is right. Yes, he is.

I never anticipated how cold and lonely it would be on the farm. Every day Sam's gone for hours, even on the coldest, bleakest days. I have no idea what he does. All the farm implements need to be in working order for the summer, so I guess he's repairing them. Our old farmhouse is so frigid; I think if Sam were inside more, he'd be inclined to fix the cracks in the walls.

Tomorrow morning, after Sam's eaten breakfast, while he's working in the barn, I'm going to sneak this letter up to Sarah so she can put it in the envelope with hers, a three-cent stamp being so dear.

Please think about coming in May. You could stay in a cozy, little room that's at the top of the stairs.

Your devoted daughter,
Polly

Sarah Wolcott Johnson

Thursday, February 8, 1934

Polly never had any common sense. More often than not she acted like a ten-year-old rather than a married woman. This morning while I was melting up lard to make soap, I looked out the kitchen window, and there was Polly running across our driveway carrying a couple of pieces of paper. No hat, gloves, scarf or overshoes, only her brown coat flung over her shoulders, not even buttoned up. Her head was down and she seemed to be looking westward, back toward their farm. She almost fell a couple of times, the driveway being so icy after the recent blizzard, followed by this morning's rain. I opened the door into our back room and led her into the parlor. Polly's eyes darted from one side of the room to the other.

"It's okay," I assured her. "Dorothy's napping, Junior and Zeke are at school, and Wesley's gone to the church for a meeting with the board. Collections are so low they need to decide whether to repair the roof. I say you can't have the roof leaking during Sunday service, but Wesley won't spend any money that's not there."

Polly's face softened. "I can't stay. Sam needs me at home, but I wanted to see if you'll put my letter to Mother in with yours again this week." She handed me the letter. Despite what she said about not staying, Polly removed her coat, flung it on the faded plaid ottoman, and sat down at one end of our old maroon davenport. I took the other end, turned, and faced her.

Polly was wearing a light-blue print dress she'd made of flour-sack that featured a flattering open neckline and a skirt that dropped down to the top of her ankles. At age twenty, she was as pretty as any screen star. Her blond hair curled around her face, highlighting her blue eyes and straight white teeth. To my envy she possessed a slender physique that only childless women own. Always Pretty Polly. Pretty Polly since she was born. I believed Petty Polly was more apt, given that she was self-absorbed, always focusing on her appearance, and rarely, if ever, was concerned about the needs of others.

Suddenly, I remembered the melting lard. "Oops, I'm making soap. I need to pull the pot off the burner." I ran to the kitchen and yanked the pot off the cookstove onto a metal trivet next to several round soap molds I'd retrieved from the attic.

"I'll give you some soap in payment for the butter I borrowed this morning," I yelled to her, immediately fearing my voice would awaken Dorothy. Luckily, I heard no noise from upstairs. I caught sight of my cup of tea sitting on the table and brought it back to Polly. She took it greedily, not aware that it had been my cup and that I was now empty-handed. Nor did she express one word of gratitude. Always a spoiled child, Polly. The sacrifices that I've made for that girl. Still, Polly's eyes were cast downward, as if she were about to cry.

"You look blue," I remarked. "Anything wrong?"

"I need to get out of the house. I can't stand my life. I never even tell Sam that I love him."

This was so out of character for my usually high-spirited, energetic little sister.

"I'm sure Sam knows how much you love him. He looks at you so fondly in church."

"Until he starts wincing," she replied. "Like being with me is painful."

I knew what she was talking about. I had witnessed those facial expressions many times. It was almost like a tic, or an involuntary flash of pain. But then he always managed to smile, as if it never happened.

"I'm sure Sam wants to be with you. He's probably reflecting on these painful days that we're all enduring. These are the hardest times I've ever experienced in my thirty-one years." I paused and Polly nodded. "You also need to remember that Sam suffered through the agonizing death of his first wife long before you ever met him. Losing your spouse can be one of the greatest challenges God can give a person."

I wasn't even sure Polly was listening, but she seemed to be attempting to pull herself together, wiping her eyes with her hand. I pulled out a handkerchief from my apron pocket and gave it to her. She never thought ahead to put on an apron, let alone carry a handkerchief. Polly was young, naïve, and used to having her own way. Adjusting to farm life would have been difficult for her during the best of times, to say nothing of a country-wide Depression.

"Polly, it's okay to admit you made a mistake," I said. "You were forced into a decision way too early. If Mother hadn't needed to leave for Connecticut, you could have had a long courtship to figure out if Sam was right for you."

I thought for a moment about my next statement, but decided to say it anyway. "Sam made no friends at church and that should have been a sign. We should have brought that to your attention."

Polly bristled. "Oh, you were vocal enough. I knew you were dead set against our marriage. So was Mother, but not because of anything to do with Sam. She needed an extra set of hands for cooking and cleaning Grandma Blessing's house. She wanted me to go to Connecticut as slave labor."

I shook my head. "No, we were concerned your happiness might turn into misery . . ." I decided not to continue.

Polly's back became rigid and she put on her angry face: lips pursed, furrowed brows, eyes staring nowhere. I'd experienced that face for many years.

"Sarah, you can see that I'm upset, and instead of comforting me, you lay into me about getting married too soon. Can't you ever be a kind, forgiving sister? You're no different than you were at fifteen, giving orders, belittling me, and always having to have the last word. Blaming me for Father's and John's deaths. I'm surprised you never blamed me for Jack's death, too."

Making absurd claims was so typical of Polly; I wished Mother were here to set her straight. Fortunately, at that moment Wesley walked in the door.

"We're going to fix the church roof," he sang out with a booming voice, unaware that he was walking into a sisterly snit. "Clarence Burland is donating the wood and shingles. He has some extras from three years ago when he put a new roof on his barn."

"What color are the replacement shingles?" Polly asked, flashing Wesley a large smile. I was glad she was willing to put aside our conflict and think about the church for a moment. Or was she indeed thinking about the church? She might be focused on Wesley. That would be more in keeping with my little sister's temperament, always flirting, even with her sister's husband, and a pastor, to boot.

Wes laughed. "I didn't even ask for a description of the shingles; I was so happy to get a donation. Most people won't even notice, anyway. You will, Polly, because you notice artistic things like design, color, and texture. That's why you're a hat-making genius."

Polly smiled brightly. Wesley could always puff her up when she felt low. She prided herself on her hats, and I agreed with Wes that she put together some beautiful creations; she had given me several. Polly loved everything that was in style, and the fashion statement of the moment was veils. Every hat she made featured at least a soft veil over the forehead, if not a long draping veil, covering the face.

"How about a cup of tea?" I asked Wes. He nodded and I rose out of my seat to go back to the kitchen, but my attention was drawn to piercing screams, almost inhuman. Twice, then once again. We all ran to the west window looking down the knoll onto Sam and Polly's farm.

"Sounds like it's at your place," Wes said to Polly. Two more screams ensued. Then silence.

"It sounds like Sam," Polly gasped, alarmed. "I need to go."

She and Wes ran to the back door and took off running down the ice-coated hill.

Reverend Wesley Johnson

Thursday, February 8, 1934

In responding to the ungodly screams, I outran Polly by about fifty yards down the hill toward their barnyard. When I saw the bloody crumpled mess that was my brother-in-law, I immediately turned and ran back to Polly, instructing her to go back to our house and call Dr. Grayson. Polly, however, continued running toward the barnyard until she could view the scene. She stared at the bloody, eviscerated body, so far gone that I didn't even try his pulse.

Polly looked and looked, shaking her head, perhaps not believing what she saw.

I grabbed my sister-in-law. "You must go call the doctor immediately."

Immobile, Polly pulled back and again looked down at the blood-covered, lifeless body. At the top of the hill I could see Sarah coming down toward us. I waited until she could hear me shout.

"It's Sam; he's injured—badly. Take Polly and call the doctor." They both headed up to our house, but in the corner of my eye I saw Polly bending over, retching into the snow. Polly started running after Sarah, then she bent over once again, heaving some more. Sarah was entering our house, but Polly started running back toward me.

"No, no!" I yelled at her. "Go in the house and wait with Sarah until Dr. Grayson arrives." I saw her stoop down, lift something up from the snow, and run up to the house. I watched until she entered the back door, and I could see through the window that she had moved into the kitchen with Sarah, who was on the telephone.

Beginning to get my wits about me, I decided I should find out what had happened. I leapt up on the cement horse tank and then jumped down into the barnyard, landing a few feet from Sam's remains. I had known immediately after looking at his ravaged body, that there was no hope. His insides had been ripped apart, blood and intestines lay open, his clothes shredded. His face was unrecognizable. Only his legs and feet were intact. My instincts told me that the perpetrator was Black Devil, but the bull was nowhere in sight.

Cautiously, I walked along the periphery of the barnyard, keeping an eye on the fence posts where, if necessary, I could make a hasty escape. There wasn't enough purchase on the wire fence to climb over anywhere; I would need to climb over at a metal post, and they were about four yards apart. I moved cautiously along the fence toward the barn until I got to the cement ramp that led into the building. Stopping, I looked in every direction, and then slid into the barn leaning against the wall. No longer protected by the possibility of a quick exit, I was vulnerable to any creature with horns. As I slid along the wall, I saw Sam's six dairy cows on the other side of the barn. On such a cold day, they were gathered together for warmth and paid little attention to me as I moved away, inching toward the bull's pen.

When I was about two yards from it, I pulled myself away from the wall and stepped toward the enclosure. Looking in I could see the bull inside, walking to his feed-trough. His horns were red, and his head was dripping with blood. I quickly closed and secured the gate to his pen. Then as a double precaution I slid the door across the gate, locking it with a large hook and eye latch. It was a door that Sam normally left open, using only the gate to pen the bull.

No longer worried that I would meet Sam's fate, I was surprised that the bull hadn't even bothered to turn around and look at me. I was shaking, cold, and confused. I wondered why Sam had opened the gate, allowing the bull access to the entire barn and barnyard. It made no sense.

With Black Devil safely penned, I returned to Sam's body, knelt and prayed for his soul. But now it was my turn to lose my stomach and I moved a few yards away. Dr. Grayson found me there. As he approached, I noticed he had thrown a camp blanket over Sam's body.

"Reverend Johnson, Reverend Johnson." Dr. Grayson put his hands on my shoulders. His touch was gentle, soothing. Somewhere around sixty-five, Dr. Grayson had been the doctor in Marshall for more years than anyone could remember. People always commented that his presence was healing. His soft-spoken voice was always even, never panicky. His face was kind. His touch, tender. Even his silvery-white hair won him the confidence of many patients.

"I'm sorry," I muttered. "What's happening?"

"Your brother-in-law was killed in a horrible accident," he answered. "But I'm concerned about you. We need to get you up the hill to your house to warm up and rest. I think you're suffering from both shock and exposure."

Only then did I notice I was trembling, which was not surprising in that I had been out in the cold without a coat for almost an hour. Dr. Grayson helped me up and accompanied me back to our house where he called the undertaker and took care of the remaining details. In a strange reversal of roles, both Polly and Sarah tended to me as I lay on our parlor davenport. I closed my eyes, but all I could see was my mangled brother-in-law in his bloodied state. To avoid this, I opened my eyes and stared at the plaster ceiling above.

After finishing his phone calls, Dr. Grayson came over to check on me.

"I served in France for two years during the Great War. What you're experiencing isn't unusual. We call it shell shock; it's a normal reaction to a traumatic experience."

I nodded and closed my eyes while Sarah pulled a crocheted comforter over me. But the recent images of Sam kept returning. Sarah had given me some warm milk to sip and my body ceased trembling. Dr. Grayson put his hand on my forehead for a moment, nodded to Sarah, and left to await the undertaker.

Sarah awakened me about an hour later from a strange, nightmare-filled sleep.

"Dr. Grayson and the undertaker left with Sam's body. We need to talk about the funeral arrangements."

I sat up and saw that Polly was sitting quietly in a rocking chair with our toddler Dorothy sitting in her lap, looking at a magazine. This was so strange. I was a preacher and used to death scenes and all the vagaries of life. Why was I so overcome? Shouldn't Polly be suffering from shell shock rather than me? What was God's plan in all of this?

Samuel Forrest Farm, Marshall Township, Calhoun County, Michigan

Friday, February 9, 1934

My Dearest Mother,

I have the difficult task of telling you about Samuel's unfortunate and untimely death, mauled by our bull, Black Devil. It happened yesterday in the barnyard by the horse tank, while I was up at Sarah's house. No one knows why Sam let the bull out or why he was in the barnyard with him. I shudder every time I think about it. The sheriff questioned us in the afternoon.

I've always been scared of that bull. He was menacing, always stomping and attacking. No wonder Sam named him Black Devil. I can count five times when he's charged one of us. I've always worried that he might get out when Sam was working in the back forty, and I'd have to get him into his pen by myself. Then the victim might have been me.

The funeral will be at the church on Monday with Wesley officiating. I understand that you won't be able to come, so I didn't make the effort to reach you by your neighbor's phone. Sam will be buried in the church cemetery over on the back left side, the area that borders the woods.

Sarah is giving me the black wool dress she wore when Wesley's father passed away. She said she'll make the alterations this afternoon. I have a black wool pillbox hat that I finished last week and I'll add a long black veil so it will be suitable. I do love veils and this situation demands one.

Mother, this letter is short for obvious reasons. I love and miss you.

Your loving daughter,
Polly

Sarah Wolcott Johnson

Monday, February 12, 1934

Today was Sam's funeral and Polly arrived at our house dry-eyed and calm, strutting in like a model. While the black wool dress I lent her was rather plain, she had added a large, shiny silver brooch, and a new black hat, detailed with a black satin ribbon and a long black veil covering her face and neck. She stood tall and in no way gave the impression of a grieving widow.

Much plainer than my younger sister, I have green eyes, brown wavy hair, and, well, I'm a bit plump, I used to be outright heavy after bearing three children, but these hard times had limited our meals. All the baked goods that normally were given to the preacher's family had trickled down to nothing. That was okay; people didn't have an extra cent and too many were losing their farms. If they could afford to give us gingerbread or a pound cake, they would. It was in their hearts, but the sugar and flour weren't in their cupboards.

I had slimmed down without even trying and most people around here had lost too much weight. We ate less so that our children didn't have to go to bed hungry. I used to worry about Sam. He was solidly handsome, but this fall he lost a lot of weight and became lanky, almost skin and bones. Polly blamed herself because she was new to the routine of making three farm meals a day, and by her own admission, she was a terrible cook. When Sam wasn't hungry, she also blamed herself. Well, in my opinion, he was too fussy and nobody can afford three meals a day, not even those of us on farms.

I decided once again to take the moral high road and asked Polly how she was doing, saying nothing about her all-too-perfect attire. She looked at me as if perplexed how to respond.

"I'm numb. I woke up this morning and couldn't believe it's his funeral. I wish Mother were here and I'm hoping she can come in May. She knows what it feels like to lose a husband too soon. You have no idea, Sarah."

No, I have never lost a husband. But I'd had my share of grieving. At fifteen I lost my father and little brother, and at seventeen, my older brother. Loss and grief were a huge component of my life, but Polly was too self-centered to even consider that. She didn't seem to recognize any suffering beyond her own. Certainly, she'd been a small child when Father and John died, but I wasn't sure it made any impact on her. She'd never displayed any grief. For me, it changed my life; I was devastated.

Unwilling to argue with Polly, I handed her a couple of handkerchiefs to put in her bag. I noticed she had a little black purse, one I had never seen before. Clearly, she was prepared for a funeral, hat and bag ready to go. In fact, it was too polished for our little unsophisticated country church. But Posh Polly had always been a clothes horse.

"Who do you think will be coming to the funeral?"

I shrugged. "Everyone from church, and when I called Mrs. Hanford in Marshall, she said she'd definitely be attending. She was such a good next-door neighbor, always willing to help us out."

It irritated me that Polly was focused on who'd be coming—like it was a party. Once again, her immaturity was palpable.

Wes strode into the parlor after cleaning up from his morning chores. He greeted Polly with a smile.

"Do you like my hat?" she asked him, turning so he could see it from the side, then pulling down the veil. It seemed like she was flirting. Leave it to Polly to play the coquette with her sister's husband. A minister. A man of God.

Wes nodded, but I was infuriated. "You're burying your husband this afternoon and all you can think about is your new hat?"

Polly's brow furrowed and she became the spitting image of our three-year-old Dorothy who makes the same face when she gets upset. "I was trying to be polite," Polly simpered. "I want this day to be over."

I immediately regretted my words, particularly since they were witnessed by Wesley. Of course, today was impossibly hard for Polly.

"Sorry I snapped at you. I'm anxious, myself. Right now, I'm worried about whether we'll have enough food for the funeral meal. Most everyone from church said they'd be coming, but only a few will be able to bring a casserole. Also, I need to check and see if I brought over enough extra plates and silverware."

Polly seemed totally uninterested in the china and silverware inventory and started picking at the fringe on the lampshade. If her goal was simply to get through the day, perhaps she didn't care. She looked up at me and judiciously picked up the Bible from the end table and thumbed through it without stopping to read anything. Putting it back down, she placed her head back on the embroidered antimacassar that covered the back of our faded floral armchair. I had embroidered it when Wes and I were engaged and I still remembered the bright, colorful little birds that now were dull with age.

"How long do you think it'll take to get the death certificate?" Polly asked, eyes closed, not directing the question at Wes or me, specifically. The conversation was interrupted by the noise of Junior and Zeke fighting.

"No, I want to be David."

"No, me. You were David last time."

They were playing with Wes's childhood slingshot, and both wanted to be David, not Goliath. I'd witnessed this fight before. Junior and Zeke, close in age at nine and eight, seemed to fight continuously. Just last week they'd fought about who could yell the loudest and spit the farthest. It wasn't an endearing competition.

"Take turns," I demanded, almost shouting. "Zeke, you be David first. Go outside to play with the slingshot. You could break all kinds of things in here. And don't hurt each other. Only shoot at your feet. Those pebbles could put your eyes out." I wondered if I'd redirected my anger from Polly to the boys, but they obediently fled outside without a word.

"Don't get your clothes dirty," I yelled after them. "You need to wear them to the funeral. We'll be leaving in a few minutes."

I felt the weight of the funeral dinner on my shoulders, worrying that we wouldn't have enough food and dishes. However, I decided to go sit down with Polly and Wes to collect myself. If they could sit in the parlor resting, I certainly deserved to get off my feet, too. The food would have to be enough; there was nothing I could do now.

"It usually takes about a month, if I remember right." Wes was answering Polly's question about the death certificate. "There shouldn't be any complications since his death was an accident. Do you even need it? Usually those documents just go in the back of the family Bible. Why did you ask?"

"I don't know," she answered. "Somehow I thought it was important."

This time Dorothy interrupted. "I need go potty." I instantly realized it was too late. The odor was overwhelming and her diaper was hanging low. I jumped up and took her hand to go into the bedroom where we kept her little indoor potty chair. How I longed for a modern bathroom rather than our frigid outhouse that was halfway to the hen house. As we walked to the bedroom I listened to the rest of Polly's conversation with Wes.

"Keep the death certificate with your marriage license. If, or when, you decide to sell the farm you may need them both. Did Sam have a will?"

"I don't know. I don't think so."

While changing Dorothy's diaper, I ruminated on Polly's marriage. We all thought that Polly was much too young for Sam, but she was blinded by the older handsome man who seemed so different from the immature high school boys she had been around. Sam had been a looker: thick, dark hair with graying temples, alarming light blue eyes, a wide smile with white, even teeth. He seemed to have more money than the rest of us and I was sure that wasn't lost on Polly who complained incessantly about needing new clothes, shoes, and, of course, hats.

During their short courtship Polly and Sam went to the movies almost every Saturday night. If there wasn't a new movie playing, he'd take her out for a play or vaudeville performance at the opera house in Adrian. No one did that any more. Every single penny was needed to pay taxes and farm loans. At that time, I figured Sam must have inherited some money. His farm was adjacent to ours, and we were struggling, so why wouldn't he be in the same straits? But of course, Sam didn't have five mouths to feed.

So, Polly fell head-over-heels in love with him. A short-lived romance, if I did say so myself. They courted for only a few weeks before Mother needed to move to Milford, Connecticut to take care of Grandma Blessing. It was immediate and necessary, as Grandma's vision had worsened to the point that she couldn't light the wood stove, cook, clean, or even walk into town by herself. So, Mother sold the Elm Street house and moved to Connecticut to create her new life there. It was one of those cyclical things. Grandma and Grandpa Blessing had ended up in Milford when they were called to take care of Great-Grandmother Tompkins, her mother, many years before.

Those circumstances left Polly in a quandary. She even broached the subject of coming to live with Wes and me. I knew that would only end in disaster. It was clear that Polly wanted to be pampered and would fail to help with meals, housework, and particularly, farm chores. I doubted that she'd even be willing to care for the children on an occasional Saturday night. So I took the diplomatic approach and explained what she already knew: Wes and I used the downstairs bedroom, the boys were in the large upstairs bedroom, and Dorothy was in the remaining small upstairs room. We simply had no space for her.

Mother, of course, expected Polly to go with her, but Polly was enjoying the good life, being showered with gifts from Sam. When he proposed, Polly not only accepted but set the date for early September, the weekend before Mother was to move. No one thought Polly should marry so quickly, but as she pointed out, she had turned twenty in August, and that was a respectable age. Polly had watched several of her friends get married directly after high school graduation, so our protests fell on deaf ears.

Perhaps Mother and I should have been more objecting to Polly's premature marriage. But Polly would have it no other way. She was planning her wedding, buying fluffy white material to make a wedding dress, and, of course, she made herself an elegant headpiece with embroidered flowers, pearl beads, and a long veil of rose-patterned white lace. It was Polly's good fortune that Mother promptly sold the Elm Street house, so there was money for the dress. Pampered Polly. Always, Pampered Polly.

I finished cleaning up Dorothy and put a clean dress on her for the funeral. It was a patched dark-gray hand-me-down from Margaret Atkins. Certainly, an appropriate color for a funeral, and no one would care what the children wore anyway. Instead, tongues would be wagging about Polly's sleek black sheath and gorgeous hat. How stylish and pretty she looked at her husband's funeral when, under similar circumstances, most women would appear haggard.

After Dorothy and I went back to the parlor to sit with Polly, I slid back into my reverie. Once Polly had married Sam, something changed. She began complaining about not having any spending money. They didn't go out on Saturday nights. Even though she was friendly with Ruth Shaw and Millicent Jordan, they didn't get together with other couples. From my perspective, it didn't feel right.

After the money concerns, Polly started in with tirades about not being able to leave the house. Then fulminations about her daily farm chores. At the same time, Sam began losing weight, joking, but not quite joking, about Polly's cooking. Then came the veiled hints that Polly was poisoning him.

I was brought back to the present when Polly started reading a story book to Dorothy. I knew the book well. It started out "Once upon a time," and ended "They lived happily ever after." Oh, if life were that easy.

Reverend Wesley Johnson

Monday, February 12, 1934

Today I presided over the closed-casket funeral of my brother-in-law, Samuel. Our tiny country church was packed full with our own congregation, many holding wet handkerchiefs. I believed this was a sympathetic response to Polly, since, frankly, no one was close to Sam and everyone loved our Pretty Polly. She seemed amazingly calm: no tears, hand-wringing or fingernail-biting. Because it was February in Michigan, there were no flowers to put around the casket or on top of the grave. There would be only dirt atop it, muddy from snowmelt and a recent rain.

Something strange happened before the service. A foul odor hung in the air near the altar and woodstove. Dorothy wasn't kind with her remarks when she came in with her brothers.

"P.U. stinky here," she said in her loudest voice. Sarah hushed her and put her in Polly's lap as a distraction for both of them. But truth be told, I smelled it, too. It wasn't emanating from the casket, positioned at the back of the altar, but near the front. Fortunately, as people started streaming into the building, the odor dissipated with the smell of the wood burning in the stove.

Preaching for your brother-in-law's funeral wasn't the easiest thing. I tried to make it special for Polly, even though it was unlikely she'd remember a single word. Yesterday I asked Polly to write out Sam's favorite hymns and Bible verses, which

I included in the service. I wondered if Polly simply used some of her own favorites. Women tended to favor "I Come to the Garden Alone" and "His Eye is on the Sparrow," two hymns that she put at the top of the list. I'd been a pastor long enough to know not to question her, because I guessed that Polly didn't know his favorites—or if he even had favorites.

The burial followed the service and I kept it short. The wind was blowing an icy rain, the kind that cuts right through you. By the time I recited the twenty-third Psalm and ended with a short prayer, people were ready to disperse. John Newson, our appointed sexton and my reliable friend, finished the burial.

Everyone attending the funeral was invited back to Polly's farmhouse where a few church women had brought soups and casseroles. Sarah had brought over baked beans, bread, butter, extra plates, silverware, and water glasses. We all gathered in the large formal dining room, where the food was laid out on the oak table that Polly's mother had given the couple as a wedding gift. It was a giant piece of furniture and shipping it to Connecticut would have cost a fortune. Sarah and I had extended the table with two extra leaves this morning, but we needn't have bothered. Everyone was generous with bringing food, but these days it was hard to provide a large meal, and there was too much empty space on the table. Sarah, who had also noticed the gaps, brought in extra pickles and jellies to fill in some of the empty space. Still looking too sparse for her liking, she brought two extra sets of salt and pepper shakers, putting one set at each end of the table.

I gave a short blessing and people made their way around the long table. Twice Sarah excused herself to wash soup bowls, items she had forgotten to supplement. I noticed a couple of her friends standing with her at the sink, drying and stacking the dishes, carrying the clean ones back to the dining room. Sarah was resourceful and had aided me immeasurably in my role as pastor, and now she was running the post-funeral gathering like an old hand. I tried to remind myself not to take her for granted.

In the meantime, Polly sat in the overstuffed chair in her parlor, right off the dining room, as people came over to express their condolences. A plate of food sat uneaten on her lap. She smiled politely to everyone who said hello and thanked them for coming, but none of her typical exuberance was on display. No one expected much out of her and I suspected she was still in a kind of stupor from the unexpected event. I was happy that several people had sat down in the parlor, so that Polly wouldn't be alone in that big room. Then I noticed Ruth Shaw and Millicent Jordan hovering over Polly, seeing to her needs. Polly undoubtedly would need these friends in the weeks and months to come.

I kept busy talking to the guests, introducing myself to a young man named Jacob Frond. Apparently, he'd known Polly since childhood, and was attending with some former neighbors from Marshall. Standing alone for a moment, I overheard bits and pieces of a conversation about farm accidents coming from the far end of the room. The voices were familiar, and I headed over towards them, where three male friends were gathered.

"When Joe Dolliver tipped over that brand-new Farmall tractor, he didn't have a chance." Tom Riley was talking to John Newsom and Fred Torquini. "Work horses, they know their limits and they'll refuse to go on those steep side hills that Joe was trying to plow. I have to admit that bright red tractor was as good a looker as any woman, but poor Joe, he just didn't know how to handle her. He was a goner."

"How's Ruby doing?" Fred asked about the deceased man's wife.

"She and the kids went to live with her parents. Right now, the house is sitting empty. Just waiting for squatters. I 'spect she'll try to keep it if she can. That boy of hers is two or three years from graduating high school. . . . I'd heard that both her daughters caught polio. How's that for bad luck? I wouldn't want to go anywhere near that place. . . . Hey, whaddya know, Reverend?" Tom greeted me as I wedged into the group.

"Not much. You?" I answered. It was a greeting I'd not heard until I lived among farmers, but these guys used it all the time and, to be truthful, I liked it. No pretenses with our farmers, good salt-of-the-earth people.

"Not easy, burying your brother-in-law," John remarked.

I nodded.

"So, what was Sam's story, anyway? He was so quiet that I thought he was kinda stand-offish. I don't want to talk ill of the dead, and maybe he was just shy, but he never seemed to wanna talk. Was he always so quiet around the family, Reverend?"

I thought about how to respond. "Sam was always polite, but quiet at family gatherings. They'd come over for Sunday dinner and he wouldn't eat much, never played with the boys. Polly said he'd had a hard childhood; his mother died young and his father went away a lot, leaving him and his brother to fend for themselves. But he rarely talked about it."

"Surprising he didn't play with the boys," John remarked. "My uncle was my favorite person when I was a kid. Uncle Dan was a fun guy, always clowning around with us. Whenever he came over, I'd get so excited. Guess Sam wasn't that kind of guy."

"Sam's eyes would always dart around at church," Tom added. "Almost like he was looking for trouble. Then he'd kinda have a pained face. It was odd."

John picked up the conversation. "Yeah, when he first started coming to church, I tried to talk to him after the service several times, but he'd say 'Fine' or 'Good,' and turn and walk away. Not the politest thing to do, but not everyone's a talker. I quit trying after a while. Don't mean to speak poorly of him, but I gave it my best shot."

I nodded. "He was definitely quiet. But when he's family, you do the best you can."

While I was a bit surprised that these men were so open about Sam, I was pleased that they felt comfortable enough to speak their minds. In truth, Sam was not simply quiet, but detached. I rarely saw him smile. I'd wondered if he married Polly just to have the prettiest woman in the neighborhood. Not a kind thought, but there it was.

The conversation switched to concerns about summer crops and the dropping meat and dairy prices, the same topics we discussed every week after church. Massive job losses. President Roosevelt's programs. The Agricultural Adjustment Act and whether it would help the farmers. It was part of the New Deal and I shared my concerns with them. The government paying us to slaughter our animals and not plant crops seemed crazy. I could read the anguish on these men's faces. They've all worked hard to support their families, but like me, had seen way too many farms go under as the Depression ravaged the country.

I was one of these farmers myself. There were arrangements like this with Methodist churches all over the Midwest with ministers who farmed to support their families. Some farming ministers even had two churches. That would be a lot of effort, delivering the service at nine a.m. at one church and again at eleven a.m. in a neighboring community, then farming and ministering to two congregations during the rest of the week. I found my weeks more than full with one small church, a dairy and chicken farm, and a large apple orchard.

Sarah had adapted well to farming, and the children loved the big yards and fields, the cattle, chickens, and all the routines of farm life. Fortunately, I had learned a lot about farming as a kid, when I spent summers with my grandparents in southern Illinois. I never knew those early experiences would come in so handy, my father being a haberdasher, selling men's clothing in Rockford, Illinois, up near Chicago. I doubted that his business would have survived these hard times. People no longer could afford ready-made clothing.

It was overwhelming, ministering to good people in impoverished times. When I went to seminary, I envisioned I'd be serving at a large stone church with ivy growing up its walls in the center of a large affluent city, perhaps Chicago. Well-dressed parishioners, women in fancy hats, like Polly's, and men in tailored suits, like my father sold, would shake my hand after the service, praise the sermon and mention a church project they'd like to take on. Everyone would be driving Model As and Ts, or fancier cars, including me. I'd be married to Sarah and the entire congregation would admire our perfectly-behaved son and daughter.

Since then I've wondered how many sins were in that vision. Certainly, pride, avarice, and greed. So here I was at this small country church with about sixty on our roll, and between thirty and forty regular attendees. We were all dressed in threadbare clothing, driving our horse-drawn buggies down gravel roads. The tiny "white" clapboard church was actually blackened from many years of bad weather. It was a spartan, single room with a platform at the front and a simple wooden pulpit. There were ten rows of wooden pews with an aisle down the middle and a wood stove near the front. An outhouse, that needed replacing, sat behind the church next to the graveyard. The church's roof was leaking, and some of the pews were in need of repair. An unfinished cellar begged to be converted into a community room for social gatherings and Sunday School classes. Sarah wanted the church electrified and a piano donated so she could start a choir. I knew that wouldn't be happening soon.

One part of my early dream was intact. I was married to Sarah and had three occasionally well-behaved children. So, God had tested me and had, hopefully, made me a better person as I had grown spiritually from those youthful days in seminary. I could relate to my parishioners, who were also being tested during our current hard times. Our sights had all been lowered. No one longed for nice clothes or a new car or fancy house. Now we struggled to provide enough for food and a warm, dry house. In these parts, the main worry of everyone was to make enough money to keep our farms from foreclosure. My parishioners' worries were my own worries.

As I looked around Polly's parlor and dining room, I noticed the guests were mostly church friends paying respects. Only Millicent Jordan and Ruth Shaw, and a few strangers from town were Polly's friends. Millicent and Ruth stuck near her, giving her hugs. They themselves looked teary-eyed, probably imagining themselves in Polly's shoes. Widowed at age twenty. Whoever would have thought that of the spirited, carefree girl I met when I started courting Sarah, so many years ago?

However I couldn't reminisce about Polly without remembering her flirting with me when she was a teenager. When Sarah and I were courting, Polly would run up and hug me. One day when I arrived, Polly answered the door and she leaned into me and kissed me on the mouth. I pulled away aghast, unclear what to do. I did nothing.

I wondered if Polly even remembered the incident. Unfortunately, that kiss had stayed with me, and my longing had increased exponentially. Frankly, I was glad when Polly got married because I told myself I never wanted a repeat of that scene. Yet, honestly, I did. My unhealthy desire for Polly had kept growing as a healthy desire seemed to have diminished for my faithful wife. I prayed to God daily to be set free from these longings. It burned like a fire that I couldn't put out.

With my ministerial responsibilities finished for the day, I continued to talk to John Newsom and some of the other church men in Polly's parlor. The topic had moved on to John Dillinger, the famous bank robber from Illinois, who had hit so many banks in the Midwest that it was impossible to keep track of all of his robberies.

"Don't know what I'd do with all that money," John said.

"Oh, I'd live high off the hog," Fred answered. "Millie and me'd take a trip on one of those Zeppelins floating through the sky. We'd look out the windows and watch the birds soar by. Then we'd wave down at you folks in your fields and you'd appear to be tiny specks."

He sported a wide grin. "Or we'd go to New York and visit the Empire State Building. Millie read some magazine articles about it a few years ago. It took over a year to build—tallest building in the world. They have an elevator in it so you can ride up to the top."

"I'd worry that it might get blown over in a tornado," John said.

"Yup, it might. Guess we'd better fly in the Zeppelin first, in case a tornado hits the Empire State Building while we're in the elevator going up to the top," Fred answered him with a grin. "Millie has lots of ideas for an expensive fur coat and fancy jewelry, too. I think she reads too many magazines."

Despite this unusual conversation, my mind wandered back to Polly and Sam. I couldn't help but wonder how that bull's gate was open without Sam's knowledge. My mind began to fill with suspicions and wandered down dark and ungodly paths. I shook my head, attempting to rid myself of these untoward thoughts.

Samuel Forrest Farm
Marshall Township, Calhoun County, Michigan

Monday, March 5, 1934

Dear Mother,

Over the past two weeks everything has been a blur, including the funeral. No one from Sam's family came, not surprisingly, since his parents are gone and he only has one brother, Mitchell, in Wyoming. It would have taken days, if not weeks, for him to travel here to Michigan in the kind of weather we've been having. Having no telephone number for him, I wrote Mitchell a long letter, but I haven't heard back. I'm not even sure I had the correct address.

Everyone is telling me that I'm "oh so lucky" having been over at Sarah and Wesley's when this horrible accident occurred—and I was. But I keep thinking about what I might have done if I'd heard Sam's screams early on. Maybe there was a way I could have saved him. I only wish I could have said goodbye. He'd been such a good husband.

Mother, please burn the letter I wrote you before Sam's death, when I was complaining about the blizzard. That was such a difficult week. I was cold, tired, and ornery. I shouldn't have given you cause to worry about me. Too many times I've acted as a spoiled little girl (as Sarah is quick to point out). I was lonely. I was tired of the farm chores and I complained too much about the cold, drafty house. Samuel was good and dutiful and treated me well. You remember how he gave me wedding money last August right before we got married? I felt like a queen when I bought Ginger with that money. Already I miss him and I have no idea how I will cope.

Wesley has been helpful with the animals and farm chores. However, I need to sell the cows and pigs. I'll keep the chickens so I can continue to make egg money. I've been checking with the neighbors to see if anyone wants to rent the land for summer crops, but no one has the extra money. If I can't find anyone, I'll let Wesley use all the fields he wants, although he already told me he won't be able to add any additional crops this year; he has so many demands on his time. I believe I'll give Jasper, Sam's workhorse, to Wesley and Sarah since their old Bessie is nearing her end. Of course, I'll keep Ginger forever, and Sailor Dog, too. These animals have become dear to me, like friends.

The sheriff and his young deputy came back last Thursday and asked me the same questions about Sam's death. So I told them the same answers. I hope that's the end of the investigation since I have so many farm obligations now.

After the funeral I asked Wesley to sell Black Devil. A few days later Wes got three church members to help him get the bull into the trailer to take to the stockyard auction. I didn't want to be around when they put the bull in Wes's trailer, so I took Ginger and went for a long ride, first down our road, then to Maple Lane and rode on and on. When we finally got home, I felt better and I spent a lot of time walking Ginger and rubbing her down. The bull's sale brought very little, but that was fine. I never want to encounter that creature again.

Mother, I want you to come visit. Please reconsider my invitation to come in May. I miss you.

Your loving daughter,
Polly

Sarah Wolcott Johnson

Sunday, March 11, 1934

Polly didn't come to church today. First, I was scared something bad had happened to her. But given Polly's predilection for sleeping in and taking hours to fix her hair and make-up, I wondered if the ten o'clock church service had become too early for her. Frankly, her absence felt like a slap in the face to the wonderful congregation members who came to Sam's funeral.

Wes and I customarily stood on the steps of the church, shaking hands with everyone as they left. Typically, Dorothy stood between us but the boys were free to run around the churchyard with the other children. "Where's Polly?" people kept asking me as they were departing.

"A bit under the weather," I answered. My sister was forcing me to lie. Right there on the church steps. But if I said I didn't know, wouldn't that reflect poorly on me, as an uncaring, indifferent older sister? How I longed for a reliable, church-going sister.

In the church yard, Wes was gathering a group of men to organize the church roof repairs and I forgot about Polly for a while. The task of feeding church volunteers always fell on me, so I quickly enlisted a few of the wives to help. Sally Adams volunteered potato soup, Martha Vincent volunteered bread, and Margaret Bomberg said she'd make scalloped onions. I myself planned to bring a crock of beans. These days everyone used beans as the back-up in case you ran out of food at a potluck. While it wasn't fancy, it was filling. Serving meat wasn't even discussed. No one had any to spare. If anyone had meat, it was always saved for Sunday dinner. Funny thing, we farmers who raised meat for others were going without. One of God's little jokes.

Also, nagging at the back of my mind was a suspicion that something weird was happening inside the church. It was such a sparse, austere sanctuary that not much could be rearranged. Almost everything was nailed down, including the pews, the woodstove, and the pulpit. But there were two benches at the very back where people sat to put on their galoshes in wet or cold weather. Last Friday when I cleaned the church with Dorothy in tow, I pushed the benches together, neatly along the back wall. Today they were askew. Also, the cushions I'd put on each bench were wrongly positioned. I'd left the dark navy one on the bench near the door and the light yellow flowered one way back in the corner, figuring it wouldn't get dirty as quickly. But already it had dark mud stains on it. Even Dorothy noticed it. "Boogeyman here," she had exclaimed.

After we settled the logistics for the roof repair, people lingered in the churchyard, talking to one another and enjoying the mild spring morning. I noticed the children were running around the wet, muddy graveyard, my own children among them, ducking in front and back of the grave markers. Viola Cross was frowning at them, and tried to catch my eye. I knew she disapproved of such behavior and I couldn't disagree. It was particularly troubling since Sam's new grave was at the back of the cemetery, muddy dirt on top and as yet no gravestone. But the kids were staying near the front, even though it was wet with last night's rain, and I didn't want to scold them. They'd sat quietly through the entire church service. As Viola sidled towards me, I turned to Margaret Atkins to ask about her ailing mother. As I half-listened to Margaret's "good days and bad days" response, I overheard another conversation not far away.

"Ray said he saw a light in the Dolliver house, and Ruby's been gone for over a month," Sally Adams was telling Martha Vincent. "He told me to stay away from there. Course I have no reason to go anywhere near the place. Even so, knowing someone was in that house makes a chill go down my spine." A quick glance told me that Viola had joined their group.

"Do you think it's rail riders?" Martha asked. "I've been told they're a rough group. The trains aren't heated, so those cars get pretty cold at night."

"Maybe," Sally responded. "But how they could even find the Dolliver place is beyond me. It's gotta be at least eight miles from the tracks in Marshall."

"Is Ray gonna go over there and check?"

"Absolutely not, if I have any say about it. I told Ray it wasn't any of our business. Those vagrants have knives. We have too many problems already without taking on any more."

This was an alarming conversation, to say the least. I now gave Margaret my full attention, asking her about the remedies she and her sister had tried using on their mother, and she promised to write down her mustard plaster recipe to give to me next Sunday. I wished I'd had it earlier this year when both Junior and Zeke had bad colds that turned into pneumonia.

I was glad it was time to go home and make Sunday dinner. Back in the day when Wes and I were first married, we got invited to dinner almost every Sunday and I loved that. We'd have plenty of time after church to talk, get the pulse of the community, and later enjoy a home-cooked meal with friendly families. Just like the baked goods we used to receive, the Sunday dinners had completely disappeared from our lives.

Wes nodded to me, and I rounded up the kids, smiled, and said our goodbyes to everyone, wishing them a pleasant week. Then Wesley proceeded to board up the church door. He put two boards into a half-pipe, mainly to prevent animals getting in the door. From the road, it looked like it was boarded up tight, but it wasn't. I wondered if someone had been coming into the church with the intention of messing it up. Perhaps it was the rail riders or whoever had broken into the Dolliver house. There wasn't much they could do inside the church other than rearrange the benches and soil the cushions. Unless they set a fire. I shook my head. My thoughts were bleak, not Christian.

The boys jumped into the back of the buggy as Dorothy and I joined Wes up front. He took up the reins and gently slapped them on Bessie's rump. "Giddy-up," he called out. She looked back at us with a tired gesture and moved out at a slow pace. This morning she was limping. I felt for Bessie. She had been such a faithful horse, doing her duty for the entire ten years of our marriage. One couldn't ask for a better animal. She had always been gentle with the children and me. Once when a wasp stung her on the way to church, she stopped cold, but didn't buck or run amok like most horses would have done. Sweet old girl. Every day when I went out to feed her, I wondered if she'd passed overnight. I sure hoped there was a place in heaven for loyal animals like Bessie.

Junior and Zeke were shouting out goodbyes to the kids in the other buggies as we plodded down the gravel road towards home. I turned toward Wes to ask him to stop at Polly's, when I saw a Model A charging toward us. To my shock, Polly was sitting tall in the seat beside Jacob Frond with a light blue scarf wound around her neck. They both waved at us as if this was the most normal thing in the world.

Needless to say, we didn't stop at Polly's. What had gotten into her? Skipping church and riding alone with a young man so soon after her husband's funeral. Was Polly out of her mind? Wes looked at me, and I shook my head. I needed to give that girl a good talking to. She should be told how a proper widow dressed, and more importantly, behaved. But darn it, Polly was smart. She already knew.

Reverend Wesley Johnson

Wednesday, March 21, 1934

"The Sheriff's pulling in the driveway," the boys yelled out to Sarah and me. We were sitting at breakfast, sharing a small cup of coffee, wanting it to last forever. Sarah jumped up and walked to the door. I quickly gulped down the last swallow of coffee and joined her. Deputy Bylowski had called us the prior evening stating that they'd be coming by this morning, so this was no surprise, although I was hoping to have a little more time to relax.

Sarah and I led Sheriff Conlin and Deputy Bylowski through the back room into the house. I had found from visiting a number of our rural church members that a farmer's back room told a lot about the family. Ours was an all-purpose room with wash tubs, washboards, drying racks, and a table used mainly for potting plants and putting up fruit and vegetables in the summertime. On the north wall was a shallow closet where I stored the shotgun and deer rifles. I was proud to say it was a room heralding a busy, hard-working family. The sheriff glanced around as he walked through.

The two officers followed us into the parlor and took seats on the davenport. Sarah sat in her rocking chair, and I sat in the sofa chair which has an annoying broken spring right in the center of the seat. I hadn't really noticed the shabbiness of our parlor furniture before; Sarah had done her best with throw quilts and crocheted coverings over the most worn pieces. The curtains, made of heavy fabric with floral designs, had faded from years of sunlight and couldn't be disguised. Nor could the worn spots in the carpet, although Sarah had done her best, placing rag rugs where she could. If the two officers noticed the well-worn furnishings, they made no comment. I suspected they'd seen much, much worse over the past few years.

"Reverend and Mrs. Johnson," Sheriff Conlin began. "We're continuing the investigation of Sam's death because there are some things that don't add up and we hoped you two could shed some light. So, I'm gonna dive right in, if that's okay with you two."

"Of course, but please call us Wes and Sarah," I answered. The sheriff nodded and Bylowski took out a pencil and tablet.

"First, we're hearing that Polly and Sam didn't have a happy marriage. What do you have to say about that?"

Sarah cleared her throat. "I'll go first since Polly's my younger sister by eleven years. I've heard the same rumors, but they're simply not based on fact. We've had Sunday dinner with Polly and Sam just about every week since September, and they've been kind to each other. No arguments. Polite conversation, that's it. If Polly's been unhappy, it's because she's young and it's difficult to endure the hard times. She'd like to have money for new clothes and go to the movies." Sarah paused for a moment. "But who doesn't have those wishes?"

I saw Bylowski nod, as he was jotting down notes.

It was my turn to speak and I was worried. I started my well-rehearsed answer. "I have counseled many couples, and I understand that the first year of marriage is difficult. You have to make so many adjustments and get used to the other person's habits. I have no doubt that Polly and Sam went through this—like every other newly-married couple."

The sheriff was persistent. "But were they quarreling a lot?"

Sarah and I both said "No" at the same time.

"Neither of us ever saw them argue," answered Sarah. "As I said, I'm sure the current hard times put pressure on my sister. She's twenty, after all, and likes nice things. She makes hats for fun; but of course, the materials are pricey."

Sarah, bless her heart, had figured out a way to tilt the subject. At that exact moment, Dorothy came toddling in the room in her long yellow nightgown, wiping the sleepy from her eyes.

"Who are you?" she asked, looking at the men in uniform.

"These are Sheriff Conlin and Deputy Bylowski," I answered. "They're here to ask Mother and Father some questions. Can you go up to the boys' room and play with them for a while?"

Dorothy nodded, but she walked into the kitchen, not upstairs.

"I'll get her settled," Sarah said as she moved quickly to the kitchen, grabbing Dorothy's hand and leading her back upstairs.

"Cute girl," the Sheriff quipped.

"Thanks."

"So back to Polly and Sam," the Sheriff began again. "Is there anything that might lead you to believe Polly was unhappy?"

"Well, beyond the hard times, it seems like Polly was having problems adjusting to farm life. Until they married in early September, she'd lived with her mother in Marshall. In September, after she got married, there were all the farm chores: tending chickens and pigs, filtering the milk, washing the eggs. In town they had an indoor bathroom, a telephone, and electricity. She was used to having more freedom, like seeing friends, reading, drawing, and sewing. Suddenly that was all gone. On the other hand, she has fallen in love with her palomino mare, Ginger, and takes her out riding every day if the weather is good."

Bylowski smiled.

"So, what about Polly's broken bones and bruises your friends and neighbors have mentioned?" Conlin asked.

My heart started racing. I wanted to be truthful. But I couldn't let my suspicions mar Polly in any way.

"Neither Sarah nor I ever saw Samuel lift a finger against her," I answered. "She said she got injured because she was clumsy and not used to all the farm chores." I was being one-hundred percent truthful, but my suspicions were far different from my words. I had long been concerned that Sam had been mistreating his beautiful wife.

Both officers got up to leave as Sarah came back. She joined me at the door to offer goodbyes.

I said a little silent prayer thanking God the sheriff hadn't delved too deeply, so I was able to answer all the questions honestly. I tried to see the best in people. I truly did, but I understood that we were all flawed. The sheriff was probably focusing his attention on Polly because he seemed to believe her husband was hurting her, and I couldn't honestly say he wasn't.

The elephant in the room, of course, was that everyone in the congregation had seen Polly's bruises and heard her story about falling off the hay wagon when she broke her ribs. I was sure it remained the main topic of conversation. Maybe Samuel Forrest was a cruel husband, but Polly, "Pushy Polly," as Sarah had often nicknamed her, should not have rolled over and succumbed to his beatings, if that, indeed, had happened. Sarah and I had always been next door. She could have come to us for refuge at any time, day or night.

As a member of the clergy, I knew the Biblical injunctions for women to obey their husbands. But in these modern times, that needed to be scrutinized, just like "an eye for an eye," as well as the references to slavery and multiple wives. I fully believed the Bible was a guidepost, not a set of laws.

Over the years I had heard rumors about wives being harmed and even killed by their husbands. Rarely do women run away, and I was sure it was because of children. I considered Sarah and our family. Knowing her, I knew she would endure a lot in order to live under the same roof with our children. But what ties did Polly have with Sam? A man she had known barely a year and been married to a scant six months.

I understood the stigma of divorce. Had Polly chosen that route, she would always carry that label. It would be difficult, if not impossible, for her to find another husband. Polly, of course, was pretty, but, truthfully, that might work against her.

Even my precious Sarah talked about divorced women in an unkind manner.

I had spent many hours trying to understand the squabbling between Sarah and her attractive young sister. Polly was the baby of the family, and I was sure that with all the tragedy in the Wolcott family, she was spoiled rotten. Mr. Wolcott and both of Polly's brothers had experienced untimely deaths. Consequently, everyone doted on young Polly, especially her mother. I knew Sarah felt diminished and was insecure.

My mind continued to wander. What if Polly, in the past few months, had fallen in love with Jacob Frond, the young man I met at Sam's funeral, and the one she'd been "gallivanting" with on the cold Sunday morning after the funeral? Did she seriously think no one would see her? I've known Polly for well over ten years, since she was eight or nine. I remembered her roller skating down the sidewalk on Elm Street, a happy girl who liked school and made friends easily. But she shouldn't be displaying, as Sarah described it, "indecent behavior."

I had always hidden my own feelings about Polly, and it was one subject I have never broached with Sarah, and never will. That would only hurt Sarah to the quick; sometimes late at night when she was quietly snoring by my side, my thoughts turned to Polly's quick smile, her laughter, her pretty face. I tried not to continue down that path to the flesh, but sometimes I couldn't help it. Polly had a grip on me.

It was true that Polly sometimes acted like a coquette, but that only fueled my desire. Sam's death was a trial for me in so many ways. Now that she was no longer a married woman, I worried about my self-control. I had no idea if Polly had reciprocal longings for me; yet my passions continued to grow. With God's help I would try to keep them at bay.

Still, nagging at the back of my mind was Polly's flirtatious manner. I had experienced it many, many times. I wondered if Polly had entrapped her high school friend Jacob into an illicit relationship. Had he become enamored with her before Sam's death? Could he have been behind Sam's untimely demise?

In the afternoon I met John Newsom at the church to dig a latrine for the new outhouse. We were building it in the far back corner of the church yard, the old one being decrepit, and more to the point, full. Last week we'd finished the roof repairs, and after this outhouse project we'd be up to date, except for sanding and repairing the pews.

John Newsom, my able helper, a man I considered more of a friend than anyone else in the congregation, took me aside as we both stopped for a needed break to drink some water. John's brow was furrowed, and he bit his lip. A tic lifted his left shoulder.

"You know, I'm not one to gossip, but this has been on my mind ever since Sam's funeral."

I looked him in the eyes and nodded, pausing for him to continue.

"Well, I grew up with Johanna, Sam's first wife. She was a sweet girl who lived on a farm just down the road from us. We went to the same one-room country school, although we weren't in the same grade, being she was a few years younger than me. A nice and kind girl and pretty like your Polly. But after her marriage to Samuel there were rumors goin' round that he was hurting her. Finally, when she died by falling off the barn roof, supposedly handing nails to Sam, people wondered if she'd been pushed."

"I'd heard that story, too," I added. "But so many years have passed, and Sam had been coming to church for over a year. Not that church-going makes you a virtuous person," I quickly added. "He was quiet but seemed to be a good man."

"But gosh darn it," John added. "There were also rumors that Sam deposited hefty amounts into the bank in Marshall after Johanna's death. Apparently, he received two life insurance payoffs."

I thought about that. "Usually life insurance is for men, not women. No wonder there were rumors."

"Uh-huh," John agreed. "Johanna's family was poor; there was absolutely no reason for Sam to carry even one insurance policy on her. He made money from Johanna's death."

John stood there in front of the latrine opening we'd been digging all morning, shaking his head. "I don't wanna spread gossip, Wes. But I cain't help thinking."

"You think he was hurting Polly and she took revenge?"

"To be God-honest, it crossed my mind, and I can't get it out of there, just like a bad song playing over and over. And if the speculation about Johanna was true, then Polly may have gotten a whiff of it and become afeared for her own life. I'm not sayin' Polly committed murder; in fact, I don't think so. I cain't imagine Polly opening up that gate to the bull's pen. But I wonder if someone, who was in Polly's good graces, thought he was doing right by her and committed the act."

Immediately Polly's high school friend Jacob Frond came to mind. I didn't know much about Jacob other than the Fronds lived down the street from Polly on Elm Street in Marshall. Sarah had always spoken kindly about the family. Apparently, they had been very helpful after Mother Wolcott was widowed. Jacob had been in Polly's class, and she had gone to the senior dance with him. I'd seen a photo of them at the Elm Street house.

"I'm so sorry to have to spill my head like this." John picked up the shovel and began to dig again. I followed suit, giving us both some quiet time.

What I hadn't told John was that I was having similar thoughts, but we both kept digging, and I focused on the present. It was a sunny, spring day and overhead the sparrows were chirping. Turning around and gazing at our little church with its newly repaired roof, I felt proud of our small community. Today even the graveyard looked and smelled of spring. A few little white snowdrops were in full bloom and I could see the crocus heads peeping out of the ground. The mourning doves cooed in the distance, interrupting the chorus of nearby sparrows.

But digging a latrine? Never in my wildest moments at seminary did I see myself doing this. Life never turned out as you expected. Truth be told, I liked physical labor. Digging and moving soil from place to place, was strangely satisfying.

Perhaps because I was feeling happy with these early signs of spring, I chose to open up to John. It was so hard to keep a professional distance from my church members and today, because I viewed John as a close friend, I broke the distance.

"I've been wondering the same thing about Sam," I confided. "But something doesn't add up. If Sam had all that money, where is it now? Polly's probably going to lose the farm; she's mentioned that over and over, and she hasn't said a thing about any savings. She says Sam was one-hundred percent honest with her about Johanna and that whole early chapter of his life."

I stopped digging for a moment. "This is the story that Sam told Polly: Johanna was sitting with her legs dangling off the side of the roof up near the top holding a box of nails, and handing them to Sam as needed. He warned her that she wasn't safe sitting there at the highest part of the gable. Johanna pulled her legs back up and got them on the roof, but she made a mistake. She stood up, rather than crawled back to Sam. In doing so, she may have been dizzy cuz she fell backwards. Maybe she didn't know she needed to crawl."

I paused. "By the way, Sam forbade Polly from ever going up on the roof. She's scared of heights so she wouldn't do that anyway. Last fall during apple picking she refused to climb to the top of the high ladders in the orchard."

John nodded thoughtfully. We went back to digging but continued slowly as the conversation became more important than the chore. Five minutes of silence ensued before John stuck his shovel in the dirt pile and looked me in the eye.

"What else did Sam forbid Polly to do, other than not go up on a roof?"

The question hung in the air like the spray of a nearby skunk. Until now I'd been totally open with John. It was now or never. I drew in a breath and chose to be truthful.

"He wanted her to stay home all the time. To not come up to our house and visit Sarah, me, and the kids. When Polly secretly walked up to give Sarah letters to mail to their mother, she always worried that he would find out."

"Not a good way to start a marriage," John commented, "sneakin' behind your husband's back."

"No, and something else," I added. "He hadn't been eating much. Polly blamed herself, saying it was her cooking. But he didn't eat much of the last Sunday dinner we shared with them at our house, and Sarah makes mighty fine goulash. Maybe he wasn't hungry, but once Polly jokingly told me that he thought she was poisoning him. You know he'd lost so much weight."

I wondered if I should go on. I did. It felt good to get this off my chest. "There's also the fact that Sam would go off for hours every day this winter. He didn't even tell Polly where he was working. It certainly wasn't a safe arrangement for him. One time she found him in the haymow, and she felt guilty for snooping in the barn. But the man must have had his reasons for keeping to himself."

"Or his demons," John added. I nodded in agreement.

Samuel Forrest Farm
Marshall Township, Calhoun County, Michigan

Friday, March 23, 1934

Dear Mother,

I am so distraught. Sheriff Conlin has been back twice this week asking me more questions about Samuel. I'm worried because he and his deputy, Zeb Bylowski, seem to think I let Black Devil out with the intention of killing Samuel. The bull's pen was open that morning. But who opened it? I certainly didn't.

I did not let the bull out. Nothing was further from my mind. Sam, poor guy, was ravaged beyond recognition. Sarah ran down to get me from the scene, and I couldn't stop vomiting as we made our way back to Sarah's house. I was shaking the entire time. I ask you, is that the behavior of a wife who killed her husband?

The sheriff has asked me the same questions over and over again. I have to tell them what happened every minute starting from the moment Sam got up that morning. Frankly, I don't remember. I've been through so much since then. I don't know how long Sam spent shaving or cleaning his teeth. I'm sure he milked the cows that morning the same as every other morning or the cows would have been bellowing. I don't know what made Sam change his routine.

The sheriff and his assistant have asked me to account for every minute of my time. I go through the long litany. Got up and got dressed, fed the chickens and gathered eggs, fed the pigs, went back into the house and filtered the milk, washed the dirty eggs, then went about making breakfast. We had bacon, eggs, toast and coffee. A pretty darn good breakfast for these times when most people are reduced to milk toast, stale bread or nothing at all. Even so, Sam didn't eat much, so I gave the table scraps to Sailor Dog.

Sheriff Conlin is the tough one. He's about fifty with rough features and graying hair. He stands tall, well over six feet, and he doesn't mince words. Rather than treating me as a young widow who has lost her husband, he barks out questions. "So exactly how long were you collecting eggs? Were you anywhere near the gate to the bull's pen? What about the horse tank? What did you hear when you were gathering eggs? Exactly when and why did you decide to walk over to your sister's place?" The questions are endless, usually a two-hour ordeal.

Bylowski quietly writes down my answers. He's a lot younger, late twenties. Slender, dark hair, and blue eyes, and not as tall as the sheriff. When I answer the sheriff's same questions over and over, the deputy smiles whenever I sigh and give the same answers. He's probably bored hearing my answers repeated over and over.

What baffles me is why Sam didn't see or know that the gate to Black Devil's pen was open. He kept that sliding door open all the time, but he could've shut it if he thought the gate was broken. Maybe he went out to the barnyard before feeding the bull and suddenly Black Devil was on him. But I'm not sure why Sam would do that. Could there have been a problem with the horse tank? It doesn't seem to have any leaks. Perhaps a cow or two was out in the barnyard and Sam needed to round them up for milking. But no, he did the milking before breakfast, and he didn't encounter the bull until hours after breakfast. I understand why the Sheriff is asking questions, but I'm as baffled as he is.

What concerns me now, dear Mother, is making the mortgage payments on the farm in late September. Sam and I planned to use the cash from this summer's crops for that. I wouldn't be the first person in this county to lose a farm. Then what would I do? I'd be a penniless widow with no skills to make a living. I still have the dream of making hats; I know I'm good at that. But that's only a dream and no one has money to buy hats. It's hard enough to scrape together enough to buy sugar and molasses.

Even though I keep trying, I've found no one who's interested in renting the land. I wish Wes could use it; he's done so much for me. It's too bad that Junior and Zeke aren't a few years older and could work the land, but at ages eight and nine they can gather eggs and feed the pigs, but not take a team out to plow, sow corn, oats, and wheat, and then harvest them. I've given Wes the silage, and he removes a wagonload every week and uses it for his cattle.

I cannot take care of the farm by myself and I'm overwhelmed. I never expected to be a widow at age twenty. Now I'm at my wits' end trying to figure out how to make ends meet. When will this horrible Depression end?

Your loving daughter,
Polly

P.S. I still want you to come for a visit in May. Of course, I understand why you couldn't drop everything and come to the funeral. But could you arrange for a neighbor lady to take care of Grandma Blessing for a couple of weeks? Sarah and I would love to see you.

Sarah Wolcott Johnson

Tuesday, March 27, 1934

"Come on in," I welcomed Sheriff Conlin and Deputy Bylowski into the parlor. I'd been expecting these two back after Polly had told me that they'd already interrogated her three times. Apparently they didn't always call before they came, in order to catch people off guard.

"Wes is at the church for a meeting but should be back soon."

"Well, our questions are mainly for you, ma'am," the sheriff answered.

"Okay, you can have as long as you want, but first let me check on Dorothy. She's taking her afternoon nap in the back bedroom."

I walked down the hall trying to compose myself. I'd been dreading this return visit, and I wished Wes were here. Dorothy was sound asleep so I closed the door quietly, hoping our voices wouldn't wake her up. The wallpaper in the hallway, once red roses on a pink background, was faded and cracked and there were scuff marks all along the baseboards where the boys had roughhoused. I mentally added the hallway to about fifty other projects needing attention.

I smiled as I entered the parlor, hoping to look less nervous than I actually was. The officers were sitting at either end of the davenport, so I took the rocking chair, my usual refuge.

"Go ahead with your questions." I tried to look casual, at ease with myself, which couldn't have been further from the truth.

"Your sister Polly had come over here to see you the morning Sam died?"

I nodded, awaiting the next question, but I saw that Bylowski was waiting for me to say something.

"Yes," I answered firmly. "We were here with her in this room when we heard the screaming."

The sheriff cleared his throat and continued. "Had your husband gone out earlier that morning? Might he have talked to Sam before the incident with the bull?"

"Well, he was out, but not over at Sam's. He went over to the church for a meeting with the board. They were talking about fixing the church roof."

"Did he stop over at the Forrest farm?"

Before I could answer the phone rang. Two long rings, ours.

"Excuse me, I should answer that."

Both men nodded.

It was Viola Cross, the neighborhood busybody, the grumpiest lady at church. If I weren't the preacher's wife, I would have had words with her long ago.

"Is everything all right? I saw the sheriff's car at your house," she asked.

"Yes, Mrs. Cross, just fine. I have to go now . . . Yes, I will. . . I really must go now. Bye." I didn't give her a chance to say goodbye.

"Now where were we?" I asked them when I got back to the parlor.

"Did your husband stop by the Forrest farm when he was out?"

My heart started pounding. I wondered if they could sense my nervousness.

"No-oo," I stammered. "If you think Wes opened that gate, then you're barking up the wrong tree. He's a Methodist minister, after all."

Conlin and Bylowski sat there silently raising their eyebrows at one another. I worried that I was being too belligerent.

"We're just trying to cover all the bases, ma'am." This time Conlin was polite.

"I'm sorry. I'm so nervous. This has been an awful situation for our entire family. We are—were close to Polly and Sam."

They both looked down at their notebooks and glanced at each other again. Next came the same old question I'd already answered, but still was dreading.

"Did you have reason to believe that Mr. Forrest was hurting your sister?" Sheriff Conlin met my eye. His voice was kind but firm.

I hesitated, perhaps for too long.

"No, I don't think so," I lied.

"Apparently, neighbors and people at your church noticed bruises and other injuries. How do you account for that?"

"She's a clumsy girl," I answered, using Polly's own words. "She's new to farm life and she doesn't always pay attention."

"But you saw the bruises yourself?"

I nodded, but I didn't ask which bruises; there were so many over the past months. I decided to respond to the last set that appeared a few days before Sam's death. "Yes, but she explained how she'd been cleaning upstairs and how she fell while she was carrying two buckets of dirty water down the stairs. The stairs are steep. You should take a look."

Bylowski wrote down some notes. I was hoping the questioning was over. My hands were clammy and I knew my voice was trembling.

"So, you were inside this house that entire morning?" Bylowski was taking over the questioning.

Again I hesitated. How was I going to answer this question? My kids knew I'd left the house. At age three Dorothy was too little to remember much from that particular morning, but Junior and Zeke had waited for their breakfasts. They knew I'd been out.

I was on the spot; I couldn't lie. "I ran over to Polly's to borrow some butter she'd churned the previous day."

"Why didn't you tell us that last time?" Bylowski's voice was even, neutral-toned.

"I don't know. I didn't think of it—it didn't seem important. I was only down there for a couple of minutes."

"Did you take your daughter with you?"

"No, I put her in the boy's room. I was only gone for a short time."

I wondered if they could tell how nervous I was. Conlin straightened up in his chair and leaned forward. "Was Sam in the house when you went over?"

"No, I didn't ask Polly where he was; I assumed he was out doing chores, working."

Then came a question I hadn't expected.

"Did you open up that gate to the bull's pen?" Conlin was scowling.

"No."

"But you were angry at your brother-in-law for mistreating your sister?" he persisted.

"No. He didn't mistreat her," I lied once again.

"How about your husband? Did he open that gate?"

"He is a man of faith. He understands that humans are not perfect, but when Polly told us how her injuries occurred, we believed her. There was no reason for her to lie to us."

"I repeat. Did he open it up?"

"No," I couldn't help raising my voice, but at this point I could envision the act of opening the gate as being perceived as an act of kindness, not murder.

A cold silent wall pushed itself between the two men and me. I didn't know how long I could continue lying. In many ways I had been thinking of Sam's death as a blessing. Yet here I was, the pastor's wife, lying to officers of the law.

I thought the barrier was as irritating to the men as to me.

"Well, that about takes care of it." The sheriff got up and put on his hat. Bylowski followed suit. I saw them to the door, and watched them looking toward Polly's farm, perhaps judging how long it would take to walk down to the barn. I knew the answer. Five minutes at a fast clip. Junior and Zeke could run down there in three minutes.

Then it struck me. One or both of the boys could have run down, opened the gate, and run back in less than ten minutes. When would all this end?

A few minutes after they left, Polly walked in. No knocking or cautious yoo-hoos, she came straight in from the back door, through the back room into the hall leading to the kitchen and parlor. Peeking in, she saw I was in the parlor, so she joined me, flopping down on the davenport after throwing her coat at the other end.

"I saw that the Law was up here bothering you."

I nodded. "Now they're asking if Wes or I opened the gate."

Polly's mouth opened wide. "No. No. This isn't right. How can they?"

"We were both outside the house that morning before . . . before you came over. No one can vouch for either of us. When I came over to borrow butter, well, you know how easy it would have been for anyone to open the gate."

"But none of us did," Polly added adamantly. "Just because you don't have an alibi, doesn't mean you're guilty." She put her arm around me. The tables had turned. Polly was now comforting me. This was a strange reversal, indeed.

I took in a deep breath to pull myself together. I needed to ask Polly about Jacob Frond since rumors were still flying about the two of them. I took in a big breath, hating to break this rare moment of intimacy between us, but the task had to be done.

"Polly, I've told you this before. Driving around with Jacob was a big mistake and continuing to be seen with him is, well, incriminating. You're not just making a fool of yourself; you're making yourself a murder suspect. The Sheriff's office is considering all possibilities, and it makes it look like you had a motive for opening that gate."

"Well, I know," she shrugged. "It's simply that Sam once told me that if anything ever happened to him, I should not waste time in finding someone else."

I stiffened my posture and raised my voice.

"No, Polly. No. You can't be seen alone with another man so soon after your husband's death. That's simply wrong. How many times do I have to tell you this?"

"I know. I didn't want to." Her lips pursed tight. "But I felt an obligation to Samuel's memory." She straightened up and looked at me.

"That's just ridiculous." My voice was louder than I intended. "It puts more validity to the claim that you might have opened that gate yourself. People will think that you and Jacob were carrying on and you found an easy way out."

Polly shuddered.

I hated to push my sister like this, but I had to tell her what was on my mind. "This puts Wesley and me in the terrible position of trying to justify your actions. People at church have seen you with Jacob more than once and tongues are wagging behind your back. What if this whole mess were to end in a jury trial?"

Polly shook her head back and forth, unwittingly moving my crocheted afghan around her. Next, she started picking at some of the yellowish stuffing that was poking out of a hole in the davenport. I didn't care about the hole. These days everybody had old, worn-out furniture, and I'd cover it up again after she left. Eventually Polly looked down, realizing what she was doing, and quit picking.

"I'm sorry," she muttered. "I didn't mean to drag you and Wesley into this. I was trying to do what Samuel wanted me to do."

"If he wanted you running around with Jacob this soon after his death, then he was plum crazy." I felt sorry for my sister, but she had to hear this. "You're a suspect and this behavior will land you in the county jail, or worse yet, the Detroit House of Corrections. Do you understand?" I set my eyes firmly on her and repeated slowly and deliberately. "Do you understand?"

Polly sunk her head down to her chest and looked up at me. Her chin was wobbling, actually shaking in a way I'd never seen.

"I understand," she whispered back. "I like riding around with Jacob in his car. It's like riding Ginger. It feels good."

I nodded. "After your marriage, you changed from being carefree with few responsibilities to a married woman with a heavy burden. But Polly, you accepted that responsibility when you said 'I do.' Whether you like it or not, the sheriff thinks you may be responsible for Sam's death. You have to act more like a grieving widow whether you are actually grieving or not."

She nodded, but soon left. Polly frequently ignored my "older sister advice" and it drove me crazy. But gosh darn it, her future was at stake.

Reverend Wesley Johnson

Sunday, April 1, 1934

Today being both Easter and April Fool's Day, I wondered what pranks the Lord had in store. Hopefully something light-hearted and gay. Normally I came to church on Easter Sunday with a heart filled with light and hope. After all, it was Easter with the promise of spring and Christ's message of eternal life. But on this day, to be honest, I felt heavy-hearted.

Too many people had left our congregation penniless. Usually they left in a wagon driven with one or two horses and what remained of their possessions. Each time, I'd gone in early morning and offered a prayer and blessing to the entire family. It was tearful for everyone. Sarah used to send some bread, dried apples, and beef jerky to help sustain them on their journey. Now that our provisions were down to rock bottom, she had sent only a few apples.

Even Junior and Zeke had an understanding of the hard times. The boys used to complain about our meager suppers, often just a slice of bread or a boiled potato eaten an hour or two before bedtime. Their complaints ended a couple of months ago when their friends, Willard and Frank Burnett confided to them that they went to bed without supper. At the same time Sarah discovered that Junior and Zeke were sneaking extra bread into their lunch pails. She knew without asking what they did with the bread. Sarah was so distraught about those poor Burnett boys that she took over two loaves of bread to the family every Friday afternoon when the bread was oven-fresh. That only lasted a month, however, because the family left to head west, uncertain of their destination. It was a hard departure for everyone. Willard and Frank promised to write letters, but of course, none ever came. I continued to pray for that family every night, as well as for all the other families that had departed.

We had an Easter tradition at our church, a sunrise service that started at seven o'clock when it was dark and ended at eight with the sun rising, lighting up our little piece of the world. Twice a year we used candles, Christmas Eve and Easter. At the Easter morning sunrise service the adults picked up the candles and lit them immediately as they came in. Later, when the sun began to stream through the windows, the congregants blew them out. I tried to give an uplifting sermon, one of hope and renewal. Later we ended by filing out to the cemetery. If the weather was mild, I talked about the message of Christ's empty tomb, and gave a closing benediction, followed by a final hymn.

Because it was cold this time of year, usually John Newsom would come early and put some wood in the stove so it was crackling by the time our family arrived. Today there was no sign of John, so the boys and I went back to the wood pile and picked up a few logs and got the fire started. Sarah told the kids that they could stand near the stove until the service was going to begin. She had already lit a candle and was standing at the door ready to welcome people as they arrived.

The truth was that I was behind in a lot of work. Sam's death set off one round of problems after the next. In addition to the sheriff's investigation, I had been questioning whether we could sustain our little church. Our loss of members had not been offset by any influx of newcomers. So far I hadn't heard from the Methodist District about any changes. However, these days, church closings were all too common. It would be devastating to board up the church, particularly for the elderly in the community who couldn't travel easily. I was thinking of Mrs. Daniels, Mr. Fogerty, and Mrs. Dykstra, as well as our next door neighbor, Viola Cross.

Sarah and I had grown fond of our community of worshippers, even those that we both first experienced as cranky or annoying. Jeremy and Josephine Gadstone wanted communion every week rather than once a month. The Torquinis thought we should worship only the first Sunday of the month during the summer and fall because of farming demands. John Douglas wanted his own pew whether or not he showed up. Viola Cross found fault with just about everything, including crying babies and adults who coughed and sneezed.

My parents, staunch Methodists, named me J. Wesley Johnson after John Wesley, the founder of our church. It had been both an honor and a burden to live up to this namesake. John Wesley, who grew up in the Church of England at the beginning of the eighteenth century, was an early abolitionist and a proponent for prison reform, a man ahead of his time. He somehow was able to maintain a solid position within the church while offering many reforms including women taking on leadership roles.

It was hard not to compare myself with this industrious man, and when I did, I always fell short. Sometimes it was difficult finding solace in my job. Instead, I became exhausted thinking about the amount I still needed to do. I went to bed tired and woke up tired. I used to think about Polly and attempted to douse the fire of longing that I had for her. Since Sam died, I prayed for her well-being. Right now, she was simply one more burden heaped onto my plate.

However, in the dark shadows this morning, watching my beautiful wife stand at the door, ready to hand out candles and share her flame, I was strengthened. Observing our children standing around the stove talking among themselves, I knew that I was at the right place at the right time. I felt the radiance of Christ's grace shine on me.

Grabbing more candles, I joined Sarah at the door. The church was beginning to warm up and John and Mabel came rushing in apologizing for their tardiness. John immediately went back to the wood pile and added more wood to get us through the hour. Then Tom Riley and his wife Carrie arrived followed by the Adams, the Vincents, the Delgados, Mrs. Dykstra, Fritz Schneider, and several others. This was my community: my family, my neighbors, my parishioners, my friends. The warmth from the little stove spread out over the congregation and we started our service singing "Christ the Lord is Risen Today."

A strange thing happened midway into my sermon, when light had begun peeping in the windows and people were beginning to blow out their candles. The door opened and in walked a stranger, a man about fifty, appearing down and out. He wore an old, dirty farm jacket with denim pants and a tattered scarf around his neck. I might have thought him a train-riding hobo except for his age and farmer's vesture. I nodded a "welcome" at him and he sat down in the back row.

When we made the procession to the graveyard, I noticed that the stranger had disappeared. Polly was standing at Sam's grave, dry-eyed, wearing a fancy dark green hat with long, sweeping feathers and a dark green veil that covered her face. Sarah told me she had talked Polly out of wearing a pastel Easter bonnet, one with pink, yellow, and light green ribbons on yellow felt. It was a duplicate of the Easter bonnet that she had made for Dorothy. Sarah, herself, was wearing one of Polly's more subdued creations, a small beige hat with a short veil that covered her forehead. We all joined Polly and I gave the benediction before we sang our final hymn, "God Be With You Till We Meet Again." Even though the weather wasn't so cold, I had forgotten to give the "Message of the Empty Tomb." I wondered if anyone had noticed.

We said our good-byes and departed. Halfway home, Bessie looked back at us and quit walking. I'd noticed that she was limping a bit this morning, and I suspected she was going lame. The boys and I jumped out of the buggy and walked home to bring back Polly's workhorse, Jasper. After arriving, I led Bessie out from between the shafts and backed Jasper in, securing the harness to the buggy. Having had a rest, Bessie was able to limp home with the boys. I said a silent prayer thanking God for taking care of my precious family. The April Fool surprises had been bearable.

Samuel Forrest Farm
Marshall Township, Calhoun County, Michigan

Tuesday April 10, 1934

My Dearest Mother,

I need to tell you that since Sam passed away I have gone out riding with Jacob Frond in his Model A. This is not a secret. Sam had told me not to waste time if anything ever happened to him. But, as Sarah has mentioned to me repeatedly, this wasn't a good idea. Jacob came over last night to tell me that he's a suspect in Sam's death. They think Jacob opened the gate to Black Devil's pen—well, you can figure out the rest. But it's simply not true. Jacob was nowhere near this farm any time before Sam's death. Never, ever.

Oh Mother, Jacob was so upset. It wrenched my heart seeing him so unnerved. Being accused of murder is not something anyone takes lightly and Jacob is so sweet and sensitive. He asked me to tell Sheriff Conlin that we hadn't been having an affair. I hadn't seen Jacob since high school until Sam's funeral, so of course, I will defend Jacob, but it's so horrible that I have to broach the subject with the sheriff.

I told Jacob that I understood his concern because Sheriff Conlin seems to consider me a suspect as well. Mother, how horrible this situation has become! Here I am at age twenty and widowed, soon to lose Sam's farm, and they think I killed him. Why in heaven's name would I kill my beloved husband whom I relied on for my livelihood?

Jacob and I will no longer see each other. He cannot be a suspect. No. No. No. He's such a nice young man, and I'm in agony that I brought him into this horrible mess. I now know that Sam's plan to keep me safe and happy was not intended for these times of hardship. Sustaining this farm will be a difficult financial battle—one that I will likely lose. I had hoped that Jacob might be able to farm some of the land and give me a cut of the proceeds. That is never going to happen. Jacob and I said our farewells last night. He says that if he loses his job at the gravel pit, he's going to head west, maybe to Colorado. That's why he hasn't sold his Model A. I wish him well whatever he does. He was kind to me, yet there have been so many repercussions.

Tomorrow I will meet with the bank and see exactly, down to the penny, how much I need to pay the mortgage. I'm afraid I'll find out we have very little in the account. Now I wish we hadn't taken that wedding trip to Kalamazoo, even if it was only for two nights. Sam wanted me to have a good time and I did, but I'm not sure we could afford it.

I'm glad that you're thinking about coming in May.

Your loving daughter,
Polly

Sarah Wolcott Johnson

Thursday, April 12, 1934

"What's wrong?" Wes asked. "You were screaming. A nightmare?"

I rolled over and faced the window trying to wake up, but it was totally dark, and I had no idea of the time. I listened for early morning sounds. No roosters were crowing and there was no early morning birdsong. It wasn't time to get up. Chilled, I pulled up the feather duvet. April was such a fickle month, sometimes warm, sometimes winter cold.

"You were screaming," Wes repeated.

"Yes," I answered. "A horrible nightmare. I was visiting Polly in jail and she was begging for forgiveness. She was crying, screaming, and banging her head against a stone wall. Her hair was a mess and she was skin and bones."

"Come here," Wes murmured and pulled me over to his side. I nestled into his warmth until I heard him snoring. Then I rolled over to my side of the bed and tossed and turned, not able to get rid of the horrible vision. Finally, I sat up, grabbed a candle from my nightstand, lit it, and proceeded downstairs to make a cup of hot tea. With only about a half-cup of tea leaves remaining in the jar, it was admittedly, self-indulgent. Even though Wes had kindly proclaimed I could have the remaining tea, I felt guilty about taking even a few leaves.

While waiting for the water to heat up, I looked out the kitchen window into the darkness. For a moment I thought I saw a moving light down near Polly's barn but it quickly went dark. Was my mind playing tricks? The teakettle began to whistle and I ran over to pick it up before the noise woke Wes and the children. After making the tea, I went back to the window. I thought I saw flickering from a window high up in the haymow. Although the tea was satisfying, my candle was burnt down to the quick, so I went back upstairs to another fitful sleep.

I was actually happy when I heard the first roosters crowing their wake-up song. Usually I was not quite ready to get up and would just as soon have some extra time to sleep. I rolled over and noticed that Wes was waking up, as usual, just before first light.

"Wes, last night I thought I saw a light down near Sam's barn. In the middle of the night."

Wes had lit his bedside candle. "Oh, you dreamed it," he answered, stretching out his arms and legs. "You woke me up and told me about a nightmare. Besides, you can't see Sam's barn from this window."

"No, this wasn't a dream. I couldn't sleep and had gone to the kitchen to make tea, and was waiting for the water to heat, when I saw it from the kitchen window."

"You sure?"

"Yes. It happened quickly; the first time was outside the barn, and the second time I saw a flickering up in the haymow."

He sat up in bed and threw his legs over the side.

"This morning I need to load up some silage from Sam's, so I'll take a look around and see if anything's missing."

"I'm afraid if I mention it to Polly, it might scare her."

Wes started getting dressed. "I'd talk to her anyway. Maybe she'd want to sleep up here. Any thief could be snooping around their barn. Or a vagrant might be trying to find a place to sleep. Sam's death wasn't exactly a secret. You definitely should suggest she sleep up here."

"Where would she sleep? The only place for her is in Dorothy's bed, and she wets through her triple diapers every night."

Wes had no answer to my question.

At noontime dinner, Wes reported seeing nothing missing from Sam's barn. He questioned whether I might have imagined the lights. However, I knew that I hadn't. It troubled me that vagrants or train riders might have been out there looking for a place to sleep. I wished the church had enough money to give meals to these down-and-out men, but all of us were needing so much more than what we had.

I started peeling potatoes right after dinner to get a head start on supper. Actually, I was doing it to relax. I had done this chore so often that I could peel potatoes in my sleep. I might even save the water and use it to make potato bread. It was funny, people often thought that potato bread was made with just potatoes, not understanding that it was both mashed potatoes and the broth that the potatoes were cooked in that made the bread so light and flavorful.

Potato "peeling," as people around here call it, (not "paring" as Mother taught us) was conducive to daydreaming. I'd been troubled about whether I should share any of my nightmares or worries with Mother if she came in May. No, I decided, I wouldn't tell Mother about my musings. What I was really afraid was that my nightmare could be a precursor of horrible things to come. The nightmare was so unnerving.

Once again, Polly was in the spotlight, but I was the one suffering. This went way back. As a child Polly would throw a temper tantrum until Mother caved in and gave her what she wanted. The first incident I remembered Polly throwing a fit was when she refused to go to bed one Saturday night. Mother and Father had invited the Thompsons over and Polly demanded that she be permitted to stay up and watch them play cards. Her outrageous behavior worked and she was allowed to stay up, even though I was eleven years older and had to go to bed.

Another time Polly insisted on keeping Clover, a kitten that a boy at church had unexpectedly given her, but Mother said no. Polly screamed and cried until Mother relented. Of course, Clover had several "accidents" in the house and Mother and I always cleaned them up, never Polly.

Polly quickly learned to throw tantrums in order to get her way. Mother simply couldn't handle the screaming. Even back then I knew that she was reinforcing Polly's unseemly behavior. However, if I opened my mouth, Mother pointed out to me that I was a jealous older sister.

I believed the conniption fit about Clover kitten was soon after Father and John had died. They had gone up to Garfield Lake on an icy cold January day with the intention of bringing back large chunks of ice for our little icehouse in the backyard. Both ended up drowning in the freezing cold water. No one knew what really happened. Mother suspected that John fell in and Father died trying to save him.

Polly had begged and begged to go along that day, but Father would not relent. That probably saved her life.

I was fifteen and Polly was four when the tragic event occurred. Mother never told Polly how obnoxious she'd been that day, thinking it would be too much stress for a young child to handle. So Polly never heard about her horrible behavior. I'd always wondered if Father's mind had been distracted at the lake, wondering about his spoiled younger daughter.

After Father and John died, Polly was raised by Mother, Jack, and me, with Mother frequently saddling me with babysitting responsibilities. Jack wasn't around much. Right out of high school he had started working with the town blacksmith for a pittance as an apprentice. It was a skill that was dying out, but no one knew it then. Everyone assumed that cars were a passing fad for the wealthy. Better-paying jobs being more plentiful than they were now, Jack soon nabbed a job at the Foundry, where he earned a lot more money and he gave a hefty portion to Mother each week. His job turned out to be a huge mistake. Within two years he had contracted a lung disease and experienced terrible breathing fits and no appetite. One quiet night, with little fanfare, Jack died in his sleep. You could imagine the guilt Mother and I both felt.

Thinking back, it wasn't surprising that Polly became spoiled. Mother was despondent beyond belief having lost her husband and both of her boys. She'd frequently run over to my grandparents next door to cry her eyes out. Sometimes she'd stay there for hours while Polly and I were in school. In the evening Mother had no energy to deal with her forceful, opinionated, younger daughter.

Naturally, I helped Mother with all the house and garden chores, but we depended on Grandma and Grandpa Blessing next door. They helped out with our expenses, until, after a couple of years, Mother started a dress-making and tailoring business. I thought the sewing helped her cope. Soon she was making money and socializing with her customers. People came by all the time either dropping off or picking up sewing items and it forced Mother to put on a happy face, whether she felt it or not.

During my senior year in high school, my good friend Caroline introduced Wes and me. His parents had moved from Rockford, Illinois to Marshall, moving into the house next door to Caroline. At that time Wes was already attending seminary in Chicago, a six-hour train ride from Marshall. My heart skipped a beat when he told me that he'd asked to be assigned to a church in Marshall to be near his parents. Of course, I had fantasies about being a preacher's wife. Some of them, I admit, were self-aggrandizing, where I was the model wife, model mother, and perfect church lady. But I did have high standards and now the people in our little country church looked up to me.

While Wesley was studying for the ministry, he would ride the train from Chicago to Marshall for holidays, ostensibly to spend time with his parents. But they knew I was the magnet pulling Wes from the big city. We were madly in love, no doubt about it. The fact that he would be a minister intensified my desire to follow a straight and narrow path. That included helping Mother and guiding Polly in the right direction. Even so, she was a spoiled, whiny child. It was about that time the Blessing grandparents moved to Connecticut to help out with my great-grandmother.

Before they left, I had a long talk with both of my grandparents. They each indicated that with their departure to Connecticut, Mother would have to depend on me for strength. Polly was too young to help Mother with her sorrow, and I was the one with maturity and resolve. Therefore, I committed to being Mother's pillar of strength. I finished high school, got a job at Miller's Grocery, and waited for Wes.

Life had those circles. My grandparents left for Connecticut to care for her parents, just like Mother left last September to take care of Grandma Blessing. Mother never mentioned it, but I knew she wanted to stay in Michigan near us. She'd suffered such overwhelming losses; she once told me that she couldn't bear to lose Polly or me. Being so far away in New England she wouldn't be here in case of emergencies. Her letters revealed her wistful, dark inner feelings. I was sure it was not her intention, but sometimes it was impossible for her to hide behind pen and paper.

I had been trying to convey to Mother in my correspondence how much I needed to have some private time with her during her upcoming visit. So far, she hadn't replied to any of my requests. I'd have to carve the time out of her schedule once she arrived.

"Sarah, Sarah, are you here?" Polly interrupted my reverie as she stepped in the kitchen. Dorothy was napping and the boys had another couple of hours before returning from school. This was my special time for myself; and truth be told, I wasn't too happy about seeing Polly.

"I'm in the kitchen peeling potatoes," I answered. "Come in.

Polly sat across from me at the table looking as fresh as springtime. She was wearing a new lavender dress that she'd been working on for a couple of weeks. It was beautifully detailed with pearl-white buttons down the front and lace around the collar. I wondered if she'd created a matching hat. Her new outfit was a far cry from how she appeared in my dream and I wondered where she got the money for the fabric and accessories.

"I want to start a hat shop," Polly announced. This came straight out of the blue.

"Where?" I asked, looking up from the potato peelings.

"Marshall, of course." She smiled like her dream had come true.

"Polly, get ahold of yourself. First, you're being investigated by the sheriff's office regarding your husband's death. Do you really think anyone would want to buy hats from you?" I said a silent prayer and decided not to share my nightmare with her. I was afraid she'd storm out of the house. "And second, who has enough money to buy hats right now?"

Polly was rarely one to be discouraged, so her response took me by surprise.

"The sheriff's investigation will blow over. Everyone knows it was an accident. But you're right about no one being able to buy hats, even if they fall in love with mine." She sighed and I felt a pang of her disappointment spilling over on me. Sisters, I thought. I could see so many of her flaws, yet I hated seeing her give up so quickly.

"Why don't you make a few hats and ask Cecilia at Sallin's Dry Goods if they can put them scattered around the store? Or maybe you could make hats for millinery shops in cities like Kalamazoo and Lansing. Have you thought about that?"

Polly shook her head. "That's a good idea. I do worry that if I opened a shop in Marshall, no one would come in and buy anything. Anyway, I need to get some materials before I make anything else. I've used up all my supplies making two hats to give to Mother when she comes."

I quit potato peeling for a moment. "I've already given you all my old hats. I wish I had more for you."

"It's not only hats; I also need feathers, ribbons, lace, and netting for veils."

"Polly, I understand you may not like big sister advice, but I need to say this anyway. Wait until the sheriff's investigation is over before you start anything. You don't want to be seen as someone who's glad her husband is gone so she can open a hat shop. You must pretend you're in mourning, even if you're not."

I expected Polly to protest, telling me how much she loved Samuel, like she had done in the past. But she didn't. Instead she nodded.

"Oh, and one other thing . . . I think I saw a light near your barn in the middle of the night. I was looking from our kitchen window." I tried to sound casual.

She looked puzzled. "Did you see who it was?"

"No, it was so dark and the light was so quick. I saw it for a second, then it went out. Later I thought I saw flickering from the haymow. If you'd like I could ask Wes to put a lock on your back door."

Polly frowned. "Maybe. But I don't want to lock myself out."

"He could put in a deadbolt, so that you have to be inside to lock it. You could lock it at night before you go to bed."

"Hmm, that's a good idea. Please ask him to do that."

"You might want to sleep up here on the sofa for a night or two as well."

"Aunt Polly, Aunt Polly." Dorothy waltzed in and interrupted the conversation. "Me wanna ride Ginger. Horsey-ride. Horsey-ride."

Polly brightened up. "Maybe."

"How about it, Sarah?"

Frankly I was happy to have the extra time by myself. They departed together and I watched from the kitchen window as they bounced down the hill to Polly's house.

About a half-hour later, Polly and Dorothy were brushing Ginger. From the kitchen window I could see Polly showing Dorothy how to give Ginger a sugar cube, one that she had made by cutting up hardened sugar. No one bought sugar cubes for animals or any other reason. It was too costly.

However, seeing Dorothy feed the sugar to Ginger under Polly's guidance was a welcoming vision since I continued to be haunted by the nightmare of Prison Polly.

Finally, in the evening after all three children were in bed asleep, I again mentioned the nightmare to Wes. We were in the parlor, both of us with our Bibles on our laps. I explained how I'd been unable to keep the dream from interfering with my thoughts all day long.

"Wes, I don't know what I should share with Mother during her visit. My concern about Polly is not that she's guilty of any wrongdoing, but the rest of the world thinks she is."

"Well, our dreams are usually more about the dreamer than the subject of the dream," Wes answered. "In seminary, we talked about this a few times. Joseph had many dreams which sustained him after he had been sold into slavery in Egypt, but Joseph's dreams involved sheaves and brothers bowing down to him. It was about him maintaining his dignity and his aspirations during a difficult time."

He paused and I kept waiting for more enlightenment from him, but there was nothing forthcoming.

"Is this nightmare more about me than Polly?" I placed the Bible back on the stand, not wanting to read any more.

"Well, you certainly are envisioning the worst outcome. Polly in jail, skin and bones, beating her head against the wall. That certainly isn't the Polly I knew when we first met. That little girl was a force to be reckoned with. What's changed?"

I couldn't answer that question. Polly certainly had survived the death of our father and two brothers and hadn't gone mad. Instead, she found love at age nineteen, a respectable age to marry. She got married only a couple of weeks after her twentieth birthday.

What had changed was Polly's deferential position towards Sam. She would never admit her frequent bruises and broken bones were anything but the result of her own clumsiness. Polly had always been a smart girl. After a few bruises she would have been more careful. But the accidents continued, as did Sam's complaints about Polly's attempts to poison him. Black Devil had intervened and I wondered if anyone had assisted the bull with his ravaging attack on Sam. The sheriff seemed to believe so.

Reverend Wesley Johnson

Wednesday, April 18, 1934

This morning, as I rambled to the barn for the early morning milking, I looked to the east at the fields I would soon be plowing. Separated by lanes and stone fences, they featured a wide assortment of shades of misty green. In the foreground, one of the meadows I'd used last year for cattle grazing was sprinkled with clover, creating a pinkish-lavender hue peeking through the early morning fog. God's handiwork was so evident in the colorful display. I made a mental note to suggest to Polly to get out her sketchbook and capture the serene beauty displayed in the eastern landscape with its dozens, perhaps, hundreds of shades of light green in the early morning hours. Yes, I had tried and tried to get Polly out of my mind, with no success.

By the time we'd all finished breakfast, the colors were different, brighter, less misty. I had often marveled how quickly nature's beauty appeared, then instantly disappeared. Rainbows, shooting stars, lightning. We must stop and savor them, because if we didn't, we'd miss them altogether. Same with children. Little Dorothy was close to leaving her baby days behind. I wasn't eager for the next phase, but I accepted God's will in the ever-changing landscape of our family.

As I started my second round of chores for the morning, Junior and Zeke were beating the parlor rugs that Sarah had strung over the clothesline. I could see the dust coming out as they swatted them with rug-beaters. This was the boys' favorite spring cleaning chore and Sarah owned a pair of old rug-beaters so each boy had his own. After they'd finished, Sarah would give them a ball and they'd pretend the beaters were tennis rackets. Sometimes their energy seemed boundless.

Once again, Dorothy was down at Polly's. I think they were good for each other. Dorothy distracted Polly from the sheriff's investigation and Dorothy loved having Polly's full attention, something she rarely got from either Sarah or me. Dorothy's favorite activity was saddling up Ginger and going for a walk in the yard. Even Sarah, who was a critical, ever-so cautious mother, mentioned how careful Polly was when taking care of Dorothy.

Sarah was taking advantage of child-free time to clean and air out the upstairs bedrooms. She reminded me that we needed to take off the storm windows and replace them with screens. That was a half-day job involving ladders; I supposed we'd need to do Polly's as well, turning it into a full-day job. In a weird way it was feeling like things were getting back to normal after so many weeks of sheriff interrogations. Even though my farming responsibilities would increase, I had to say I welcomed spring and summer wholeheartedly.

To my surprise John Newsom dropped by this afternoon, visibly nervous. I immediately invited him into the little room where I wrote sermons. It only had room for two chairs and a tiny writing table. Dorothy named it "Daddy's Dollhouse" since it was so tiny. I called it my sermon-writing room and the children were usually not allowed in. John's demeanor suggested that he wanted to speak to me in private, so I shut the door.

"Whaddya know?" I asked, trying to lighten the mood.

"Not much. . . I have to . . .tell you. . .somethin'," he stuttered.

I sat silently and nodded for him to continue.

"Someone's been taking wood from the pile at church."

"Oh, don't worry about that," I answered. "I put a lot in the stove before you arrived on Easter Sunday and I may have done so last week as well."

John shook his head. "No, I'd been thinkin' for a few weeks that we'd been using too much, so I started keeping track and it seemed like it was going missing way too fast. So, after church on Sunday, I deliberately pulled a couple of small logs off to the side. Sure 'nuf yesterday when I drove by to check, they'd gone missing, along with several big ones. Someone's stealing our wood."

John and I sat there in silence. Anyone in the church needing firewood could simply have asked for some. Also, most farms backed up to at least a couple of acres of forest, a ready supply of firewood. Who would be taking it? All the neighbors along Cornfield Road attended our church, except the Caccinis, who went to St. Mary's Catholic Church in town and they owned at least forty acres of wooded land. No one in the neighborhood needed to steal firewood. The thief must have been someone from town. But why drive a car or buggy all the way out here? Surely there would be a closer place to pilfer firewood.

"What do you think is happening?"

"I think someone's sleeping in the church at night," he answered. "There's not much traffic on Cornfield Road after dark. We farmers are ready to hit the sack as soon as we've had supper. Anyone could take down the boards we have on the doors. Then they could put 'em back up in the morning before anyone sees what's goin' on."

"Why do you think that?"

"Cuz I saw him boarding the door up this mornin'," John replied. "I couldn't sleep so I got up early and told Mabel I was going out for a constitutional. It'd been weighing on my mind for a few weeks now—the woodpile goin' down so fast. Also, the matches are close to gone."

"Who was it?" I asked, keeping my voice quiet in case it was a church member.

"I think it was that guy that came into church on Easter Sunday and sat in the back row. It was still kinda dark this morning when he was putting the boards back on the door with his back to me, so I cain't say for one-hundred percent, but it looked like him. Same kind of jacket and pants."

"Hmm, did he see you?"

"Nah, I skedaddled. I wasn't about to start a commotion with Mabel having no idea where I was. I just turned round and headed home."

"I wonder what he does during the day? It's hard to believe he has a job wearing the same clothes every day."

"I was wonderin' the same thing," John replied. "Where does he get food? He could get water from just about anybody's well, as long as a dog don't start barkin'."

"Let's both go over tonight," I suggested. "Not with the idea of throwing him out, but to hear his story."

I harnessed up both Jasper and Bessie to the buggy and picked up John right before sunset. Bessie was doing much better and acted as though she wanted to get out. When I walked in their pen, she lifted her head and whinnied, like always. She was a tough one, that Bessie.

We parked the buggy out by the road so the stranger wouldn't hear us. Both Jasper and Bessie were used to waiting at church, so they were quiet. Sure enough, we could smell the wood burning. It wafted over our heads, a pleasant fragrance like ham baking in the oven.

"Must be burning hickory," John whispered. I nodded in agreement.

We both walked up to the church door and I knocked. "This is Pastor Wesley Johnson, checking to make sure you're okay. Just wanted to talk to you." I opened the door about an inch and peeked in. A shadow of a man was lying down on the floor near the stove. He sat up, squinting his eyes.

I walked in, followed by John right behind me. John left the door open to allow some of the waning sunlight to flow in. We both strode up near the stove and sat side by side in the nearest pew. The grimy, disheveled man slowly got up off the floor and hefted himself in the pew across the aisle from us. My first impression was of a man who hadn't bathed in weeks, reeking of body odor so foul that even the hickory smoke wasn't able to cover it up. I could see that he'd been lying on Sarah's cushions taken from the back benches. The man's jacket and pants were marked with grime and dirt marks covered his face. His gray hair was matted and overgrown down to his shoulders and his beard was desperately in need of trimming. We all stared at each other in silence.

Finally, John spoke up. "Charlie, it's Charlie, right? I hardly recognize you. It looks like you fell on hard times."

"I'm sorry," the man answered, his head slumping down in front of him. "I was cold and needed a place to sleep. I need to find my Ma and Pa. I cain't find my parents."

John took over the conversation as we heard the man's story, broken and punctuated with pleas for his parents. I surmised that Charlie had been a farm hand who traveled from farm to farm, living with whoever needed extra help. John knew him from neighborhood gatherings, although he'd never hired Charlie for any jobs. Charlie would sleep in an extra bedroom, or if need be, in a hayloft during the summer. In late fall he'd always leave Michigan and go to Florida where there were jobs picking citrus fruit. But this year he just couldn't scrape up enough cash to make it to Florida. He spent his days foraging in the forest for food and had stumbled upon the church with its wood stove for nighttime warmth. It seemed as if the winter had taken a toll on his mental capacity or, perhaps, he'd always been slow.

"Charlie, we'll see if we can find your parents tomorrow, and let you sleep here now." John ended the conversation.

"We'll come back at sunrise with some food for you," I added. "Don't leave until we bring you some breakfast."

"Much obliged."

John and I made our way to the buggy, jumped in, and headed towards John's place. "Do you think his parents are alive? He seems a bit long of tooth himself."

"Don't know. I'll do some checking tomorrow."

The next morning Charlie gobbled down his bread and butter, thanking us profusely for the food.

"Where do your parents live?" I asked. "Are they in Marshall or Battle Creek?"

"No, they lived off near Detroit, but they both passed away several years ago."

John and I shared furtive glances.

"Last night you said you wanted to find your parents."

"I get confused at night. I get scared, too."

"Well, now that the weather is warming up, I bet you could sleep in my barn," John said. "You might be able to help out with some chores, too."

Charlie's face brightened and a smile appeared.

I said a little prayer of gratitude for my friend John. I hoped Mabel would be okay with this arrangement. Charlie sorely needed a bath and his clothes washed. Hopefully this would work out until we found a safe place for him.

Samuel Forrest Farm
Marshall Township, Calhoun County, Michigan

Thursday, April 19, 1934

My Dearest Mother,

Sarah and I are both so happy that you're coming the first two weeks in May. We'll walk down to the woods along the bridle trail, have lots of picnics, knit, crochet, and, of course, sketch and paint. Oh, I do hope I can find my sketching pad and water colors up in our attic. I checked this morning where I thought they should be, but alas, they weren't there. Wesley had suggested to me a particular landscape of fields for watercolors, and I'm saddened I couldn't find my painting supplies. When I moved here after the wedding, the attic was crowded with so much of Samuel's stuff that I didn't look at much of it, not wanting to go through any remnants of his first marriage.

Back then I thought I could buy anything, Samuel having his own farm and means. It seemed like his pockets were lined with money. But the sad reality is that I am as broke as everybody else. I can neither afford to buy a new sketch pad nor water colors. These days no one can afford anything that isn't food or farm supplies.

You asked how I am doing. I miss Samuel so much and most days I feel an ache in my stomach. Several times a day I look out toward the barn longing to see him come up the lane, either bringing Jasper up from plowing, or coming back from sowing oats, or bringing the cows up for their evening milking. Sam and I were so much in love. He was the kindest, dearest husband a girl could have. Now I recognize I was fortunate to have him as a husband, if only for a few months. I learned so much from him—how to be patient, kind, and generous to a fault.

Sam, too, was a cautious man. That's why he asked me to watch the yard in case the cattle got out. For many months I thought it was silly, but now I understand. The Lechmans, a family who lost their farm a couple of weeks ago, couldn't recover after their beef steers were rustled from the field that borders Smith Road. They never did find the thieves. I don't know why Sheriff Conlin is spending so much time investigating Sam's death when there are cattle thieves at large.

You asked me if I had heard back from Sam's brother, Mitchell. No, not yet. I do have a wonderful collection of condolence letters from cousins Ruth and Addie, as well as from our old neighbors on Elm Street, Mrs. Hanford and her two daughters, Irene and Belle. Those little girls wrote the sweetest letters.

Mother, going to church without Sam is so hard for me. I have so little energy that I don't want to get out of bed in the morning, particularly on chilly days. It seems like so much effort to wash up, get dressed, and find something to eat. But I must. I force myself to get up because the chickens depend on me. They're hungry. Thankfully I was able to sell the cows and pigs to Tom Riley who lives about five miles away and goes to our church. I practically gave them away, but they needed more care than I could give them. As part of the deal, Tom and Margaret Riley are giving me butter and cheese every week. They were happy to get the extra livestock. Any leftover butter goes straight to Sarah. I don't know if it's like this in Connecticut, but around here nothing goes to waste. Not a drop of milk, a grain of sugar, a teaspoon of flour.

The sheriff's investigations are exhausting. I used to want to go to town with Sam, to get out of the house and sit by his side in the buggy, but now it's simply too much bother to gather up all the tack to harness and hitch up Ginger. For a few Sundays I couldn't do it and just stayed home from church. Sarah, however, told me that is unacceptable, particularly since it makes me look guilty. So, I've taken to walking up to Sarah's on Sunday morning and riding with them. It's crowded, so Dorothy sits on my lap along with the boys in the back of the buggy; I love having her wiggly little body, squirming and yet pressing tight against me. Unfortunately, I'm a bit rumpled by the time we get to church.

I find myself alternating between crying and feeling excited that you're coming. Please don't change your mind. During this gray spell, you're my one ray of light. Sam loved me so much and I miss him dearly. I simply cannot abide the fact I will never again look out the window and see him repairing the fence or building a trellis.

Mother, I must tell you this because there are people in the neighborhood and church who think I'm happy to be released from my "older" husband and want to find someone much younger. First, Sam was forty-one. Of course, that's significantly older than me, but he wasn't sixty or eighty. There were many advantages to being married to Sam. His maturity inspired me. He spent time thinking about the future and providing for me. We both wanted to start a family. He frequently mentioned a tree that would be good for a tire swing or a portion of the pond for summer swimming or winter ice skating. We talked about converting the rooms upstairs into children's bedrooms.

So Mother, dear, let's count the days until you're here with Sarah and me. I will mark each day off the calendar until you arrive.

Love,
Polly

Sarah Wolcott Johnson

Friday, April 20, 1934

Once again I woke up with a bad feeling. First, that god-awful nightmare and now, this feeling of impending danger with premonitions of Polly facing frightening situations. As Wesley had often said, I have an anxious and nervous personality, and all of Polly's problems seemed to be feeding into it. Ironically she'd been telling me that she'd been sleeping fine. But I didn't think I'd had one uninterrupted hour of sleep for a week. I'd been trying to take naps with Dorothy to restore my energy.

Today's weather matched my mood: cold, gray, and drizzling rain. Right after breakfast I looked down at Polly's farm and saw the sheriff's car parked out by the toolshed. Dorothy was awake and running around our house, so I was distracted with her until I looked out and saw Polly walking with Deputy Bylowski, headed to his car. Oh, how I wished we had a car. I could have jumped in it and driven to their driveway blocking their access to the road. No way could I do that with a horse and buggy, even if Bessie were already harnessed up.

Instead, I grabbed Dorothy so hard she squealed out. Then picking her up close to my chest, I ran down the hill, yelling out to them. They both looked up and waited for me.

"What's happening?" I asked breathlessly as we approached.

"I'm taking your sister down to the office for more questioning," Deputy Bylowski answered.

"No," I responded. "Don't do that. People will think she's being arrested. There's already so much gossip going around. It's a favorite topic of Mrs. Cross."

"Your sister already agreed to go."

"It's okay." Polly spoke slowly and calmly. "It'll be good to get out of the house, and I need to clear things up with Deputy B." Her comment suggested a tone of familiarity that was not appropriate.

Bylowski's face turned beet red. I looked back at Polly who was waiting patiently. A lavender hair ribbon matched her new lavender flour-sack dress and she looked amazingly pretty with her perfect blond hair, blue eyes, and flawless skin. It never failed to amaze me how we shared the same parents, yet a stranger would never recognize us as sisters. I also made a mental note that no new bruises had appeared since Sam's death.

"Okay," I answered, placing Dorothy on the wet ground. "Go answer the questions. If I don't see you tomorrow, come over for breakfast before church on Sunday." That was my way of ensuring she'd get to church. I yanked Dorothy's hand and we raced up the hill to our own house. But I couldn't help looking back and seeing Zeb Bylowski helping Polly into the passenger side of the car. In my mind's eye, I could see Polly flashing her widest, prettiest smile at him. Once again I was feeling helpless as my little sister was digging her own grave. Flirting with the sheriff's deputy. This was a new low.

I decided to make a stop at the privy before Dorothy and I went back inside, instructing her to do her business like a big girl.

"Big girls don't wear diapers. Only babies do."

"Me wanna be baby."

"No, you need to be a big girl now."

"No. No. No." She defiantly pulled at her diapers and ran to the house with the soggy cloth around her knees.

⁓

The weather, so miserably cold and wet, necessitated the boys playing inside after they arrived home from school. They started with a loud game of hide and seek, resulting in much running, yelling, and commotion. Dorothy joined in the game after one of the boys hid under her bed and woke her up. With all this going on, I hadn't been able to tell Wes about Polly's new escapade with Deputy Bylowski. The rain finally let up, and the boys decided to go play in the haymow and, at my suggestion, Dorothy started a quiet, pretend tea party with her doll, Josephine.

"No, you big girl," Dorothy admonished her doll. "You bad girl. Bad girl."

"Be nice to Josephine," I said.

I had already alerted Wes that I needed to talk to him. He caught my eye and we went into our bedroom and shut the door.

"It's Polly again," I muttered. "She was flirting with Zeb Bylowski."

Wes groaned and shook his head in astonishment. "First Jacob and now this. You had your big sister talk with her, correct?"

"Yes, in no uncertain terms. But Wes, she doesn't listen! I'm so glad Mother doesn't know about any of this. I don't know how much to tell her when she visits in May."

Wesley nodded but said nothing.

"Something else doesn't add up. Polly is overly careful with Dorothy whenever she takes care of her. She may be more protective than I am. But Polly has had so many broken bones and bruises because of her self-admitted carelessness."

Wes squirmed around uncomfortably and finally spoke. "All those accidents and injuries? Do you think they really happened? Could Sam have been so two-faced that he actually hurt her and then brought her to church on Sundays as if nothing had happened? That could make a young wife want to hurt her husband."

"Wes, I don't know. She's adamant that he has never touched her in an uncaring way. I want to believe her, but it's hard." I drew a breath to calm myself. "No, I don't believe her."

"I don't either," Wes agreed.

Reverend Wesley Johnson

Tuesday, April 24, 1934

Ever since Polly sold her cattle, I'd been getting silage from Sam's farm two or three times a week. Polly offered it to me as a favor for helping her out, as she no longer had need for it. So far, I'd kept the boys away because when the silo was more than half-full, you had to access it from the exterior ladder. It was a long hike up to the top and it wasn't a safe place for young boys to be horsing around. Now that the silo was down to about a third capacity, it was accessible from a door inside the barn with a short ladder up from the manger.

Around sixty feet high in total, the silo was made of concrete slabs with metal staves around the sides reinforcing its solid structure. The dome-shaped metal roof had a rooster weathervane atop it, the highest point on the farm. At the top of the exterior ladder was a window opening, about four feet square that I'd been using to get into the structure.

This silo was built against the side of the barn for ease and convenience, with the barn feedlot at the base. All Sam had to do was pitch the silage down to the manger and the cattle could come eat. For me it was different since I needed to haul the silage back to my barn. I used two wheelbarrows near the manger to catch the silage, taking home the contents of six wheelbarrows in the wagon every few days.

Today I took Junior and Zeke with me to help since they'd gotten home from school early. I showed them how to go through the milk house to the barn and over to the feedlot, and then climb the six-foot ladder to the door. Before they jumped in, I warned them that their feet would sink down several inches into the moist, stinky silage. Sarah had wisely told them to wear overshoes.

The first thing the boys did was to hoot and holler, enjoying the strong echo inside the canister-like cavern. "Hip, Hip, Hooray," yelled Junior as I took the large pitchfork and shoveled silage out the opening and down to the wheelbarrow. "Hip, Hip, Hooray," the echo circled back.

"Hooray, Hip, Hip," responded Zeke. The sounds continued to reverberate.

The boys ran around hollering and listening to the echoes for several minutes as I pitched silage down the opening to the wheelbarrow below.

"What are those things up at the top?" Junior asked me. I looked toward where he was pointing, but I couldn't see very well, it being dark up there.

"Those square things on the wall," Junior clarified, and I saw what he was pointing at.

"Oh, I don't know. Maybe to reinforce the wall up there." I turned back to my pitchfork.

"Hallelujah," was the new echo. "Hallelujah, hallelujah, hallelujah," fell down from the walls and roof.

"You should get a choir to sing in here," Junior yelled to me. "In here, In here, In here."

"What is this silage made of? Made of? Made of?" asked Zeke.

"Cut up cornstalks, alfalfa, and clover. The cattle love it. Love it. Love it."

"Well, it stinks to high heaven. High heaven. High heaven."

The boys started playing Blind Man's Bluff.

"Blindman, Blindman."

"Blindman, Blindman."

By now the wheelbarrow was full.

I interrupted the game. "Okay, Junior, go down and move our wheelbarrow out of the way, then push Uncle Sam's underneath." Junior exited, scurried down the short ladder to the barn's interior, switched wheelbarrows, climbed back up, jumped through the door, and resumed the game. I loved the energy of youth.

"Blindman, Blindman."

"Blindman, Blindman."

Soon the second wheelbarrow was filled. I needed to go empty both of them into the wagon before refilling them.

I climbed down to the barn floor and wheeled the first one out to the wagon, followed by the second. Bessie was looking sickly again, and I immediately wished I'd harnessed Jasper instead. I made a promise to myself that this job would be Bessie's last, even if she rallied, as she had a couple of weeks ago. She had served us well over the years and now that Polly had given us Sam's workhorse Jasper, Bessie could enjoy herself in the meadow. I took my time pitching the silage from the wheelbarrows into the wagon and gave old Bessie some tender strokes.

When I re-entered the barn with the empty wheelbarrows, I heard Junior calling me for help. With my heart racing, I climbed up the ladder to the open door and leapt into the silo. Zeke was lying prone, head down in the fetid silage while Junior was screaming and pulling at his brother. I hoisted up Zeke's small limp body and rushed down the ladder, through the barn and milk house out to the grassy yard, positioning him on his back. Junior followed right behind, white-faced.

I was praying every second that elapsed. I was sure it was only a few seconds that Zeke was unconscious, but I was unimaginably terrified. To have this boy's life at risk shook me to the core.

I put my hand on Zeke's chest and could feel the rise and fall of his breath. For reassurance, I put my hand on his temple to feel his pulse. It took a minute for Zeke to come to, coughing and gagging. In a moment he sat up, but immediately bent over vomiting. Once finished, his eyes watered and he started crying. I rolled him on his side so if he started to vomit again, there was less chance of him choking.

"I dared him a penny to stick his face right down into the silage," sobbed Junior. "I didn't know it would hurt him."

"You can't do that because the gasses can kill you. Silage is fermenting, rotting, and it creates poison gas. Never put your head in silage, ever."

Zeke continued to choke and cry and I pulled him close and placed his head in my lap while he sobbed.

"Zeke, can you talk?" Junior asked his brother.

"Yeah, I don't want that penny," Zeke answered, pulling himself up, his color returning.

I decided to give the boys the rundown on other silo hazards.

"Silage made from cornstalks, alfalfa, clover, and other green grasses will make poison gas. Never put your head down in the silage like Zeke did and never stay in the silo for more than a half-hour. If you need to be in the silo, then go out for a few minutes and come back in and finish up your work." They both nodded.

"Also, if you store wheat or oats in a silo, you have to be careful because it pulls you right down to the bottom and you could suffocate. It's like quicksand. You can't stand on top of grain when it's in a silo nor when it's in a wagon. It sucks you down and you can't get back out, no matter how strong you are."

I looked at both Junior and Zeke whose eyes were open wide, terrified.

"Always be careful if you go into a silo. I shouldn't have left you there alone."

They nodded.

"Are you gonna tell Mother about Zeke?"

"We don't have to. She gets scared enough about you two running around both farms as it is."

Junior looked relieved. He seemed much more worried than Zeke, who sat up and began to pet Sailor Dog. Polly's large black and white Collie had wandered over to Zeke when he was crying, and now was lying belly up, encouraging Zeke to scratch him. As he rubbed the dog's belly, Zeke started chattering away, his usual self. All three of us coddled and played with Sailor Dog until I looked toward the sun and realized it was getting late.

After instructing the boys to stay there on the grass, I quickly filled up the two wheelbarrows again. As an extra safety precaution before we left, I nailed up the interior door to the silo so the boys wouldn't be able to open it. I used the same type of U-shaped staples that Sam had used on the small window at the top of the exterior ladder. With the staples in place neither Zeke nor Junior would have the strength to pull them out.

We returned home and the boys started target practice with their BB guns, one more farm hazard. I let them do it since I planned to teach them how to hunt deer in the fall. I gave them one more lesson in gun safety and, not surprisingly, the two boys followed my instructions to a T.

Samuel Forrest Farm
Marshall Township, Calhoun County, Michigan

Tuesday, April 24, 1934

My Dearest Mother,

This will be my last letter before your visit. You can't imagine how excited I am to have you here staying with me. We'll have a jolly time visiting Sarah and her family and we'll go to Wesley's church services, just like old times. I'll introduce you to my new friends, Ruth Shaw and Millicent Jordan who've been so good to me since Samuel's death.

The warm spring weather will be so welcome and you'll see the tulips that I planted last fall along the meandering path to the hen house. My daffodils are in bloom now, so they will be gone, but I can see the iris buds coming out and the red poppies sneaking up. The spirea bushes under the kitchen windows should be in full bloom so we can make some beautiful bouquets to take up to the cemetery.

However, dearest Mother, I must warn you about the hoopla that is still rampant after the unfortunate demise of my dear husband. You must arrive with the understanding that you'll take my lead and develop a thick skin regarding the endless interrogations. The sheriff's office has been relentless in their continual questions, and to my utter amazement, they still consider me a suspect. Also, anyone around me, including Sarah, Wes, and Jacob are suspects. It's so absurd that I wonder if dear little Dorothy, toddling around in her fat triple diaper, will be next on their list. Haven't they heard of farm accidents? Accidents occur every day and murder is the farthest thing from anyone's mind.

Mother, I await your visit.

Love,
Polly

P.S. Please bring all the letters I've written to you since you've been in Connecticut. If I have to go to trial I will need evidence about my marriage.

Sarah Wolcott Johnson

As Dorothy and I sat in the parlor mending clothes, I could hear the rain splattering against the windows. Why did it have to rain today? I instinctively knew that Polly and Mother would be late coming over. Polly wouldn't want to walk in the rain, so of course she would deprive me of time with Mother. I made a silent vow to myself that I wouldn't get mad at Polly this morning. My goal was to make Mother's stay as pleasant as possible, particularly since we wouldn't be going into town or picnicking as originally planned. In fact, I wasn't sure what we'd do if it continued to rain.

So far Mother's visit had consisted of her spending time with Polly, punctuated with coming over here for meals. Polly had some lame excuse that her cookstove wasn't working quite right, but it was so like Polly to shirk any responsibility. Mother, in turn, had enabled this behavior saying that Polly needed extra time with her. Well, she was my mother, too, and I craved some special, personal time with her.

Glancing out the window, I saw that the sky was getting darker and darker, so I lit the kerosene lamp.

"I think it'll be a while before they come because of the storm," I told Dorothy. "Let's see how many clothes we can get patched."

"Okay, Mommy."

Dorothy's job was to hand me shears, thread, and fabric patches when I needed them. I'd chosen the hardest job first:

a pair of Wes's overalls that had holes in three places and needed strong denim patches. Fortunately, I had plenty of denim patching material and was already working on the third patch.

Dorothy's constant companion, her doll Josephine, was on the floor next to the sewing materials. She was teaching the doll how to mend clothes between my requests. "Hand me shears," she demanded of her doll. "I want blue thread. No, no, no, that's wrong," she scolded Josephine. "Pay attention. You bad girl. Shame on you."

Then she started spanking the doll. "Bad girl. Bad girl," she shouted, as she struck her doll's backside with both hands. Then to my astonishment, Dorothy got up and jumped up and down on her doll and started kicking her.

I looked at my daughter in horror. How could she transform a peaceful mother-daughter activity into this abomination? Had I been too hard on Dorothy during the ongoing potty training? Once she turned three I was determined to be done with diapers. Maybe I'd been too harsh with her.

"Dorothy, Dorothy," I cried. "You're hurting Josephine. You don't want to hurt your doll."

"Yes, I do," she snapped back. "She bad girl. She need spanking."

Sure, Wes and I spanked our kids now and then, but only when they were naughty or doing something dangerous. We were never cruel and never had a gentle spanking ever resulted in a bruise. Dorothy's interpretation was way beyond the pale. How I wished Wes were here. I wasn't sure how to handle the situation, but I picked up Josephine and said, "It's okay, we know that you were doing your best. It's okay. It's okay, Josephine."

"Hello, hello," I heard Mother and Polly in the back room. I groaned. Such bad timing.

"We're in the parlor; come on in," I responded, and Dorothy ran out to greet them. I wondered if my daughter had absorbed anything I'd said. "We left our coats and umbrellas in the back room," Polly sang out, sounding disgustingly cheerful.

I jumped up and gave Mother a big hug.

"So what are we doing today?" Polly asked, as she flopped into my rocking chair, where I'd been sitting and had all the mending piled on the floor.

"I'd like to sit there since I'm mending," I said to her. Polly got up and moved as far away from me as possible, to the end of the davenport across the room. Mother, in the meantime, had plopped down in the overstuffed chair across from me.

"Well, we're here at ten o'clock just like you wanted," Polly announced. "What are we doing today?" She repeated her question then turned to Dorothy. "Dorothy come here and sit on my lap." Dorothy bounded over to her and jumped in her lap like a silly puppy.

"Had the weather been nice, we were going to town and then have a picnic, down at the fountain. But since it's raining pitchforks and hammer handles, I suggest you both help out with the mending."

Mother reached down and picked up Zeke's shirt. "How 'bout this?" she asked.

"Fine," I said. "He's only got two shirts and he's wearing the other one today. I'll thread a needle for you."

Mother picked up some patching material, then grabbed the shears off the floor, and cut out a patch and inserted it inside the shirt again with a couple of pins. I handed her the threaded needle and she began a clean overstitch around the patch. Mother always had neat, precise stitches.

"How about you take this one, Polly." I got out of my chair and handed Dorothy's old wrinkled, brown gingham dress to Polly.

"Are you kidding?" Polly answered. "First, this thing isn't worth saving, and second, why are we wasting Mother's precious time doing your work?"

I looked at her in disbelief.

Polly held the dress up in front of my daughter. "You don't even like it, do you, Dorothy?"

"Quit egging her on," I exclaimed. "Shame on you for making fun of her dress."

"I wasn't making fun of it. I just don't think Dorothy likes it. Do you Dorothy?"

Dorothy, smacking her lips together, moved her head slowly and deliberately side to side.

"Can't you see, you're trying to make Dorothy into a fussy, ornery little version of yourself?" Forgetting what I was doing, I accidentally poked my needle into my thumb, and a pop of blood appeared.

Glancing at Mother to back me up, I saw that her eyes remained on her sewing.

Polly shot me a piercing glance. "I don't know what you're getting at, but I would think you'd be happy if she became a little version of me. A creative girl who wants to look nice and takes pride in her appearance."

"I take pride in my appearance," I shot back as I wrapped my handkerchief around my bloody thumb. "But have you noticed there's a Depression? No one has money for new clothes. Everyone has patched up clothes and that includes Dorothy."

"Girls, girls, settle down," Mother urged, finally looking at me.

"No, I won't," I answered. "Polly, you come over to my house and immediately start a fight. Shame on you. Shame on you."

Polly's face froze with a scowl.

"Mother, this is what I was telling you about Sarah. She always treats me like I'm four years old. She blames me for Father's and John's deaths. She never quit blaming me and she's always shaming me. Shaming me for what? Being alive at age four?"

"Now, now," Mother responded, but Polly paid no attention.

I answered. "Well, perhaps you should take the blame. Maybe you deserve some shame. You were acting so badly at home that day, yelling and screaming, begging Father to take you to the lake. Probably Father needed to spank you and was so distracted when he got to the lake that he cracked the ice and fell into the lake right after John."

"Sarah, please," Mother interjected.

"No, it's about time she knew the truth." I turned to Polly. "You had behaved badly all that morning. I suspect you didn't even care that Father and John drowned. You continued on with your nasty flare-ups, even at their funeral. You ruined the rest of my childhood, being selfish, throwing one temper tantrum after another."

"Mother," Polly shouted back. "Tell her I was merely a four-year-old acting as any child would."

Mother said nothing.

"Mother," Polly shouted again. "Tell her I was acting like any small child would."

"I'm sorry, Polly," Mother responded. "You were a handful. You had a huge outburst that morning. Sarah's right about your behavior, but no one knows what occurred out at the lake and no one blames you."

Polly turned her head from Mother to me. She wadded up the little brown dress around the sewing shears and threw it at me. I dodged it, as it fell to the floor.

"Come on, Mother," she shouted out. "We're going home and going to do something fun. Maybe we'll go to town if the rain lets up. Until then, we'll play rummy or bake some cookies."

Mother looked uncertainly at both Polly and me.

"Come on, Mother," Polly said impatiently. "I need you."

Slowly Mother got up, placed the half-patched shirt neatly on her seat and walked out with Polly.

"Sarah, you shouldn't blame her," Mother muttered to me as she left.

Reverend Wesley Johnson

Saturday, May 12, 1934

Warm sunshine poured over our farm this morning when Mother Wolcott walked over from Polly's to help Sarah manage the picnic, today's family activity. I knew that Sarah and Polly had been on the outs, but I hadn't even asked why, figuring it was one of those sisterly things that frequently came up between them. I was pleased that they'd settled it and were back to planning activities together again before Mother Wolcott left.

Today we were going to have a picnic under the maple tree in our side yard. Sarah and I had moved a table from the back room to underneath the tree and the boys were carrying chairs. After completing a list of chores Sarah had asked me to do, I harnessed up Jasper to go over to Polly's to bring back yet another wagon full of silage for the cows. Frankly, Sarah and I would have been in serious trouble without Polly's generosity. Our supply of hay was nearly gone, and the little we had left needed to be saved for Jasper. The taste of the milk was a bit different with the cows eating all that silage, but it didn't take long to get used to it.

Unexpectedly Polly ran out from her house when she saw me coming up the drive. I pulled Jasper and the wagon to a halt, and jumped down to say hello.

"Can you come in the house and look at the cookstove?" she implored.

"Sure, what's wrong?"

"It gets way too smoky and everything I make tastes like smoke. It's so bad my eyes burn every time I use it. Even when I only want to heat up the tea kettle."

We walked through the small back room and I noticed that the only items in the room were a couple of hats and coats hanging on hooks. No gardening items. No Ball jars for summer canning. No laundry supplies. No jars of popcorn kernels. It looked like Polly was making no provisions for her future, although I knew she had a garden out back. In fact, I had plowed, cultivated, and even planted most of it.

In contrast, last week Sarah had reorganized our back room into a frenzy of kitchen tools, gardening tools, and washing supplies. She'd had the boys help her put everything in order, all set for when she needed it. The boys could identify a coffee grinder, a food mill, and the ice cream churn, even though they'd never used any of them.

Walking into the kitchen, I turned my attention to Polly's wood stove, an old, black boxy apparatus, with raised letters *Quaker Social*. "When was the last time you used it?" I didn't want to be sticking my arm into red hot metal.

"Oh, not for a couple of days," Polly answered.

"You fasting?" I grinned at her.

Polly flashed her prettiest smile at me, the one that always melted my heart. "No, with Mother here, we've been eating over at your house, so she can spend every minute with the children. Haven't you noticed?"

I nodded. "I'll take a look, here."

I opened the firebox on the left. Lots of ashes remained from her last use. Next I opened the ash bin, which was overflowing.

"First thing we do is get all these ashes out and then we'll look for the problem." She quickly came up with a galvanized bucket and I pulled the bin out and dumped the ashes.

"Where do you control the flue?"

She looked at me confused.

"The air control," I clarified.

"I don't think there is one."

I looked at a couple of dials at the back of the stove top. "Looks like this is it," I answered. It seemed to be closed.

"Oh, I thought that controlled the amount of heat," she answered. "I turned it off last week when the weather got warm."

"No, it has nothing to do with that. When you're cooking, you need to open it up totally so that the smoke goes up the flue. That may be the problem, but it may be something else. Show me how you make your fire."

She picked up an old newspaper and threw it into the fire bin, then put several pieces of wood on top of it, and pulled out a match.

"No, don't light it yet," I warned. "You need to lift up the kindling, so the paper can burn under it. Otherwise it'll smolder." I propped up the kindling and then asked her to light it underneath.

"We'll see how much smoke we get now."

"No smoke so far."

Polly brought over a pot with some eggs in it and put it on the burner that was directly above the fire. "I'm going to make deviled eggs for the picnic," she explained.

"Having the flue opens makes a huge difference," I chided her.

Once again she flashed me her prettiest smile. But then Polly came close and wrapped her arms around me. "You're so wonderful; I couldn't survive without your help."

I held my breath, not moving. Polly didn't let go.

Suddenly I felt my lips against hers and all thoughts abandoned me; I felt only an overwhelming desire for her. Nothing else. There was no past nor future, only the present as she pressed her body against mine. I was melting into a deep abyss and I was inundated, unable to pull away. My body was on fire, my breathing rapid as I was swept into pure desire. Her body was taut against mine and I could feel her breasts pushing into my chest. I was in a trance, one beyond my control.

I would like to say that I ended it right then. That I woke up from my trance, broke away from her and left her house.

However, mesmerized in those heated moments for far too long, we shared kisses, deep and long and passionate. My mind vanished, leaving me in the moment of delicious longing. My heart pushed against hers, beating in unison. All self-control was eradicated.

Polly, however, pulled away, bringing me back to the bright light of day in her kitchen, the window open for the world to see, the repaired cookstove behind us.

"We can't ever do this again," she whispered.

"No, we can't," I murmured as I guided her closer, for another kiss.

"No," she uttered more decisively, jerking away. "Never. That's final."

"I could leave Sarah. We could be married in the church."

"No, Wesley. You have a family."

"You and I could raise the kids. You already spend more time with Dorothy than Sarah does."

"Wes, no. You need to leave now."

"But Polly. . . ."

"You should leave now." She walked to the door, adjusting her hair.

"I'll leave, but my heart is with you." I got up and turned to the door.

"Thank you for fixing the stove and I'm so sorry." She had tears running down her face. I guess she blamed herself.

Sarah Wolcott Johnson

Monday, May 14, 1934

Mother had been visiting for almost two weeks now and during her entire stay I'd been trying to carve out some private time with her. Instead, I'd spent my days preparing meals for everyone, while Mother played with the children. Until yesterday, Polly and Mother showed up daily at mealtimes, Polly saying her stove was on the fritz, apologizing for not bringing anything.

After our altercation on that rainy Tuesday, I'd kept all my concerns about Polly to myself, but Mother needed to know. Finally, today, only one day before she was scheduled to leave for her return to Connecticut, Mother came up for our special visit. Wes was plowing an addition to the garden, the boys were in school, and Dorothy was over at Polly's "helping" her with her housework.

Mother sat at the kitchen table while the sun streamed in from the east window. I was in the middle of breadmaking. I decided to broach the subject that I'd avoided during her visit.

"It's been two weeks and I didn't get a chance to talk to you in private until today." I looked seriously at my mother while I kneaded the dough on a breadboard, which I'd placed on the table across from her. Normally I stood and kneaded the bread dough on the counter, but today I wanted to sit face to face. "I've been trying to talk to you since you arrived, but to no avail."

"I haven't been avoiding you," Mother replied. "Polly may have been monopolizing my time, but since she is so recently widowed, I thought I should spend my time with her. Also, you have no idea how much I enjoy being with my grandchildren; it's a special time that won't last forever. I've loved all of our walks, picnics, and trips to town. And, you have to admit, Dorothy has been so proud of her potty training—I spent a lot of time getting her to this point. I'm leaving you with a much lighter laundry basket." My mother smiled at me, much like she had done for years when I pointed out Polly's selfish tendencies.

"Yes, and I appreciate that," I said. I caught her eye. "I think it's good that Polly knows the truth about her temper tantrums and the lake deaths. She's always said that I've blamed her, but of course, I didn't. However, she was a holy terror that day. She has no idea what an ill-behaved child she was that day."

"She was four years old being a four-year-old."

"You have no memory of her tantrums that day?"

"Of course I do. But you had temper flare-ups at that age and Dorothy will too."

After Dorothy's treatment of her doll last week, I didn't consider her a virtuous three-year-old. She had potential for some gigantic conniption fits in the upcoming year.

"Children need discipline. Polly was never disciplined after Father's and John's deaths."

Mother shook her head, but said nothing more.

I continued. "You have no idea how appalling Polly's behavior has been since Samuel passed."

"She's struggling, dear."

"Struggling or not, please, please suggest to Polly that she lead the quiet life of a grieving widow before she gets thrown in jail. I've had such terrible nightmares about her. Even my daytime hours are fraught with nervous worries."

"Sarah, you'd best focus on raising your own children and let Polly be."

"But the sheriff won't let her be."

"It won't last forever."

"It's dragging on for a long, long time."

"It'll all work out in the end. God will take care of Polly."

"But Mother, you're blind to the circumstances. Polly is in serious trouble with the law. The sheriff doesn't believe Sam's death was an accident. You have no idea how many times he and his deputy have questioned her. This week while you were over at Polly's, they came here and questioned Wes and me one more time." I tried to keep my voice level and calm.

She simply nodded.

"And who were those two strange men who were talking to Polly on Friday?" I asked. "I thought I knew everyone from the sheriff's office. I saw them pull into her driveway Friday afternoon."

"She introduced them as Mr. Blackwell and Mr. Smith, if I remember correctly, but I was upstairs reading most of the time, so I really don't know."

"What did they want?" I persisted.

"It wasn't my business."

"How long did they stay?"

"About an hour, plus they walked out to the barnyard."

"So, it was about Sam's death?" I couldn't believe Mother's lack of curiosity.

She shrugged. "Could be. I don't know."

"Probably insurance investigators. Last week she hinted that Sam left a policy."

I pounded the bread dough back and forth on the table. Finally, I stood up to make a point.

"You have no idea how outrageously Polly has been behaving in the wake of Sam's death. While I know she would never intentionally do anything to harm Sam, I wonder about her wild nature, rambunctious attitude, and capacity to forget things." (I'd rehearsed this little speech for a few days.)

"If you had come for a visit while Sam was alive," I continued, "you'd have seen some terrible bruises all over her arms and legs. She said they were from various accidents."

At long last Mother looked up at me. "Are you suggesting that Samuel hit her?"

"Beat her up is a more accurate description."

I grabbed the bread dough and slammed it down into the large bowl. Then I covered it with a wet dish towel, my eyes watering. I found myself sobbing.

"Mother, you haven't been here to witness everything that Polly's been involved in. We are in these horrible times and people around us are losing their jobs and their farms. Wes and I can barely scrape by. Every week the collection plate yields less and less. Last week it was thirty cents and, had they not been donated, the roof and outhouse repair supplies would have cost five dollars. Polly keeps harping on not being able to make her mortgage. Well, we may not be able to make ours either. Yet our kids keep growing, needing bigger clothes, bigger shoes, and more food. When is it going to end?" I sat back down, laying my head down on the table, my body shaking.

"It will end when it ends," Mother spoke up. "God is testing us. We must be strong. Remember that our family has always been challenged. A hundred years ago Grandma Blessing's parents arrived in this country penniless, not knowing a single soul. They struggled to survive. PawPaw worked in a hot, stinky shoe factory to earn enough to live in a tenement. MawMaw was home with eight kids to raise in a tiny three-room apartment in New York City. One of those rooms was a kitchen so tiny only one person could be in it at a time. Think about that. The living room was also the dining room and bedroom for six of the kids. MawMaw and PawPaw slept in the other room with the two youngest kids. They had to walk down six flights of stairs to go to the communal outhouse.

"You and Wes have friends and family. Right now, you have a roof over your head and you have food in your pantry.

I understand the situation could change and your pantry could be empty. Have you asked the church members for help?"

I nodded. "We're all helping each other. Wes has told the congregation over and over to keep coming to church even if they have to pass an empty collection plate. Every week we have an exchange after church. I've been giving Dorothy's outgrown clothes to Sally Adams who has a girl a year younger than Dorothy. Junior and Zeke are about the same size so I'm handing down their pants to Martha Vincent. Shoes are a big problem and I've been putting cardboard in their soles, just like I do for Wes and me. But soon their feet will be too big for their shoes and I'll be giving them away." I tried to collect my breath. "Nothing, Mother, nothing goes into the burn barrel anymore. There's no reward for all this penny-pinching. We all get poorer and poorer. Our family could end up in bread lines like everyone else."

"But you're making bread today. With the butter that Polly got from Mr. Riley, we'll have a delicious treat."

When did Mother become such a pie-eyed optimist? Maybe living with Grandma Blessing was making her addled. Sure, we'd have bread and butter, but what Mother didn't understand was the lack of meat and vegetables.

The only food that remained in our cellar was last fall's potatoes and I was having to sort them daily, throwing out the rotten ones, and splitting up the good ones into two piles. One for eating and one for spring planting. Most of them had already sprouted, so the decision was easy. For planting I would cut up most of them into quarters, leaving an eye or two in each section. When we moved to this farm I'd learned to plant the cut side down. In fact, we'd be doing this in just a couple of days.

I looked out the window and could see Wes plowing the garden with Jasper leaning into his collar. Polly had been generous to give us Jasper; I wasn't forgetting her good qualities. But undoubtedly Polly would be eating much of the bounty of our garden over the next year. I turned to Mother to give her our latest news.

"Last night our sweet horse Bessie died. I cried for hours. She was like a dear friend who served us faithfully for all ten years of our marriage. How much more can we endure?" My eyes watered up again, thinking about our gentle Bessie.

"You'll endure what you must. I see Wes plowing your garden. What a joy that will be for the children to raise their own food."

Mother didn't understand that a huge garden was a whole family affair, not the kids raising watermelons for a treat. She'd never grown more than a few tomatoes and cabbage. Perhaps that amount of working in the ground was a joy for her. But our half-acre garden required weeks and weeks of sweat, toil, and aching muscles. Even Junior and Zeke complained about their sore arms after hours of hoeing onions.

But I decided I needed to be more positive for Mother and began to tell her about the apple orchard, which in many ways, was less of a burden than the garden.

"God willing, there will be a bountiful apple harvest in the fall. It depends on the amount of rainfall over the summer. Last year our crop was so big that we kept the boys out of school to help. They were able to pick the low hanging ones, sort out the wormy ones, and carry the peck baskets. This year they may be able to jointly carry a bushel basket. But again, it depends on the rain. The older varieties tend to produce every other year, instead of yearly."

Just then Polly appeared in the doorway. "Ready to come and pack for your trip back tomorrow?" she queried Mother.

"I suppose so."

"I'll bring up some asparagus for supper. What else are we having?" Polly asked.

"We'll also bring some potato salad and baked beans," Mother added. I guessed she had understood at least part of my concerns about Polly.

Reverend Wesley Johnson

Wednesday, May 23, 1934

Struggling to find the right words for this Sunday's sermon, I sat back in the chair in my tiny study, looking at the blank sheet of paper in front of me. Empty save for one word in the top right corner: optimism. Seemed like every Sunday I used the same theme. But how many ways could you deliver the same sermon week after week?

The house was quiet, but I could hear sounds from outside. In the distance I discerned a whirring noise. A few years ago the county had bought three road graders, big noisy vehicles that roared as they came close; however, they did a great job of smoothing out our potted gravel roads. Sarah hated when they went by, because they kicked up a lot of dirt that created a dust film over all the furniture and floors. I figured the grader I heard might be on Gorsline Road, about two miles away. Was this distraction something I could use in a sermon? I couldn't connect it to optimism in any logical fashion. Then I heard our back door open and shut.

"Hello, I've brought Dorothy back." Polly's voice sounded cheerful, coming from the next room. I walked into the kitchen where Polly was pouring Dorothy a glass of milk.

"I'm missing Mother already and she only left yesterday." I could tell she was avoiding my eyes. Our interactions had been awkward, almost like we were making amends after an unpleasant fight instead of an intimate interlude.

My guilt had kicked in ten-fold. I was so angry with myself for those weak but wonderful moments. How I wished I'd been strong enough to turn my back and walk out Polly's door. Was God testing me once again? If so, I'd failed miserably.

Bringing myself back to the present, I commented, "Sarah's still at Sally's house with the church knitting circle." I leaned over and gave Dorothy a kiss. "What did you do with Aunt Polly?"

"We look for treasure," Dorothy answered. "I find smelly stuff."

"The smelly stuff is a bottle of perfume that Sam gave me for Christmas," Polly chimed in. "Dorothy and I both put some behind our ears."

I leaned over and smelled Dorothy's left ear. "Oh, you smell so good, just like a princess." She grinned from ear to ear.

"We told each other some stories and later went out to the barn to look for Goldie Cat, but we never found her," Polly said. "So, we played fetch with Sailor Dog and took a nap."

Polly got up to leave, giving Dorothy a kiss.

"Thanks, Polly. She has such a good time with you."

Polly nodded and quickly took her leave.

While my guilt was palpable, Polly wasn't forthcoming about her feelings. I knew I needed to get beyond the awkward pauses.

I looked down at Dorothy. "Okay, girl, let's go write a sermon," I said, picking up Dorothy and carrying her into my little study. Instead of jumping on my lap, Dorothy sat on the floor and started whimpering.

"What's wrong?"

"Me bad girl."

"No, you're not. You're a good girl."

She was crying softly and pulled out a folded piece of paper from her pinafore pocket and handed it to me.

"What's this?"

"Treasure. I stealed treasure."

"You took it from Aunt Polly?" I asked. "Did she know you took it?" I already knew the answer as she pursed her lips and shook her head.

I unfolded it and started reading. Dorothy lay on the floor whimpering.

Dear Polly,

I'm trying to write this with better penmanship than usual. You know that wasn't my best school subject. If you've found this in your bloomers drawer that means I've died. I told you before we were married I'd been fearful of the stomach cancer curse that took pa and grandpa. It's a horrible disease with no cure and years of suffering. A couple of years ago I had a little pain but not bad. But this year around Thanksgiving the pain got fierce. So I took to going to the barn to be alone. I kept hoping it would go away.

This letter is to give you instructions because I want what's best for you.

My death can't be judged a suicide or homicide. No one knows about my dreadful illness and you wouldn't be able to collect on either of the life insurance policies if it was either of those. You may get accused of poisoning me. Remember my joking about your cooking and how it'd poison me. Don't ever mention that to anyone. Don't worry. I won't leave bottles or anything behind.

Right away find someone young to court and be seen in many places with him. People need to watch you. Make it look like you didn't take our marriage seriously and now you are going to enjoy yourself. Then people won't be thinking about suicide. Instead, they'll wonder about your motives, but you'll quickly clear yourself and suicide will be long forgotten.

Don't pay the mortgage. With these depressed times, you won't be able to eke a living from the farm. You want it to look like I left you without a cent. Rich young widows get hit by thieves and money-hungry male suitors. Make it look like you're struggling. You should have enough money in the Marshall Savings Bank to live for about a year. The garden should produce enough food to allow you several more months if the foreclosure is slow. I doubt if you'll be able to find anyone to rent the land, but try.

Then cash in the life insurance policies. One's from a company in Boston and the other's from New York. The papers are in the top drawer of the roll top desk near the farm deed. The insurance companies will probably send investigators. Answer all their questions without extra information. When the checks come in the mail, take them to the Lansing Savings Bank and place them in a savings account. It's a long train ride to Lansing, but you don't want the folks in Marshall or Battle Creek knowing about your money. Then don't spend any of the money for at least a year. Two years is better. You don't want to open any cans of worms if the pretty widow suddenly has lots of money.

Then you can move to San Francisco and start that hat shop.

Love,
Samuel

P.S. Burn this letter. You can't have anyone find it.

PART 2

Polly Wolcott Forrest

Thursday, May 24, 1934

From the first time he hit me, I was scared of Sam. He said he beat me because I deserved it, and I believed him. The more he hit me, the more I tried to behave differently. I quit asking for money. I tried to make better meals, getting recipes from Sarah and other church women. But his appetite for my food waned, no matter what I made. He might come in from the barn, angry for some unknown reason, and slug me in the face. Most of the time, he'd hit me in the torso, so the telltale bruises wouldn't appear above my collar.

Sam, my husband, who vowed to love, comfort, and honor me, turned out to have the cruelest heart. I had no idea of the extent of his violent nature before our wedding. I'd only been around kind, benevolent men like Father and Wes, and had no context for his extreme brutality. Post-wedding Sam was a far cry from pre-wedding Sam. His last kind gesture was buying me Ginger as a wedding gift. After September 8th, Sam turned into a barbarian, torturing and tormenting me for no good reason.

His excuses were rampant. You forgot to wash my overalls. You spent too much time at your sister's house. You don't know how to make a decent pot roast. You wasted too much water on your bath. It was humiliating, and I wanted to be a good wife. Sam went to church with me, but all the way home he would poke fun of Wesley. Then we'd go over to their house and eat their food. I'd go home seething with anger, getting painful headaches that no amount of aspirin powder would relieve.

Most nights I'd go to bed late, after Sam was asleep. I'd crawl into my side of the bed and wait to hear his snoring. Then I'd silently cry myself to sleep. On the nights when sleep wouldn't come, I'd try to figure out how to run away. But as if reading my thoughts, Sam would threaten me. *Don't even think of leaving. If you ever run away, I'll find you, and that'll be the end of you. I won't be crying at your funeral.*

I wanted to reclaim my life on Elm Street, when I was the prettiest girl in my class, and I could have the pick of all the boys. Back then life was fun. Now I longed for pretty new clothes and time for reading, sketching, and baking sweets. Farm life was tediously uncreative, and ending up with such a cruel monster was antithetical to anything I'd ever desired.

Then, one day, after hearing a few agonizing cries from the barnyard, it was all over. At first I couldn't believe my good fortune. Sam was dead and I was free. But my tearful nights continued. I continued to be wary, worried about what was around the corner. My reflexes that caused me to flinch with pain still kicked in. All those ugly habits remained.

I guessed my feelings had labels: guilt, shame, sorrow. But instead of being honest, I continued the falsehoods. I simply couldn't admit to the world, particularly Sarah and Mother, that I'd been wrong. I chose the wrong man. I wanted someone like Wesley. Wesley who was smart, articulate, and admired by all. Wesley who inflamed my passion. Wesley, the man who was wed to my sister.

During this dreary winter when Sam wouldn't allow me to leave the house, Sailor Dog and Ginger became my closest friends. Farm dogs slept in the outbuildings to protect everything on the farm, so I only saw Sailor Dog when I was outside. But I put his food and water dishes on the back stoop, which was convenient for me, and since I was the person who fed him, he adored me. He'd roam around the farm all day guarding the buildings and livestock. When I was out in the yard, he'd come running up, jumping and giving me kisses, sniffing for a treat in my pocket.

Sam, of course, limited the amount of time I could ride Ginger, but since his death, I'd taken her out daily, going down the country roads, letting Ginger set the speed, often at a gallop down the straight part of Cornfield Road. Of course, I knew that rumors were flying. I'd see Viola Cross in her window watching me ride by. Sometimes she'd have the telephone receiver up to her ear, shaking her head as if she were describing me as a strumpet.

This morning I looked around the farm, assessing what I'd need to endure this life a few more weeks until my name was cleared in the sheriff's investigation. I might go to Paris and visit millinery shops, observing all the latest styles in women's hats. Then I'd purchase enough supplies to get my own shop started, probably in San Francisco. I'd seen pictures of the city in magazines. Of course, I couldn't share any of this dream with Sarah who thought I was far too worldly already.

Mother's visit went well, except for Sarah's provocations. I thought I was able to convince Mother that Sam was a good husband. I wasn't sure why I wanted to keep up the charade. Perhaps because Sarah had been so persnickety and self-righteous. At least Mother remembered to bring the letters I'd written to her since September in case I ever needed them to defend myself. It gave me chills when I thought I could be put on trial for Sam's murder. Even in his death, Sam haunted me.

I hated lying to my mother, but both she and Sarah belonged to the "I told you so" club. It was not that I didn't harbor some doubts about Sam. I did. Something didn't feel quite right, even when we were courting. But Sam lavished me with gifts and the vision of becoming a lady of leisure had much appeal. What a stark contrast to the reality my life would become after our wedding.

⌇⌇⌇

After collecting the eggs this morning, I figured that Sarah and Wes would soon be appearing at my door. They would have read the letter and stewed about it for several hours. I sat down at the kitchen table, nibbling oatmeal cookies that I'd made yesterday with Dorothy. Not unexpectedly, the knock came immediately and with intensity. Four long, hard thumps.

At the door Wes cleared his throat. "We need to talk to you."

I wondered if he, too, was thinking about last week here in my kitchen: our intimate embrace, the long kisses, the unencumbered passion. But right now he seemed a bit awkward, almost school-boyish in his approach. I also wondered if Sarah had any suspicions—if she noticed any changes in Wesley or me.

I asked Sarah and Wes to come in and led them through the back room, where they tossed their jackets onto hooks, and we proceeded to the kitchen table. I took my place in front of the little plate that held only a few cookie crumbs.

"I wish I had coffee to offer you."

Both nodded. Everyone in the neighborhood had run out of coffee, and no one had the means to buy more. Of course I did, but revealing my financial situation would be at odds with the sheriff's investigation, and these days any jury would be unsympathetic to a wealthy, young widow accused of killing her husband. Hopefully it wouldn't come to that, but I had to be careful.

Without fanfare Wesley pulled out "The Letter."

"Yesterday Dorothy had this stuffed in her pinafore pocket."

I grabbed the letter and produced the biggest smile I could muster.

"How I've worried that this piece of paper had gotten into the wrong hands! I was so afraid that Sheriff Conlin or those two insurance investigators from Boston, Mr. Blackwell and Mr. Smith, had found it." I paused a second. "Did Dorothy take this out of my treasure box?"

Sarah and Wes both nodded.

"What happened yesterday?" Sarah glowered.

"I showed Dorothy my treasure box, that big round hat box that Aunt Millie had given Mother. It has pink and red roses on it—a perfect box for keepsakes. Do you remember it?"

Sarah nodded, but continued to frown.

I decided to give a lengthy description of my time with Dorothy. "Dorothy and I played a game with it. She shut her eyes and pulled out one item at a time, trying to guess what it was. First she drew out a linen handkerchief that Aunt Millie had made me; it has bluebirds embroidered in the center and blue tatting around the edges. I've favored it since way back when I was Dorothy's age. Do you remember that handkerchief?"

Sarah nodded again. "Keep going. You can omit the details."

"Well, Dorothy pulled out a rolled-up set of drawings Sam had created for me. He was such a good artist. We looked at the drawings, mainly of things on the farm, one of the red barn and tall silo, another of the horse tank with the willow tree bending over it, a cardinal perched on one of the branches, and then, my favorite, Ginger grazing out in the meadow, down the lane, near the lilac bush. Do you want to see them?" I was deliberately adding details that would irritate Sarah. I seemed to have a talent for getting under her skin and it often gave me pleasure.

With grim faces Wes and Sarah both shook their heads. "As I said you can omit the details."

"I believe she pulled out the perfume next. There were other things in the box, but we quit the game to make cookies. She didn't pull out the letter, and it wasn't until later in the evening when I was rearranging the hat box that I noticed the letter was missing. I had no idea how long it had been gone. I was afraid someone had broken into the house and taken it."

What I didn't say to Sarah and Wes was that Dorothy had indeed pulled out the letter, and I told her I might give it to her someday. I said it was a treasure map, revealing candy and toys, all hidden near her house. Dorothy had watched as I had opened the red flowered hat box and placed the letter on top, then left the box on the floor near the old walnut armoire, its lid askew.

No, I didn't tell Sarah and Wes that I'd left Dorothy alone in my bedroom for her afternoon nap. Later, when the cookies were baking I looked to see if the letter was missing. Sure enough, it was gone and there was a bulge in the pocket of Dorothy's pink pinafore.

Sarah was sitting rigid in the kitchen chair, while Wes was hunched over the table on his elbows, his chin resting in his hands. Neither said a word. They were both waiting for my comments about the letter.

I let them wait another long minute before I broke the silence. "So now you know Sam's plan and why I rode around with Jacob, and why the sheriff's investigation needs to end."

"Yes, but is this really what you want to do?" Wes asked. "Sam was clearly taking advantage of the insurance rules, if not the law."

Sarah sat there with a straight face and nodded.

"He did it out of love."

"Polly," Sarah squirmed in her seat, "Wes and I were up almost the entire night talking about this. We believe you should reconsider whether you want to follow through with Sam's instructions. You're a good person, but your actions have been deceptive and self-serving." Sarah was reacting exactly as I expected: pompous and self-righteous, the preacher's wife to the end.

"His death was not intentional," I muttered. "Sam would never choose to tangle with Black Devil. I was scared of him and Sam was ever so cautious around him, always. That's not something Sam would do. It was an accident."

Sarah stared at me, her eyes glaring and mouth open.

"But there are so many innuendos here regarding suicide," Wes said. "If he took his own life, surely you know that you aren't eligible for any insurance claims."

I had expected his statement. It was time for my speech. I frowned and shook my head.

"Oh, how could I have been so blind to not recognize that the stomach cancer had come back and was consuming his every moment? I thought those long spells in the barn were to avoid me. Instead, he was trying to hide his terrible sickness. Why didn't I recognize that?" I dabbed my handkerchief underneath my dry eyes, and managed a sob. "Did the two of you know that he was so ill?"

They shook their heads.

Wes answered, "You were newly married. You didn't know his habits, his customs. You blamed yourself for the times he distanced himself from you. It wasn't your fault, Polly."

Not surprisingly, Wes was much more comforting than my own sister. He continued, "You've been through a horrible ordeal. No one should become a widow as early as this. But Polly, his intention was spelled out in this letter. If those insurance guys were to get ahold of this, they would deny every penny."

I bit my lip as if in contemplation. "I can't say that I haven't been struggling with this. I have. But my struggles have led me to a decision to follow Sam's instructions. He bought the insurance policies when he was in good health. He paid the premiums. Then he died prematurely. It was not his desire, nor mine, nor anyone else's, that he would pass at such an early age, from cancer or a farm accident." I looked over at both Wes and Sarah. They were both looking at me with long faces. Sarah had her eyes closed. I wondered if she was praying for my salvation.

She opened her eyes. "Polly, if you go along with this, you may get away with it, but God will know." She was shaking her head and wrinkling up her nose the way she did when she encountered a dead fish or smelly outhouse.

"Sarah's being a bit harsh," Wes said. "We can't pretend to know God's will. But it seems as if this letter indicates that Sam was considering suicide when he wrote it."

"You need to do the right thing," Sarah piped in. I wondered if she had even listened to what Wes was saying. "You need to tell the insurance agents the truth."

"I *have been* telling the truth." I pulled my arms around each other clasping my shoulders, hunching over. I was putting on a good show for them.

As I looked up to Sarah, she was pursing her lips and pointing her finger at me, shaking it. "Shame on you."

Once again Sarah was treating me like an errant child. How well I knew that finger shaking from my childhood on Elm Street. If I were running in the house, yelling too loud, or taking the last cookie, there was her index finger pumping up and down. I cleared my throat to respond. "Well, this has been weighing on my mind from the moment I found the letter."

"When did you find it?" Wes asked.

"A couple of days after the funeral when I was going through Sam's things in the rolltop desk. It's where he kept all the important documents."

That brought a hushed silence.

"But the letter said that you'd find it with . . . your clothing," Wes answered, his cheeks turning red.

I nodded, but Sarah seemed to be getting more and more agitated, tapping her feet. I wondered for the millionth time how she ended up with Wes. He deserved so much more.

"How could you do this to our family?" Sarah screeched. "Your actions have all the tongues wagging at church, in Marshall, and the entire county. Sheriff Conlin is out here every other day trying to get you to confess. Then you acted so stupidly by cavorting with Jacob Frond. Father must be turning in his grave. I have no idea why Mother didn't give you a good rawhiding when she was here."

I kept my voice calm and even. "I let her read the letter."

Sarah's eyes widened.

"Mother believes Sam's death was an unfortunate accident."

Sarah was now shaking her head, pursing her lips, and glaring at me. Finally, she looked at Wes, "We should be getting home. Polly's not going to change her mind."

Wes shook his head at his wife. I knew that any good pastor would refuse to leave when tensions were this high. Sarah, in her typical fashion, sat up straight in her chair, lifted her chin, and again pursed her lips. It was another one of her opinionated postures, her way of telling me that she was right and I was wrong.

The first time I ever observed this behavior was after Father and John drowned in that horrible, icy lake. I remembered that instead of crying, Sarah sat there with her dry eyes piercing me. She told me I was a spoiled baby. She had sat there glaring at me with her chin lifted, just the same as now. She blamed me for their deaths. Unfortunately, back then I was a scared little kid, and I accepted the blame.

No more, Sarah. You can keep your shame and blame. You're no longer going to foist it on me.

After Father and John passed, Mother frequently asked Sarah to take care of me. Since she was fifteen and I was only four, it made sense. But I truly believed that Mother had no inkling of Sarah's hold over me. Mostly I tried to stay away from my sister when Mother was out of the house on errands. Mother took in sewing so she wasn't gone all day every day. However, she was out of the house at least a couple of hours daily for fittings and deliveries. During those times Sarah was in charge. She watched me like a hawk and if she deemed I had gotten out of line, I had hell to pay.

Wesley had been strangely silent. Once again, I thought about our intimate encounter and wondered how he felt about me. There was a powerful bond between us. I had expected him to offer a prayer, but instead, he looked at his wife with confusion. I wondered if she had ever exhibited this supercilious behavior with him; perhaps she saved it solely for me. After a long moment, he spoke up.

"I understand your position, Polly. Both you and I witnessed the aftermath of Sam's death. No one in his right mind would choose to fight with that bull. The doctor said that his death was an accident. I, for one, believe that to be the truth."

Sarah continued to scowl at me, while Wes maintained an even tone.

"Even if Sam pondered suicide it doesn't mean that he committed it. There are too many things amiss: you found the letter in the desk, not with your clothing, then the hints about poison, and my apologies, Polly, the horrible mutilation of his body. I think we all should leave this for what it was: a horrible accident."

With that Wes nodded to Sarah, pushed his chair back, and stood up to leave. Sarah followed suit. Wesley wished me goodbye and offered an invitation to come up to their house anytime. "We want our house to continue to be your second home," he said. Sarah, true to character, said nothing.

Once they left, I reached into the back of the cupboard in the canister labeled "sugar," pulled out the coffee I had ground last night, lit the cookstove, and filled the little coffee pot. While I was waiting for the coffee to brew, I burned the letter, holding it over the kitchen sink, watching the flames turn the paper to ash.

Sarah Wolcott Johnson

Thursday, May 24, 1934

Any other time I might have enjoyed the crisp spring air, blue skies, and freshly planted fields, but today my teeth were clenched and fists knotted as Wes and I trudged up the hill to our house. I pondered Polly's reaction to our visit. She had been petulant, like a three-year-old, much like Dorothy. It was clear she had no intention of coming clean with the insurance companies or the sheriff. Also, I couldn't believe she had shown the letter to Mother. It reeked of her smug, self-centered nature.

Wes and I made it up the hill, but before we started on the path to the back door, he turned to me, a huge frown, furrowing deep into his forehead. "We shouldn't have left Polly in such an awkward situation. You're her sister and you were unkind. We both need to go back and apologize."

"For what? Telling the truth? You know that Polly's always been self-absorbed, headstrong, and money-hungry. She married Sam for money, nothing else. When she was a little kid, she talked about marrying a king so she would have lots of gold and rule over everyone, particularly me. Later, her only goal in life was to be rich. I know this is true—I lived with her."

Wes shook his head. "That's kid stuff. Sure, she wants more money. We all do. I'd like to be witnessing grander renovations for the church than a patched roof or new outhouse. I know you'd like our house electrified and an indoor bathroom added. But that's the way it is. These are the times we're living in."

Wes put his hand on my shoulder and continued. "Frankly, I haven't seen greed in Polly since she's been married. When she was in high school, maybe. Certainly Polly acts immature, and she wants nice clothes. She rides Ginger like a wild woman, but, remember, she's only twenty years old. She's young, energetic, and this Depression is hard. She lost her husband and is about to lose her farm. Her husband gave her instructions and now she's following them. He wanted the best for her. Show a little compassion."

Compassion? I'd been showing my sister compassion for months. I'd witnessed all those injuries that Polly received from "accidents," and then there was another "accident." One that killed her husband. Was it an accident that Polly was ready for the funeral with a new black hat and bag? Polly was in it for the money. Sisters have a sixth sense about these things. Of course, Polly was young and immature, but also avaricious. Maybe she viewed Sam's death as a payoff for all the abuse she'd received at his hands. That's the Polly I knew, but telling Wes would only provoke him more.

Wes had turned around, gazing down at Sam's farm, instead of continuing up the path to our house. The sweet scent of lilacs was in the air, but neither of us was enjoying these spring fragrances. I put my hands on my hips and turned toward the house but Wes didn't follow me.

"What are you doing?" I scolded him. He hadn't moved an inch.

Wesley's voice was loud and firm. "We're going back to Polly's and we're both going to apologize."

"No, I won't. You don't understand her the way I do. I practically raised her. She's selfish and greedy. This is all about her wanting and getting more. I wonder if she even loved Sam. She certainly felt unsure of it before he died. You know how he was: silent and unfriendly."

As we were standing in our yard, I could hear the cows bellowing to be milked, but Wesley appeared oblivious to their cries.

"You need to milk the cows. I bet you don't even hear them."

Wes's face turned red and his face contorted. "You're my wife and you'll do as I say."

I couldn't believe my ears. This was not my husband. Wes always spoke so slowly and deliberately, thinking through each word. A few times I had witnessed him getting angry at parishioners who were frankly, narrow-minded. But this was directed at me.

"You're treating me like Sam treated Polly."

Wes yanked my arm, ignoring my comment. "We're going back there right now. No arguing."

I found myself stumbling back down the hill with Wes beside me, grabbing my arm as if I were going to run away. My arm hurt where he was pulling me and I guessed I would have a large Polly-sized bruise the next day.

When we got to the door, Wes knocked first, but then walked right in. I followed. Polly was still sitting at the kitchen table. She jumped up, holding a cup of coffee in her hand.

"Coffee!" I yelled, smelling it before I actually saw it.

"Yes, it's coffee," she snapped. "You can despise me all you want. There it is."

Wes interrupted. "We're here to apologize, not to criticize you."

Hearing the word "apologize" Polly jerked backwards towards the cookstove, but carefully caught herself with her left hand on the counter, regaining her balance.

No one made a sound as we three stood there looking at each other.

I couldn't hold back. "Polly, you're such a liar. You kept making excuses for all your bruises and now you're still hiding stuff from us. Sam's letter. And now the coffee. When will it all end? All these lies. All this deception."

Contrary to what Wes said, I was not going to apologize for anything. She was the one who needed to make amends.

Polly stiffened, put the coffee cup on the table, and stood rigid, arms crossed. I looked out the kitchen window and could see Sailor Dog in the yard a few feet away, probably drawn close by our voices.

Polly wrinkled up her nose. "Well, sometimes deception is the best course of action. Fewer people get hurt." She was making no sense.

"I think not," I responded. "Deception only builds and builds until you have such a mess you can't get out of it. Oh, what a tangled web we weave."

"That's enough, Sarah," Wes said to me. He was speaking as if I were a misbehaving child, which perturbed me even more.

Polly stood there, her pretty face screwed up in anger, arms still crossed. Wes and I were also both standing, the kitchen table between us, creating a huge divide.

"Polly, we came back to apologize, not to spy on you and your coffee," Wes reiterated. "I, for one, understand why you feel you should carry out Sam's instructions. He was your husband, and you're being obedient." He then looked icily at me. The Wes I didn't know, making me feel more and more uncomfortable.

Over the years I had wondered about Wes and Polly. She flirted with him endlessly, often making casual remarks about her dress or hat. She fished for compliments and he always obliged. When she married Sam, I was so relieved. But now, I was beginning to feel that tension once again. If she were to set her claws into Wes, I guaranteed it would be the end of her.

Polly continued to stand, hands now on her hips. The veins in her forehead were visible as she bit her lip, like Mother did when angered. Finally, she spoke.

"I've omitted a certain piece of information, but it needs to be told. I thought holding back was useful, particularly when children are involved." She gazed straight into my eyes. "And particularly when our family can be hurt. Yes, I have been deceptive, and I admit to being selfish by not offering you the last little bit of coffee that I possess, but I have definitely chosen the right course by not bringing my nephews into this investigation."

I gasped, startled. I couldn't believe she said the word *"nephews."* "You have been devising a plot to hurt Junior and Zeke? You good-for-nothing. . . ."

Wes put his hand on my shoulder shaking his head at me. "You're only making matters worse."

He turned to Polly. "What do you mean?"

"Your sons—my nephews," she stuttered. This was typical Polly drama. "I love them dearly. I didn't want to bring Junior and Zeke into this horrible mess. But if you want the god-awful truth, well then, okay."

I couldn't imagine what my sister was talking about. I was ready to grab her coffee cup and throw it at her.

But again, Wes put a hand on my shoulder. "We all need to calm down. Let's hear Polly's story."

Wes turned to her. "We need to clear the air. Please go on."

It infuriated me that Wes was being so polite to Polly. After all, we'd just caught her in a lie, but she looked directly at Wes, snubbing me, and started speaking.

"The morning of Sam's death, when Sarah and I were running up the hill to your house to telephone Dr. Grayson, I started retching. I couldn't stop, then I kept having dry heaves, so Sarah ran ahead to make the call. Once I finished, I stumbled over the boys' slingshot in the snow. At the same time, I noticed both boys' boot prints going down to the horse tank and coming back up the hill. I picked up the slingshot, put it in my pocket, and kept it."

I heard myself gasp. Was she suggesting that Junior and Zeke were responsible for Sam's death? That was preposterous.

Polly walked over to the cupboard and pulled out the slingshot from an upper shelf and handed it to Wes. "Here it is."

He took the slingshot and looked it over, passing it back and forth from one hand to the other.

I found myself shouting at my sister. "You actually think the boys shot Black Devil to provoke him to kill Sam?" I couldn't believe she was blaming Sam's death on our boys. "You blame Junior and Zeke?"

"No, I'm not thinking anything like that," Polly answered. "But I do think there are times when we keep things to ourselves so innocent children aren't brought into the fray. Maybe you think that's deceptive, but I think it's the right thing to do. I've kept this to myself and believe me, I've lost sleep over it. I didn't mention it to Sheriff Conlin, which was a deliberate decision."

I felt my knees going weak, grabbing towards Wesley for support, but he had stepped back. I grabbed onto a chair and stood with both hands on it, righting myself, trying to breathe normally. "I'm feeling sick. I need to go home," I stammered, and headed for the door, bracing my hands against the wall as I left the kitchen. Wesley uttered a quick goodbye to Polly and followed me out.

Reverend Wesley Johnson

Thursday, May 24, 1934

After the second visit with Polly, Sarah and I walked quietly back, neither of us saying a word. I was extremely late starting my early morning chores so I first proceeded to milk the cows, then fed the chickens and pigs. Despite Sarah not feeling well, I noticed that she filtered the milk and supervised the boys who were cleaning off the dirty eggs. When we met back for breakfast, the boys were waiting and Dorothy was attempting to dress herself. It didn't feel like a normal day; all our routines were off schedule.

Helping Dorothy put on her dress, I prayed silently for our family. If we ever needed God's love, it was right now. The boys raced into the kitchen, looking surprised that breakfast wasn't ready. I could tell by Sarah's somber demeanor that she expected me to do the talking. She sat down at the kitchen table, her eyes on me.

"Sit down, boys," I began, "we need to have an important talk." Both boys sat at their places at the table, looking at me expectantly. Dorothy wandered off to the parlor, looking for her doll.

"You absolutely must tell the truth," I said, "no matter how bad you feel about this. Do you understand?"

The boys nodded in agreement. Both were fidgeting. Junior wrapped his fingers around the corner edge of the dark blue oilcloth, and Zeke pumped his feet against the legs of the chair. For the first time I noticed several worn spots on the oilcloth. Sarah wasn't even attempting to hide them. I looked at the boys until I had established eye contact with both.

"You must tell the truth," I reiterated.

"We understand," Junior replied. "What's this about?"

"Did you boys see Black Devil the day he killed Uncle Sam?"

Both boys squirmed in their seats, looking down towards the floor. Sarah began fidgeting with the gold tatting on her handkerchief, her head also bent down.

Junior sat up and looked me in the eye. "Zeke saw Black Devil in the barnyard, so we snuck down to Uncle Sam's horse tank. We hid behind the horse tank and when Black Devil came over to drink, we took turns shooting pebbles at him. He didn't like it."

"Shooting pebbles?"

"With the slingshot."

"But we didn't open his gate," Zeke added. "We didn't let him out. Black Devil was already in the barnyard. We didn't want him to kill Uncle Sam."

Sarah started crying. I looked at her and shook my head, but she acknowledged nothing.

"And then what?"

"The bull got so angry that he was running fierce around the barnyard. We got scared and ran home."

Sarah continued to cry, tears running down her face, making only a small attempt to wipe them with her handkerchief.

"What else?"

"Nothing else."

"Were you in Uncle Sam's barn that morning?"

Both replied, "No."

"Did you see Uncle Sam that morning?"

"No."

Sarah's convulsive weeping pierced the silence between the questions.

"Zeke, do you have anything else to add?"

"I'm sorry we shot pebbles at Black Devil."

Both boys wore scared faces: eyes open wide, furrowed brows, and limp lips.

Sarah attempted to ask a question between sobs. "Was this before or after I went to Aunt Polly's to borrow butter?"

They both shrugged.

"When did you go for the butter?" I interjected.

"Right before breakfast," she managed to answer, her chest heaving.

"We went down first thing in the morning," Zeke said. "I saw Black Devil when I was going out to the chicken house."

"After you came home, what did you do?"

"The chores," Junior answered. "Then we came in and waited for breakfast."

"Did either of you see Black Devil after that?"

They shook their heads.

"Did either of you see Uncle Sam any time at all that morning?"

They both answered, "No."

"And where did the slingshot end up?" I asked.

"I don't know," Zeke answered. "I took the last shot, cuz Junior had the first one. I looked for the slingshot later but couldn't find it. Maybe I left it at the horse tank or it fell out of my pocket when we ran home. On the funeral day, I looked for it in Aunt Polly's yard down by the horse tank, but it wasn't there."

"Did either of you see Aunt Polly that morning?"

Both said no.

"Okay," I said to them. "Thank you for telling the truth. Now go play, and we'll call you for breakfast."

The boys both ran out the door faster than I'd ever seen them run.

Sarah, no longer crying, went into one of her silent moods. It took me a long time and several prayers to still my heart.

Polly Wolcott Forrest

Friday, May 25, 1934

After my morning chores I made myself another cup of coffee, perhaps just to wallow in the memory of my mistakes. Once again I'd suffered from tortured nightmares all night long. Last night I dreamt that Sam was pushing me off a cliff. Not the ravine that resulted in broken ribs. But a high mountain cliff where survival was impossible. I saw him grab and push me before I woke up screaming. Even the knowledge that Sam was no longer alive didn't keep me from reliving many of these horrible memories.

Succumbing to Wes's passion was a huge mistake, the height of stupidity. I would never do that again. Sure, I had always admired Wesley and wondered how he ever could have been interested in Sarah. But it was so wrong. So wrong in so many ways. My bad decisions were mounting up and I was quite ready to cash in Sam's policies and leave this place behind. I had had enough of Sarah's criticism to last a lifetime. She spoke harshly of Viola Cross, but she was just like her— a nosy-parker meddling in the affairs of others.

Thinking about yesterday's encounter with Wes and Sarah, I was angry at myself. I hadn't planned to bring Junior and Zeke into yesterday's brouhaha, but once again Sarah was acting superior, and her coffee remark was so smug. So what if I didn't want to serve them coffee? I had only a handful of coffee beans left, and I couldn't be seen in town buying such frivolous items as coffee, even though now I could afford it.

Last Tuesday, I found a can of money hidden on a dusty window sill in the milk house. It was in an old Skoal chewing tobacco can with its lid on so tight I had to pry it open with a screwdriver. I only found it because I was looking for an empty jar to store some buttons. But there it was right under my nose, forty-eight dollars. That find spurred me to keep looking for more, and I hit gold. Sam, I presumed, had hidden money in small jars, boxes, and tins out in the barn and outbuildings. Six containers, all told. All bills, no coins. He hadn't hidden a cent in the house. Believe me, I'd searched all over the house when he was alive.

It was clear that Sam had no intention of sharing any money with me, and I had fallen for his "hard times stories" hook, line, and sinker. I buried the secret money in tins around the yard, since under the mattress or in the sugar jar or anywhere in the house was too risky in case of fire or theft. Every day I made a mental note where each of the jars was buried. If I got even a few dollars out of my loathsome marriage, I wasn't going to lose a cent because of a faulty memory.

In the week after I'd discovered the hidden money, I'd gone through the barn and all the outbuildings trying to find a clue as to what Sam was doing out there all fall and winter. Something seemed a bit "off" right from the beginning. Sam's secrecy made me suspicious, as well as his habit of taking food with him out to the barn every day, even though I made him a big farmer's dinner at noontime. It didn't add up. Why had he stashed away all the money?

I now wondered if the "other woman" theory might have some credibility. Maybe he was saving up to leave with her. Or perhaps, he was saving to buy her gifts. The pain no longer pierced my heart. I was lucky to be rid of Sam, and I certainly wasn't torn with jealousy that he might have fallen prey to someone prettier or more worldly. But the presence of those hidden jars of money did pique my curiosity.

Early last fall I thought Sam might be using the time in the barn to make a surprise for me, perhaps building new kitchen cupboards or a wooden swing for the front porch. God knew I'd complained enough about the current cupboards and hinted repeatedly about wanting a porch swing. Sam was handy and could do that; he'd made the rose trellises. About a week before our wedding he'd presented me with the two trellises, one for the front of the house and one for the back. But in the fall, after waiting weeks for a surprise, I gave up. At Christmas he gave me perfume, nothing handmade, and I disliked the perfume with its overpowering scent that would better serve a lady of the evening.

After the holidays, I spent my time inside our house, drinking tea and trying to keep warm. I still wondered what he was doing in the barn, but the first time I wandered out to find him, I was rewarded with some hard blows to the head and chest. Sam would deliver them wherever he found me, in the milk house, granary, or behind the barn. Sometimes I was innocently going out to brush Ginger, but since Sam hadn't authorized it, I was in violation of his unwritten rule that I stay inside the house.

I was sure he didn't want me finding his extra piles of money around the farm. There was only a little money in the bank account. The life insurance policy money from his first wife remained a mystery, perhaps a myth. If he once had received any money, he'd hidden it far beyond my reach.

As I sat at the kitchen table drinking my coffee, I regretted bringing my nephews into the fracas. I should have controlled my temper. Those boys were nice kids, but full of piss and vinegar. Boys being boys. They would've never intentionally hurt Sam.

The warmth of the coffee wasn't lifting me up this morning. Perhaps a ride with Ginger would do the trick. I'd go down the lane through the fields avoiding the roads and nosy neighbors. It was a pretty ride down a long lane along the creek and the last piece on a bridle trail that stretched out over a mile.

In my mind's eye, I was already in the saddle. The lilacs down along the way were in bloom and on the ride back I'd stop and pick a bouquet. I planned to go all the way till I got to the fence at the Dolliver property and then I'd turn around. It was all back in the lanes along the fields, no roads, some of the trail ran along the creek and there would be no one who could see me and pass judgement.

Everybody knew each other's business in this rural neighborhood. I thought a small town was bad. Well, living on a farm was a hundred times worse. Everyone made the excuse they were looking out for one another, but really they were meddling types, Sarah being among the worst. She openly listened in on the party line and said that Wes had never reprimanded her for it. She claimed that all the neighbors eavesdropped, especially Viola Cross, who monopolized the phone line with her gossip. Then they all put up the pretense of being good Christians every Sunday morning.

While I was finishing my coffee, I heard a knock on the front door, and at the same time, Sailor Dog started barking. No one ever came to the front door of Michigan farm houses. Either the driveway ended at the back door or continued on to the barn. If you ever got a knock on the front door, you knew it was someone selling something or someone totally unfamiliar with farm life, usually both. I took the last gulp of coffee and hid the dirty cup in the cupboard. Then I burned a match to hide the smell. I didn't want anyone to know that I had coffee—salesman, friend, or neighbor.

I was hoping it might be a Raleigh salesman coming by with his suitcase of herbs and spices. I'd ask if he had coffee and tea, and I'd buy a bottle of vanilla flavoring, and packages of cinnamon and nutmeg. I enjoyed making snickerdoodles with Dorothy, and my spices, like most of my other supplies, had dwindled to nothing.

By the time I got to the front door the knocking was louder and more persistent. So was Sailor Dog's barking. He was at his usual position midway between the driveway and the house. The front door hadn't been opened since I'd been living there and I wasn't surprised to find it stuck tight. I pulled and pulled, but it wouldn't open, so I went to the side window and shouted through the screen. "Hello, the door's stuck. Are you selling spices?"

"No, ma'am. We wanna question you about Sam Forrest. Are you Mrs. Forrest?"

I could see two men standing, still facing the door, not realizing I was at the window. I walked back to the door and shouted out, "Yes, but Sheriff Conlin handled the investigation. You should talk to him."

"This is about som-thun' else, Mrs. Forrest. Do you got another door?"

They had to be idiots. Of course there was another door. Looking out the south window, I saw they had parked a shiny, new car in the middle of the driveway, totally blocking the way, also idiotic. No one did that, particularly when milk, hay, and silage wagons needed clearance to get to the barn. These guys knew absolutely nothing about farm operations.

Their car was not to be forgotten, a Plymouth touring car, light green with a cream-colored top, and stylish white walled tires with red rims. The spare tire hung right in front of the passenger door, making it even more attractive, like a red and white button on a pale green linen dress. I thought these colors would make a great summer hat. The car, however, was much too fancy for farm country. Even Doc Grayson drove an old, dilapidated Model T.

Were these men mobsters or thieves? Friends of John Dillinger? My God, could Sam have been involved in bank robberies? Would that account for the cash I'd found?

"Come to the back, but bring your car around back so you don't block the driveway." I was thinking that Wes might be coming to get some silage today. As soon as I told them to come around back, I regretted it. If they were unsavory business associates of Sam's, then they could rob me and hold me hostage for the money I'd found, and their car would be hidden from view.

I walked out to the backyard before the two men got out of the car. They were middle-aged, wearing black suits and hats, looking incredibly out of place. Both were stocky, with round fat faces, the kind you didn't see any more—long, hungry, gaunt faces now being far too common. One man was about two inches taller but otherwise they could have been twins. The taller one was carrying a briefcase.

I walked outside to the driveway.

"Good morning," I said, reminding myself I needed to act like a proper grieving widow.

"Good morning," they replied in unison.

The taller one spoke: "I'm Jack Stimson and this is Clem Cavanaugh."

Both held out their hands, so I shook them, repeating my name, "Polly Forrest."

What followed was an awkward moment. They must've thought I was going to invite them in. But Wes, in particular, had warned me about the perils of being a young widow living alone, particularly in these hard times.

"May we come in?"

"Well, my house is a mess and I need to clean up before my morning visitors come." (As if I were going to clean up or even have visitors.) "You can get the information from the sheriff's office."

"We're U.S. Gov-ment officials. We need to investigate another matter."

"U.S. Government," I answered. "I paid our taxes on time." I was trying to figure out some ruse to get rid of these guys. My mind was racing. I had buried the first of Sam's life insurance checks in a tin can under the yellow rose bush, so it wouldn't get stolen before the second check arrived. However, the second check came in the mail yesterday and was still lying on top of the roll-top desk. I didn't want anyone seeing that check, least of all these strangers. The amount was huge: five-hundred dollars. I scolded myself for not burying it yesterday the moment it arrived. Even with the checks buried, I worried that someone might find them. My plan was to take the train to Lansing to deposit both checks. I'd buy some coffee beans when I was up there, too. No one in Lansing knew me.

I wondered if Sarah and Wes had seen the car come up the drive. I wished I'd told these officials to leave their fancy car where it was originally parked. Then Sarah would certainly see it and send Wes down here in a split second, if only to make sure I wasn't carrying on with a male friend.

"How do I know you're from the government and when did government officials start driving fancy touring cars?"

The smaller guy looked at his companion and rolled his eyes. Stimson reached in his pocket and pulled out an official looking badge, then Cavanaugh followed suit, both handing them to me. The badges were identical, gold colored with the words *WHITE HOUSE* on top and *POLICE* on the bottom. In the middle was an engraving of the White House with an Eagle Seal above it. I handed them back.

"White House Police? I don't understand. Is President Roosevelt coming for a visit?"

Presidents and presidential candidates had made whistle-stop tours giving speeches from the cabooses at the train stations in Marshall and Battle Creek, but they never made their way out to farm country. I wondered if a special trip was being planned. Neither agent batted an eyelash.

"No ma'am, Roosevelt's not acomin' here, but we gotta question you about Sam."

This guy didn't speak like he was a police officer, and why was he referring to my late husband as "Sam" and not "Mr. Forrest?"

"Well, this is unexpected," I answered. I stepped back toward Sarah's house, and to my relief I saw Wes making his way down the hill toward us.

"That's my brother-in-law coming down the hill; please wait a minute until he arrives." I walked toward Wes to greet him while I heard the two muttering in anger. For once, I was relieved that Sarah was a nosy busybody and had sent Wes down.

I rushed toward him. "They say they're U.S. Government, White House Police, with official looking badges, but they could have stolen them. I'm afraid they're here to see what I have in my house and come back and steal it," I whispered.

Wes scowled, and as we reached the driveway, he deliberately kicked the gravel, shuffling along. I could tell he wasn't happy to be dealing with government officials. He introduced himself as "Reverend J. Wesley Johnson" and they, in turn, introduced themselves.

"We gotta search the premises," they told Wes, completely ignoring me.

"I'll need to check with the sheriff before you can do that. My sister-in-law has been through a lot and we don't need any more investigations."

"We have papers saying it's okay." Stimson pulled them out of his briefcase.

Wes riffled through the papers. "They don't look official to me."

Both men looked dumbstruck. Neither said a word.

"Tell you what," Wes paused. "I'll check with our local officials and if you're legitimate, come back Monday morning at nine. Otherwise, don't ever show up here again." I'd never seen this side of Wesley; he was usually so friendly and companionable.

Without speaking the two turned around and jumped back into their fancy car and sped down the long driveway.

I thought I was prepared for any eventuality but now I was at a loss. Wes, however, knew exactly how to handle the men. It was clear that they thought they could coax me into letting them into the house. But with a man on the scene, they quickly departed. What would I have done if Wes hadn't shown up? Right then I decided to have a phone installed as quickly as possible, whatever the cost. That meant I'd be digging up a can of money this afternoon.

"Are you okay?" Wes asked me. The tenderness in his voice once again left me smitten. Here he was watching out for me, even after I'd practically accused his sons of being involved in Sam's death. I wanted to jump into his arms but I restrained myself.

"Yes, I'm okay. Thank you for getting rid of them. Do you think they were crooks looking for stuff to steal?"

"Hard to tell. That car certainly isn't government owned."

Wes had come to the rescue and now everything was better. I was angry at myself for not handling the situation on my own and I was irritated at the men for ignoring me after Wes arrived. Why did Wes deserve more attention and respect than me? Life, as Mother frequently pointed out, was not fair. My many long months with Sam had shown me that being a woman without means in a bad marriage was a million miles from fair.

"Come back with me and I'll call Sheriff Conlin and ask him to check on these guys," Wes suggested.

I wasn't ready to face my sister so soon, but I had no choice, so I told Wes I'd come up in an hour. That would give me enough time to bury the second life insurance check. I'd already decided it was going to go under the red rose bush on the other side of the house from the yellow one. No reason to hide them both in the same place. I dug a hole and put the check in an empty Clabber Girl baking powder jar that I'd been using to store string. The red roses were climbing up Sam's trellis. I loved the trellis, reminding me of happier times. However, I couldn't stop thinking that Sam's mean-spirited, nasty moments outnumbered the kind ones by a hundred to one. Maybe a thousand.

Sarah Wolcott Johnson

Friday, May 25, 1934

I spotted today's trouble when I noticed a fancy car blocking Polly's driveway. Fearing it was a new suitor, I alerted Wes who went over to check. He was gone only about ten minutes, but came back and went straight to the phone and called Sheriff Conlin. Listening in on Wesley's side of the conversation, I figured out what had happened. Wes gave him names, descriptions, and mentioned the two men were "rough around the edges." Sheriff Conlin told Wes that he'd call back once he got information from Washington DC.

Next, Wes left to make his sick calls. That allowed me time to ponder the situation. What had Polly gotten herself involved in? For the past several weeks we were dealing with hints that she'd killed her husband—or Polly's suitor had. Then came the veiled innuendo of suicide in Sam's letter and yesterday the implication of Junior and Zeke. Her behavior simply wasn't one of a grieving widow.

Now, with the arrival of the White House Police, I wondered if Sam had been plotting to kill the President. And why? Sam never talked politics; he was extremely quiet, actually secretive. I certainly never heard him say anything about the President, positive or negative.

From my point of view, Mr. Roosevelt seemed to be going all out to get the country afloat. Last year he started three government programs to help farmers. Sam should have been aware of that. Frankly, it was too soon to know if the programs would be successful. Did Sam have complaints about Mr. Roosevelt? It was quite unnerving that my brother-in-law was a suspect of the federal government.

My mind kept wandering back to President Roosevelt. One of the few things that Polly and I had in common was that we both loved the President's fireside radio chats and Mrs. Roosevelt's newspaper columns. They were a frequent topic of conversation when Polly and Sam came over to our house for Sunday dinner, Wes would explain current events to the kids using topics that the President had discussed. Had Sam been sitting there seething behind our backs? Had he been quietly plotting an assassination during our Sunday dinners? The thought left me cold.

"Hello, Sarah are you here?" Polly's voice wafted from the back room. "Can I use your phone?"

"Yes, of course. Come in." I was taking the moral high road with Polly. Despite her selfish behavior with the coffee and her insinuation that the boys were somehow involved in Sam's death, I'd decided to put aside animosity and display a friendly face.

Polly arranged to have the telephone company, Michigan Bell, hook the phone up next week. The telephone wires were already in place, so it wouldn't take long. When we got our phone, the workers set up poles and a line down to Sam's house, but Sam didn't want a telephone.

"Too many snoopy women listening in on the party line," he had joked. At the time I wondered if he was directing his comment at me. However, as a bachelor it seemed that Sam had little need of a phone. He could get news from Burt Kalmbach, who came by with his horse and wagon and picked up his milk cans every day, right after he picked up ours. If he didn't hear the local gossip from Burt, he could get it from Henry Fountain at the grist mill where he made his weekly trips.

I'd noted over the past two years that Sam made other trips to town; I never knew what they were for. Nor did Polly. I always asked her, but she shook her head in exasperation. Wes told me that once he saw Sam using a pay phone in town. The next day Wes made a point of telling Sam he could use our phone anytime. Sam politely thanked him, but he never once came up to use it, not even after he and Polly were married. Now I wondered if he had been planning something unsavory on the public phone in Marshall.

If Sam was plotting to kill President Roosevelt, I really doubted that he would have told Polly. Maybe she found out, and that's why he was hurting her. Some kind of physical blackmail. But why wouldn't she have told the sheriff? There were so many unanswered questions.

I couldn't get my mind off the subject. President McKinley was assassinated by an anarchist from Alpena, Michigan, up near Traverse City, a guy with an unpronounceable last name, Leon Czolgosz. I wondered if Sam was also an anarchist and if he was in cahoots with others either in Alpena or, perhaps, in Calhoun County. I'd never known any anarchists and didn't understand their motives. I highly doubted they were religious people.

After Polly hung up with Michigan Bell, Viola Cross called me to ask about the fancy car she'd seen drive by. I told her what had happened. Viola was positively up in arms about anarchists.

"Those people try to shut down the government," she told me. "They build up arsenals of weapons in unlikely places, like barns or empty factories, and aren't afraid to shoot any governor or legislator they don't like. They sometimes call themselves militia. You've gotta be real careful if Sam was harboring anarchists. They're crazy and violent. They might even be using Sam's barn as an arsenal."

"Well, we don't know anything yet," I tried to assure her. I knew she would be listening in on the party line for more information.

Polly had settled on the floor to play with Dorothy who was talking to her doll. I walked over and looked down at Polly.

"Do you think Sam was involved in a plot to assassinate the President?"

"What's assassinate?" asked Dorothy.

"Dorothy, go to your bedroom and find me your blue nightgown right now," I demanded. I'd put the nightgown in the back room laundry hamper this morning, so I figured this would buy Polly and me a few minutes alone.

After Dorothy ran away, Polly looked down at the floor and shook her head. "I have no idea what he was up to," she answered.

"Well, did he despise Mr. Roosevelt?"

"He never talked about him one way or another. We did listen to some Fireside Chats but Sam never commented."

"Well, they say it's the silent types," I added and told her what Viola Cross had said.

She shrugged. "I wish this was all over. Sam spent most of his waking hours out in that barn. At the time, I figured he had chores to do, like fix equipment. But now I wonder."

Dorothy returned. "I no find it, Mommy." She looked up at Polly. "Aunt Polly, play Lincoln logs."

Polly got back down on the floor with Dorothy and began assembling a small log cabin. Dorothy was "helping" Polly by handing her the logs. Both seemed totally engrossed in the project when Junior and Zeke ran into the house.

"Aunt Polly, Aunt Polly," they screamed as soon as they saw her.

Junior ran up to her and pulled on her sleeve. "Come out and do target practice with our BB guns. We'll show you how."

"No, she with me." Dorothy faced her two older brothers with bravado, standing up and putting her hands on her hips, elbows out. I was afraid Dorothy had seen this posture too many times. Once again she was mimicking me.

"I'll come out after I help Dorothy finish the log cabin," Polly told them, and they rushed out the door. Soon I could hear them firing their BB guns.

Even though Dorothy was back, I needed to speak to Polly. "I suggest you go through your house and the barn to see if there's any evidence Sam was planning an assassination."

"What would I even look for?"

"Papers, receipts for things like guns, ammunition, copies of the President's schedule, information about getaway cars, maps. Stuff like that."

"I read an article in the Chronicle a while back that the Michigan Militia was holding meetings over in Albion. Did Sam go to any of those meetings?"

Polly looked at me with incredulity. "Sarah, you have a vivid imagination. You believe that old windbag Viola and everything she says? All she does is pass on gossip. Pick up the phone right now and you'll hear her passing this anarchy and assassination stuff on to the neighbors."

I slipped over to the phone and stealthily picked up. Sure enough, Viola was telling someone about one more unsavory event at the Samuel Forrest farm. I dropped the receiver back down into its socket and nodded to Polly.

Suddenly we both broke out in laughter. It felt like old times. Polly and me having fun together. Unfortunately, it wouldn't last long.

Polly went out in the backyard to join the boys while I stayed inside putting Dorothy down for a nap. A few minutes later I heard Sailor Dog barking. When I went outside to check on things, Polly, Junior, and Zeke came running around the corner. Sailor Dog was a decent watch dog and barked only when something was wrong. Occasionally there was a stray rabbit or coon that caught his attention, but otherwise, barking meant strangers.

"Where's Dorothy, and where's Wes?" Polly asked.

"Dorothy's napping in her bedroom and Wes is still out making sick calls. The last one was going to be Doris Dykstra, the widow who sits on the left side of the church, midway back. She was coughing all through last week's sermon which drove Viola crazy. Frankly, I thought Doris should've stayed home and not exposed all of us. Occasionally Viola is right."

Polly nodded.

We kept looking around but saw nothing amiss but Sailor Dog continued to bark.

"Okay, boys, you go in the house and play upstairs in your bedroom. Keep your door open and don't let Dorothy go downstairs if she wakes up. This is serious. Don't let anyone go downstairs until we're back," I commanded.

Polly grabbed both BB guns from the boys before they left and handed one to me. Was she crazy? Any thief would look at a BB gun and laugh. But wanting to get this finished, I took the gun more to appease Polly than anything else.

Polly said to the boys, "We're going to see what's bothering Sailor Dog. Probably just a squirrel or rabbit, but it might be mobsters."

I wondered for a moment if Polly was joking about mobsters but she didn't crack a smile. Again, I wondered about her grip on reality. BB guns and mobsters. This was as absurd as anarchists.

"I'm not sure we should be doing this," I said as we walked down the knoll toward her house. I immediately worried that the boys would get curious and come over. We both adjusted the BB guns, carrying them pointed at the ground, but I wondered if there were any BBs in them. Probably not—neither Polly nor I had checked. When we got to Polly's driveway, Sailor Dog came running toward us, still barking.

"What's wrong?" Polly said, looking from the house to the barn to the various outbuildings. Nothing unusual. "Come, show us," she urged the dog.

Sailor Dog, yelping even louder, led us toward the old granary that Sam had been using as a shed for small tools. Polly and Sailor Dog continued walking toward the building as I pondered our safety. Polly turned around, looking at me, putting her index finger up to her lips, blowing a "shh" sign. As if on signal the shed door opened and two men emerged, both stocky, wearing tailored shirts and pants. I wondered if they were the "White House Police" from this morning. They certainly fit the description

Suddenly the shorter one pulled out a handgun and pointed it at us.

"Get out of here now," Polly shouted at them, ignoring the gun. "There's no money here. Get out right now."

Sailor Dog growled menacingly at the men.

What happened next was beyond my comprehension. The guy with the gun pointed it at Sailor Dog and, without hesitation, shot him in the head. Sailor Dog fell on the grass. It was so fast I couldn't believe it happened. Polly ran to the lifeless dog, hugging him and dropping the BB gun. Beginning to comprehend what had just happened, I froze. The short guy grabbed the BB guns while Polly continued to hug Sailor Dog.

"Take the dog back behind the barn, near the car," the short guy instructed the taller one. "You two, go into the shed until we're done with our search." He kept the gun pointed at us as Polly got to her feet and we started walking toward the old granary.

My heart pounded wildly and my breath came in spurts. I needed to pray but no words came to mind. Finally, a distant voice from the back of my mind prompted me: "Our Father, Our Father, Our Father," but I couldn't recall the rest. My attention was focused on following Polly into the old building without stumbling. When we got to the door my hands were on my chest trying to slow both my heartbeat and breathing.

Stepping up into the granary I steadied myself with my hands, placing them against the doorframe.

Once inside the shed, Polly turned over a couple of pails and we both sat down without asking. I wondered if Polly was as terrified as me. The short guy held the gun on us. I wiggled a bit, which elicited a gruff, "Don't move." When the taller guy returned, the other one put his gun back into the side of his pants. I realized not enough time had elapsed to bury poor old Sailor Dog; the taller guy must have left him lying on the grass behind the barn.

We were in the front room, which held shovels, axes, crowbars, sledge hammers, and gardening tools. In one corner sat a severely damaged milk can covered with dust and cobwebs. Smaller sized items such as nails, screws, and sandpaper lined the shelves of a dilapidated pie safe.

A rough wooden sliding door opened into a windowless dark rear room. Polly simply sat still on the overturned pail. I wondered if Sam had kept guns and ammunition back there. Was this the room where a presidential assassination had been planned?

The short guy with the gun turned his head to look at the taller guy searching the room. Polly looked at me and mouthed, "Same guys from this morning." Sensing something was going on, the shorter guy pulled out the gun again and kept it on Polly while the taller guy proceeded into the back room. From what I could see, there wasn't much back there, and it didn't take him long to determine that.

Walking back to us, he turned to Polly. "Where are the plates?"

Polly looked confused. "The plates?"

"Where are the plates?" he shouted louder this time.

"In the house. The china cabinet in the dining room," she answered with an even voice.

The short guy's body went rigid and his scowl lines deepened as he clenched his teeth.

"You know what we're talking about. Tell me where they are."

"But I don't." Polly looked straight at him. "If this has anything to do with my late husband, believe me, he didn't tell me anything."

"Huh, you don't know nuthin', do ya?" he sneered. "Well, tell me where he hid stuff. It was supposed to be back there in that stupid room."

Polly shook her head. "I really don't know about that filthy room, but there's definitely no money hidden in the china cabinet. Believe me I have spent enough time washing those dishes."

"You're the wife, and wives are snoopy and know everything. You gotta know where they are."

"No, I don't. We got married last September. He only wanted a young wife for bragging rights, nothing more. He didn't even tell me how much we owe on the farm, where the deed to the farm is, or why he never bought a life insurance policy. The son-of-a bitch."

I'd never heard Polly speak like this about Sam. She'd always defended him while new bruises appeared on her face and neck each week. But, of course, I'd known it was a lie all along and now she was lying again. She'd already told Wes and me the farm deed was in the rolltop desk, and, of course, we'd been disputing whether she should make claims on Sam's insurance policies. But I was worried for my life so I kept quiet.

The shorter guy shook his head in disbelief.

Polly straightened her torso without leaving the perch of the overturned pail. "Believe what you want. And search everywhere. I know nothing about where Sam hid plates or anything else."

"The plates were supposed to be stacked along the wall in this back room," the taller guy added.

"You're welcome to search the room but I didn't take anything and as far as I'm concerned, go ahead and take the plates from the china cabinet. They belonged to his first wife. Nothing sentimental there for me." Polly sounded angry. As for me, I was scared.

She reached into her dress pocket. "Look, here's thirty dollars, the last of my husband's money. Take it and leave."

To my surprise, both waved her off and the taller guy continued to search in the back room, and once again, the shorter one held the gun on Polly. She and I sat silently on the overturned pails while she continued to hold the thirty dollars in her hand. Wes and I could have used thirty dollars for a whole lot of things: shoes and boots, cloth and sewing supplies, a new davenport, a new mattress, but more importantly, the mortgage due later this summer.

I couldn't understand it. Why did Polly have thirty dollars in her pocket and why didn't the thieves take it?

Reverend Wesley Johnson

Friday, May 25, 1934

With Jasper pulling the buggy, I drove back from my round of sick calls, observing the meadows, tilled fields abundant with hay, oats, wheat and corn. In every direction there were pine forests in the distance. I marveled at the beauty of God's work as I noted veils of layered sunshine creating differing shades of brown and green as fluffy cumulus clouds floated above. This spring day must have been God's compensation for the bitter, difficult days we'd experienced over the winter. I pulled on the reins for Jasper to slow down a bit as I wanted to savor the moment. I'd gotten used to Bessie's slow pace and Jasper, being younger and more spirited, was a bit hasty for my liking.

I wanted to use the time to reflect on the situation with Polly which I'd been deliberately avoiding, shutting it out of my mind whenever possible. Years ago, I had decided to keep Polly at a distance. Oh, yes, I'd had fantasies, but they were solely figments of my imagination—until two weeks ago. Now, I wondered if I married the wrong woman. Polly was the one who made me happy. Polly was the one who made me whole. Once again, as I had so many times previously, I offered a prayer asking God to help me gain control.

Since Polly seemed dead set on cashing in on Sam's insurance policies, I suspected she wouldn't be living next door to us much longer. I might need to act fast—if, indeed, I was destined to act. I wondered if Polly's plans included a move to Connecticut to buy a new house for Mother Wolcott and Grandmother Blessing. That would make Sarah happy, but would limit my time with Polly. Oh no, I was thinking crazy thoughts; after all, Sarah was my wife.

Sarah. Sarah. Sarah. Could I leave Sarah and our beautiful children? I was tormented. In the cold light of day could I ever leave her? The Methodist District certainly would have none of it. I agonized as Jasper automatically turned the corner onto Cornfield Road westbound. Storm clouds were swirling in the distance blowing their way eastward toward our farm. No, I concluded, it was not in God's plan for me to leave my wife.

After cooling down Jasper, watering him and giving him an extra portion of oats, I walked into the house to find no one there, at least not until I went upstairs and found Dorothy napping, and Junior and Zeke staring out their bedroom window. I could tell by their expressions that something was wrong.

When they saw me, both of them started yelling at once.

"Junior, what's going on?"

"They shot Sailor Dog and dragged him behind the barn."

"Sailor Dog?" I questioned.

Both boys nodded. Zeke started crying, and Junior chewed on his fingers.

"Where's your Mother?"

"Sailor Dog was barking so she and Aunt Polly went to find out why."

"They took our BB guns."

"Who took them?"

"Two guys wearing black. They didn't look like farmers."

I was beginning to understand what happened or at least I thought so. "Go hide under your beds and stay there," I ordered, then changed my mind.

"No, first go wake up Dorothy and bring her in here to stay with you. Shut your door and don't let her wander off. Stay away from the window and try to stay under the bed until I come back." I drew down the roller shade, yellowed with age.

Next, I flew downstairs to the telephone and called the sheriff's office, thanking God that the Methodist District provided each of its ministers with a telephone. The sheriff's office answered after only one ring and said there'd be someone coming between thirty minutes and an hour. That was too long to leave Polly and Sarah with strangers who had a gun. I walked to my gun closet in the back room and took out my shotgun.

As I set out the back door to go down to Polly's place, the fancy Plymouth touring car from this morning tore out from behind Polly's barn, sped down her long driveway and turned left onto the road away from our house. I squinted to see if Sarah and Polly were in the car. I saw nothing; it was all too fast. With my heart racing, I started running toward the barn, yelling their names over and over.

"Sarah. Polly. Sarah. Polly."

The door to the old granary opened, and Sarah and Polly staggered out. Both shielded their eyes from the sun.

"They told us not to leave until an hour after they left," Sarah said. "But I was worried about the children and then we heard you calling."

Looking in the distance to the boys' window, the shade still appeared to be drawn. I praised God for my obedient children and offered a silent prayer that my loved ones were safe. Taking Sarah's arm, we walked back to the house to wait for the sheriff. I could feel Sarah trembling as we climbed the steep hill to our house; she was sniffing back tears and stumbled a few times. In stark contrast, Polly walked stiffly, her face drawn tight.

Of course, the boys were as upset as I'd ever seen them when they found out that Sailor Dog was indeed dead, and that the strangers had taken off with their BB guns. Sarah began to console them, and Polly played with Dorothy, so I took on the unpleasant task of burying the dog. A soft green patch in back of Polly's barn by the old grapevine looked to be the best place. As I dug, I wondered why Polly had insisted on taking the BB guns. They might as well have taken my old slingshot.

By the time I finished, Sheriff Conlin and Zeb Bylowski had arrived and were questioning both Polly and Sarah. The sheriff told the boys he'd try to find their BB guns but couldn't make any promises. The boys both shrugged and ran out to the barn to play. Oh, if only I could shrug off this crisis so easily.

Polly Wolcott Forrest

Monday, May 28, 1934

I cried all weekend, mourning my beautiful Sailor Dog, remembering all the comfort he'd given me over the past weeks and months. Sometimes after Sam hit me, I'd sit on the back stoop, and Sailor Dog would come sidle up and lick me. He seemed to know when I was upset and he'd turn up at my side. The day that Sam pushed me off the wagon and I fell into the gully below, Sailor Dog came and comforted me, whining until Sam ordered me into the buggy and took me to Dr. Grayson, who taped up my ribs. I was in pain for many long days, and Sailor Dog hung around the stoop until I was well enough to come out and sit with him. What a precious friend, Sailor Dog.

In his absence the only thing that could cheer me up was a good long ride on Ginger, but yesterday I was sobbing all the way down the bridle trail. Afterwards, I'd spent most of the day dragging around the house feeling weepy, wondering if I'd been better off if Sam had successfully killed me the late October day he pushed me off the wagon. Instead of Sam being absent from my life, he was still here, sending his thugs to scare and intimidate me and to kill my dear dog.

I sat on the wooden stoop, trying to recreate warm memories when the sheriff came up the driveway. He was by himself and sat down next to me.

"You doing okay?"

I nodded. "Sarah and Wes are next door and have been helping me out, particularly since this last incident."

"Well, you might want to spend your nights up there with them, for peace of mind, anyway."

"I've been thinking about that. Any news on the two White House policemen?"

"Those guys weren't White House Police, as you'd probably already figured out. Funny thing, though, they used actual names of real White House agents who were in Cincinnati last Friday."

"What are their real names?"

"We don't know yet. That's why you shouldn't be spending your days or nights alone in this house. It's possible your late husband was involved with some rough fellows. Be careful."

I recited all the details of the incident again and he took his leave to go up the hill to talk to Sarah. I was feeling much more comfortable with the sheriff who now seemed to be focusing his investigation outward rather than at me and my family.

Retreating to the house to force myself to eat some supper, Sailor Dog kept penetrating my thoughts. Every time I shut my eyes he was there looking soulfully at me. I tried to eat a slice of bread, but my appetite failed me; instinctively I got up to take the uneaten bread out to Sailor Dog's bowl and found myself flooded with tears one more time. Finally, I called Sarah to ask if I could spend the night on their davenport.

"Sure," she said. "I'll get out some sheets and a blanket, but bring your own pillow; we don't have any extras." I grabbed a pillow from the bedroom and ran up to their back door.

Sarah was waiting for me, sheets in her arms, leading me into the parlor. "You'll have to get up early with the kids; I don't want them getting any ideas about sleeping late. Now, go into Dorothy's room and quietly change into your nightgown. I'll make sure Wes stays in our bedroom."

Somehow it didn't surprise me that Sarah was giving me orders, not consolation. When I came back downstairs, she was waiting for me with the davenport already made up.

"I'll come wake you up in the morning after Wes has gone out."

"Thank you," I said. She was treating me like a four-year-old once again. Making sure I got up with the children. Acting as if I was one more chore for her to orchestrate. It saddened me. After what we'd been through, I didn't want this division between us to continue.

"Sarah, whatever those two men were looking for, I'm not involved. If I knew, I never would have gone over to the granary looking for them. You saw them kill Sailor Dog. We were in terrible danger."

"Yes," she sighed. "We were lucky to get out alive. You're right; this isn't a time for us to be snapping at each other. Let's start fresh. I'm glad you're here."

I gave her a big bear hug and she took her kerosene lamp and went down the hall. Briefly I wished I was going down the hall to Wes's bed, but I cleared those thoughts from my mind. If anytime, I needed Sarah and Wes right now, as a sister and brother, to help me.

Lying down on Sarah's davenport, I shut my eyes and breathed in her clean sheets. They smelled the same as when she brought them in from the clothesline—fresh, clean, cottony, unlike my pillowcase which I hadn't laundered in weeks. I'd hoped to fall asleep immediately and wake up refreshed, a new person.

However, it turned out there were three lumps in the davenport that were hard as rocks, and there was no way of avoiding them. I willed myself to fall asleep anyway, despite the lumps. But they poked harder and harder into my chest, stomach and thighs. When I could no longer endure the pressure, I got up and turned the cushions upside down, but the result was no better, perhaps worse, with more springs sticking up in different places. I then tried putting the cushions on the floor, but they still were jabbing me. Finally I put the cushions back on the davenport, and I stayed on the floor with the sheets, blanket and pillow. I managed to fall asleep for a few minutes, but kept waking up because the floor was so hard.

A few hours into the night, I migrated back to the davenport and sat up with my feet up on the ottoman, drifting into a nightmarish hell where Sam slugged me so hard I fell unconscious. The nightmares recurred every hour or two. Twice Sam pushed me off the wagon and I'd see him standing up above, laughing, looking down at me in the ravine. I was in horrible pain, wondering if I'd manage to get out.

"Polly, Polly, wake up time," Sarah cried out. I'd heard Wes go out the door earlier, but I'd fallen back asleep.

"No, I just fell asleep; I need an hour or two more."

"No. You can go to your house and sleep some more, but you have to set a good example for the children." She stood her ground, waiting for me to get up.

"Okay, okay." I took my clothes and quietly got dressed in Dorothy's little room, not making a sound.

"Thank you," I muttered to Sarah as I took my leave out the back door, hugging my pillow. I was genuinely grateful to my sister for her kindness, but I was exhausted.

As I walked down the hill to my house, I concluded that something was wrong with me. Even though Sam's death had given me a reprieve, all I could see was the negatives in my life. How lucky I'd been that Black Devil committed his revenge on that evil man. But instead of reveling in my new-found freedom, I was afraid of my own shadow, crying my eyes out for days on end, losing sleep every night. I couldn't even enjoy my sister's hospitality. Everything in my life was like Sarah's davenport, lumpy and painful.

When I arrived back in the house, I took out a pad and paper from Sam's roll top desk and wrote:

1. *Sarah is my sister, not my enemy. We survived a horrible experience together. I will do nothing to drive a wedge between us. That includes Wesley.*

2. *I will not be passive. I am alive, not Sam. I will not feel hopeless. I will find a way to take care of myself and I won't let his ghosts haunt me. No more fear of Sailor Dog's killers. I have a deadbolt lock and a telephone, and I will ask Wes to teach me to shoot real guns, not my nephews' BB guns.*

3. *I will search the hayloft high and low to find clues about what Sam was doing out there, even if he was storing weapons, meeting with anarchists, and planning unthinkable deeds.*

After writing that down, I went out to the barn to begin a thorough search to find Sam's secrets. I wondered if I'd find a tube of lipstick. Perhaps I'd find receipts or Presidential documents. However, after searching up and down for three hours, I found nothing. What had Sam been doing up in the hayloft? Or in the dingy, dark back room of the old granary?

I had regained my resolve, but had no answers to any of the questions.

Sarah Wolcott Johnson

Thursday, May 31, 1934

Normally, I would have been happy and calm. The setting was perfect: I was sitting in the rocking chair by the south-facing kitchen window darning Wesley's socks. The sun was just right for darning; it flowed over my shoulder, allowing me to see the stitches clearly. Dorothy sat on the floor playing with the eggbeater, pretending to whip up some egg whites. But my nerves were on edge. It had been six days since Polly and I were held at gunpoint, and I still couldn't relax. When Dorothy shouted up to me, I jumped to the ceiling.

"Mommy, Mommy, I wanna do flowers."

I counted to ten and then spoke to Dorothy. "Turn the crank and finish your egg whites, but don't put your fingers in the beater. That would cause an ouchie. We need to wait for Aunt Polly before we can take the flowers to the cemetery." I transferred my little wooden block to another sock that had a small hole. The block spread the threads flat so I could darn it evenly and not create a rumpled mess. I'd be teaching Dorothy to darn socks soon enough.

Dorothy jumped up and dragged her three-legged stool underneath the phone, picked up the receiver, and dialed the number seven—Polly's number on our party line. Was this the same baby girl who wasn't even toilet trained a few weeks ago? So much could happen in such a short time. Polly taught her numbers last week and showed her how to dial. Would Polly be teaching her to read next week?

"Aunt Polly, I wanna do flowers," Dorothy yelled into the phone.

There was a short pause.

"Dec-or-a-tion Day," she answered.

"Okay." Then she put the receiver back and scooted the little stool back to the sink.

I reminded Dorothy that she should always say goodbye before she hung up the phone.

In a flash, she retrieved the stool, picked up the phone again, and spoke into the dial tone, "Goodbye." Then she hung up a second time.

I was so grateful that the Methodist District had provided us with a telephone so Wesley could stay in touch with church members. As much as I got irritated with the District on other things, like not letting us know the length of Wes's appointment, I was happy that we had that phone in case those thugs showed up again. I was feeling more protective of Polly these days. I knew that the veneer she put on for those two thugs was pure bravado, that underneath she had been as scared as I was.

Soon after Dorothy's phone call, Polly appeared with a picnic basket full of flowers and Ball jars in the back of her buggy. Every Decoration Day, the two of us took flowers to the Wolcott graves at the Oakridge Cemetery in Marshall. Today we were starting with Sam's grave at our little church graveyard.

"You're sure the water pump outside the church is working?"

I nodded. "John Newson performed some magic with it. I'm not sure what, but Wes is happy the well hasn't gone dry. One less problem that needs fixing."

Polly had already harnessed Ginger to her buggy, so we hopped in, put Dorothy between us, and drove over to the church. Once we got there, Dorothy stuck to Polly like glue while she pumped water into the jars and arranged the flowers.

I noticed that the Torquinis and the Rileys had already placed bouquets on their family plots. So had the Newsoms.

Polly made a huge bouquet of red poppies with foliage for Sam's grave. I made two large arrangements of irises, poppies, and spirea for the entrance to the cemetery, and we saved the rest to take into town to put on the graves of our father and brothers.

By the time we'd gotten to the cemetery in town and arranged the flowers on the gravesites, it was getting a little cloudy. Still, Polly insisted on stopping for a moment at Miller's Grocery. She came back with two small bags.

"Coffee—a bag for you and one for me." She smiled broadly and gave me a sisterly hug. By the time we started heading back, Dorothy was asleep with her head on my lap.

"Sarah…" Polly hesitated like she was afraid to ask me something. "Did you ever see Sam with another woman?"

"No, not even once. Why do you ask?"

"A few things. Now that I have a phone, I get calls, and the person hangs up as soon as I answer. Millie Jordan told me that's what the *other woman* does."

"It could be anyone, even those thugs, trying to find out if you're home," I suggested.

"All the time that Sam spent out in the barn made me suspicious. But what woman would meet a man out in a barn?"

"One who was getting paid," I answered. "But don't you think you would have seen somebody coming up the driveway?" I added. "I keep an eye on both our driveways. I can see anybody driving up, and I'm always looking out the window, watching the boys." My voice dropped. "Clearly, I miss a lot of things. I didn't see the thugs drive up and park in the back of your barn."

"I guess someone could sneak in now and then, not regularly. But there's Sam's trips to town. Sometimes he'd be gone half a day or more. How long does a trip to the grist mill take?"

"About an hour or two depending on how many people are ahead of you. But Polly, why would Sam have wanted another woman? You're young and beautiful. It's more likely he got entangled in some anarchist's plot."

Polly sighed. "That would be worse than a fallen woman. Can you imagine being married to someone who tried to kill the President?"

She turned to me. "I keep wondering if that's what he was doing out in the barn all those days. Remember the assassination attempt last year on President-elect Roosevelt when the mayor of Chicago was killed. Do you think Sam could have been in on that?"

I couldn't offer an answer. Sam was so quiet. For all I knew he might have been using a wireless radio out in the barn, planning something illegal. All this speculation was driving me crazy.

Polly was pulling the buggy up to my stepping stone. She pulled Ginger to a halt, and looked at me.

"Wes doesn't want to teach me to shoot," Polly announced. "I understand that as a minister he's concerned about how the guns would be used, so I respect his decision." There was resignation in her voice. I was happy Wes wouldn't be in personal contact with my sister, but at the same time troubled that Polly was in a situation where she feared for her life. If I knew how to shoot, I'd teach her.

Polly Wolcott Forrest

Monday, June 4, 1934

Deputy Zeb Bylowski came by this morning, not unexpectedly. It had been a week and a half, and the ruffians who killed Sailor Dog hadn't been apprehended. When the deputy walked in, I offered to make some coffee, and to my surprise, he said yes. Instead of the formal parlor where we'd always met with the sheriff, we sat at the kitchen table, waiting for the coffee to percolate on the cookstove.

With a handsome face and dark brown hair and eyes, Deputy Bylowski was tall and slender. I'd already noticed the absence of a wedding ring, but that didn't mean much to people around here. Most farmers didn't wear rings—if a ring got caught on something sharp, it could take off a finger or even a hand. Needless to say, farm equipment had lots of sharp edges, so it was rare to see a man sporting a ring.

"Are you feeling better today?" he asked.

"I'm having trouble sleeping and I miss my dog terribly. Do you have any idea who those thugs are or what they wanted?"

"Well, Sheriff Conlin told you, they're not Stimson and Cavanaugh, Mrs. Forrest."

I interrupted him. "Oh, please call me Polly."

He smiled but didn't use either name. "Those two men were impersonating two actual agents with those names. You said they had gold White House Police badges. Did the badges look like this?"

He pulled out a sketch of a badge that matched perfectly. I nodded.

"You have no idea who these two really are? Their real names?"

"No."

"Did they show you anything with names—like a driver's license or government card?"

I shook my head.

"Do you know why they wanted plates?" I asked.

"I can't tell you right now. The White House Police seemed very interested when Sheriff Conlin called them; I suspect they'll send someone to interview you."

I raised my eyebrows. "How strange that the White House is interested. I figured the two men created a hoax to look inside my house with robbery in mind."

Zeb nodded and changed the subject. "Did you ever meet Sam's brother, Mitchell?"

"No, I wrote him a letter after Sam's death, but a few days ago it came back returned, address unknown."

"What do you know about Mitchell?" he asked.

Just then the new telephone rang. Zeb nodded indicating it was okay to answer it. I caught it after the third ring, but when I answered I heard a click and no one was there.

"Do you think that was those guys checking to see if I'm home?" I asked Zeb.

He shrugged. "When you leave the house, just take the phone off the hook so anyone calling will hear the busy signal. Then they'll think you're home."

"Oh, but that would tie up the whole party line. Sarah would be infuriated, and Mrs. Cross, down the road who spends a good portion of her day on the phone, both talking and listening in, would soon be over pounding on my door. She seems to think the telephone was invented just for her."

He smiled. "Let's get back to Mitchell. What did Sam tell you about him?

"Only that he has a ranch in Wyoming. I never met him."

"Anything else?"

"They weren't close. Mitchell had been living in Wyoming for many years. Sam said he'd made a trip out there to visit him before he started farming here in Michigan." I paused for a moment. "Hmm, if you think one of the impersonators was Mitchell, I have to say there was absolutely no family resemblance. If you ever met Sam, you'd know he was tall and thin, dark hair, longish oval face, clear blue eyes. These guys were short and heavy with full round faces and double chins. Actually, they looked a lot alike. Not twins, but perhaps brothers."

He nodded. "Did you ever see Sam making sketches?"

"Well, yes; he occasionally would sketch farm scenes. He was a good artist, much better than me. An amazingly talented artist." I was surprised that I had anything good to say about Sam. "He sketched my horse Ginger. It's my favorite one."

"Can I look at the drawings?"

I ran upstairs to my treasure box and pulled out the sketches. Zeb thumbed through them until he came to the sketch of Ginger.

"Beautiful horse."

"Do you want to see her?" I didn't expect him to say yes.

"Absolutely."

We went out to the barn and I led Ginger out in the yard with a rope. "What a beauty," he said, rubbing her sleek neck.

I nodded in agreement.

"Do you like to ride?"

He nodded. "I practically grew up on horses. I have a dark brown Quarter Horse named Jackson at my parents' farm. When I can afford it, I'm going to buy some land and raise horses. I'd hoped I'd be there by now, but these times are hard on everyone, even those of us who still have jobs."

"What a nice dream. Myself, I'd like to raise horses and own a hat shop." I'd never said that out loud before. Sure, Sam knew about my dream of a hat shop, but raising horses wasn't part of it.

Zeb raised both eyebrows and started laughing. "That goes together like salt and pepper. Raising horses and selling hats. Have you considered cowboy hats?"

I started laughing.

"Well, I know the two don't exactly fit together nicely, but there you have it. Eenie, meenie, minie, moe. Raise horses or start a millinery shop."

Walking back to the house from the barn, we stopped in the old granary and Zeb and I looked around the back room again. There was some dirt-covered lumber, a rusted-out wash tub, and a couple of straw brooms that had seen better days. No plates. No money.

"Would you like a couple of worn-out brooms?"

Zeb shook his head and laughed. He was so handsome when he laughed. I'd never noticed. I guessed it was because Sheriff Conlin overshadowed him. Or perhaps I'd never seen Zeb laugh.

Before he left, Zeb asked something that stayed with me.

"When this is all over and your case is closed, would you like to go out to see a movie?"

I smiled at him and said yes. It felt good to be one hundred percent certain I was telling the truth.

Then I wondered what had just happened. I pondered the fact that I'd told Zeb my dreams of raising horses and owning a hat shop. Zeb, who was investigating whether I opened the gate to Black Devil's pen with the intention of killing my husband. Zeb, who had power over whether I went to jail or not. Life used to be carefree. Now I had to think through every sentence I uttered, every action I took.

When Sam died, hallelujah, I thought I'd been given a second chance. I'd take his money and run. Create a new life. Maybe visit Paris and then make a go of it in California. But today, talking to Zeb, I visualized a different life. I loved horses and I loved making hats. That vision wouldn't require a move to San Francisco. I felt so totally, unbelievably, happy. How amazing that I was pondering a future right here at home.

My good feelings were short-lived. After Zeb left, Sarah called to check on me. I reassured her I was okay and told her about Zeb's questions. Thinking about the thugs who killed Sailor Dog infuriated me, and I wondered if Sam had been in cahoots with them. They both seemed to think what they wanted was in the back room of the old granary. As far as I knew, Sam was the only person who used that building.

Frankly, I was worried that my life was at stake. Would they have killed me if Sarah hadn't been with me? And what were the plates they were looking for? They seemed more like thieves than religious zealots, but I'd heard the story of Mr. Smith finding gold plates buried on his farm in New York state. Those plates had been engraved with religious instructions, and Mr. Smith started a new religion based in Utah. Maybe Sam had found some gold plates on our farm. It's unlikely that Sam would have wanted to start a religion, but he would have tried to sell anything made of gold.

Gosh darn it, life got messier and messier. It seemed fitting when Sam met his end with Black Devil. Divine retribution. But why didn't I see all this coming? I knew Sam was evil from the day he first hit me: October 2, only one month after we were married. Why didn't I walk away that day? Sarah was right next door. I could have left him, easily.

My bruises and other injuries kept piling up. It was my fault, he said. I asked for too much. My cooking was terrible. I was trying to poison him. I complained too much. Later when Sam pushed me off the wagon, it became clear that his intent was more than to intimidate me: it was murder disguised as an accident.

But now those creepy sinister men had entered my life. It seemed like Sam was laughing from his grave. "Polly, it's not over. They got Sailor Dog and they can get you, too." I could hear his voice saying that I deserved the extra punch, that extra bruise, those broken ribs.

Thank God, Sam was dead.

Too bad, Mr. Samuel Forrest, you may have won some battles, but you lost the war. Signing off, Perturbed Polly.

Sarah Wolcott Johnson

Tuesday, June 5, 1934

Polly showed up at the house this morning and asked if I would drive her to the Marshall train station the next morning. She wanted to visit a millinery shop in Lansing. When I asked her what hats she was going to take, she looked at me like I had asked her to fly to the moon.

"None. I don't have any to sell. You, of all people, should know that. I'm going to ask them if they want me to make any for them to sell."

"Okay, Polly, let's start over," I answered, wanting to avoid one more squabble. "I'll drive you to the train station tomorrow morning. Afterwards, Dorothy and I will pick up the Ball jars from the cemeteries. Next year, if times are better, let's buy urns and plant some geraniums. They're such pretty flowers and we don't have to worry about losing our canning jars."

Polly wasn't paying attention to what I was saying, looking out the window toward her farm. "There's some strange things going on," she said. "I think someone goes into the barn and the outbuildings and moves stuff around."

"What kinds of things get switched?"

"Oh, shovels and axes. Things like that. A couple of pails are missing and so is a scoop."

"A scoop?"

"Yes, one that I use when I feed the chickens shelled corn."

"You remember where all those things are?" This was so uncharacteristic of Polly.

"Well, maybe it's a friendly ghost moving Sam's stuff around in the middle of the night." Polly laughed out loud.

Me, I had trouble laughing about Sam's barn, particularly if he had been using it to stir up trouble for the White House.

Polly Wolcott Forrest

Wednesday, June 6, 1934

Finally, I was off to Lansing to deposit my two insurance checks. No one would know me there, and I couldn't rest easy while the checks were buried in my yard. I told Sarah I was going to a millinery shop, which wasn't the entire truth, but I needed an excuse so she'd drop me off at the train station. I wore my navy blue suit and hat, and to my surprise, Sarah complimented my appearance. The hat was exactly like the one I made her for Christmas, plain and dignified, yet elegant, with a small veil over the forehead. I wanted to appear to be an affluent widow who needed to make bank deposits.

After arriving at the station, I wondered if I'd made a mistake by dressing up. Men in dirty, tattered clothing filled up the waiting room. Most stared idly into space; I doubted if they were waiting for a train. This observation made me fear a thief might grab my purse and run off with it. Inside my bag were the two checks I was going to deposit into two separate Lansing banks, hoping that if one bank failed the other would remain open. My nerves were frayed from worrying about losing the checks. Clutching my bag close to my stomach with both hands, I walked up to the ticket window.

As I pulled out my wallet to purchase a ticket, I looked to see that both checks were still in their respective envelopes. Reassured that they were, I bought my round-trip ticket. Then, breathing a sigh of relief, I looked up at the large clock in the station and realized it was going to be another twenty minutes before my train arrived, so I looked around for a place to sit.

At first I only saw more filthy men who never looked up to acknowledge me, let alone offer me a seat. Finally, I settled on a bench beside a woman wearing a soiled, green-checked gingham housedress. Two small children sat at her feet. They too had distant looks on their faces and I wondered if the hard times had taken them from their home. I chose to say nothing. Another day I might have given the children each a penny for a candy, but I didn't want to be opening my purse, and risk losing the checks.

My experience with trains was limited. Mother took me with her once when she went to Connecticut to visit the Blessing grandparents. I was probably seven or eight and I'd wanted to sit in the dining car and choose food from a menu, but Mother had packed a dinner for us, claiming it was too expensive to eat in the dining car. I begged and begged, so she relented and we went after the dinner rush. She ordered me a Coca-Cola and she had a cup of tea. We talked about the nice appointment of the dining car with white linen tablecloths and little vases of red roses in the center of each table.

That day, I decided I wanted to be rich. The waiters were polite in asking each person what they'd like to eat, and it seemed so much fun reading the menu and deciding. The few people remaining in the dining car were eating and chatting away happily, expecting to be treated like royalty. In a booth across the aisle from Mother and me sat a man, woman, and little girl about my age. She was wearing a frilly, pink dress and she had a chicken dinner with mashed potatoes and gravy. Even though she had a drumstick, her mother cut up the chicken for her and the girl ate it with her fork.

I remembered that scene like it was yesterday. After they'd finished their dinner, a waiter brought a tray of desserts and told the little girl to choose which one she wanted. I watched every second, deciding what I would have chosen: a chocolate ice cream sundae with whipped cream and a big red cherry on top. But no, the girl chose a plate with three ordinary sugar cookies. Then she only ate one half of a single cookie. To my surprise her mother didn't wrap the remaining cookies to save them in her purse. Instead, the waiter took them away and dumped them into a garbage canister. It was that day that I decided I wanted to be "well-to-do."

With Sam's death, my luck had changed. The two life insurance checks were in my purse. I made a mental note to go to the dining car on the trip home and order anything I wanted. Perhaps even two desserts, and certainly a chocolate ice cream sundae, if they had it.

I hadn't told Sarah about the cans of money I'd found hidden on window sills and shelves around the farm. That was how I noticed that things had been moved. I'd paid attention to every single item in every outbuilding. Surprisingly, I'd found nothing in the haymow even though I'd searched that whole area several times.

Instead, I'd found cans of money in the toolshed, milk house, smokehouse, and icehouse on shelves along with cans of nails and screws. I was enjoying being this new Polly, the one who could find money and then bury it in the soft earth, hidden from all.

I had called the Lansing banks and gotten directions from them so I knew exactly where to go once the train arrived at the station. It would be an easy walk to the Lansing Savings Bank on Grand River Avenue, then another ten-minute walk down to Michigan National Bank on Michigan Avenue. To my dismay, when we arrived in Lansing it was spitting rain and I hadn't even thought to bring an umbrella.

Rushing as fast as I could, I managed to get to the first bank before the downpour. I walked into the large cavernous room with marble floors and six teller windows. When I got to the window and told the teller what I wanted to do, he took me to a stark little room to meet with Mr. Carlisle. I sat at the polished wooden table that had a high-finish shine. On the far wall were two pictures of sailing ships; otherwise the room was empty.

Mr. Carlisle walked in and introduced himself. The banker was all smiles and asked me how I was doing.

"Fine," I responded crisply. I wanted to get this business completed and on to the next bank.

"So why are you starting an account with us if you live near Marshall?" he asked. I hadn't anticipated that question, figuring they'd be happy to get the money, no questions asked.

"I'll be moving here in a few months," I lied.

"Do you have a new address in Lansing?" he inquired.

"Not yet. I'll be looking for a place soon." The lies were piling up and I felt a pain in my stomach. Mr. Carlisle started talking about different neighborhoods including the one he lived in. He was wearing a wedding band so I figured he was just being friendly, but I was anxious to get the second check deposited. Mr. Carlisle took a crow's age with all the paperwork, making mindless small talk as he did. He was as bad as Mrs. Cross.

We both looked up when the thunder became louder and louder. "My goodness," he said. "Sounds like quite a storm."

"I forgot to bring an umbrella. I was so focused on keeping the check safe." I said nothing about the second check, which was still weighing heavily on my mind.

He nodded knowingly. Why was I saying this? Nerves, I suppose. He didn't need to know I'd forgotten an umbrella.

The banker finished the transaction, gave me a small dark-blue savings account book with the date stamped on the first page and the amount of the deposit written beside it. Mr. Carlisle thanked me for using their bank, and wished me well with the move. I wasn't even sure I thanked him. I waited by the large glass doors with several other patrons until the rain subsided. Then I sloshed through several puddles and a light rain until I got to the second bank. My navy suit and hat were wet, but there was nothing I could do about it.

The transaction was easier with the second banker, who was younger than Mr. Carlisle, and was all business. Asking me no personal questions, he handed me another savings account book, this one maroon-colored. So now I had two of them in my purse replacing the checks. Finally, I could relax.

The rain had ceased and I felt a sense of euphoria as I walked to my next destination. This was a reward I had planned for myself after depositing both checks. Soon I found myself looking into the window of a fancy millinery shop, only two blocks from the second bank. As I gazed in, my eyes were met with the most delightful treats: hats in all shapes, sizes, and colors with a myriad of accessories. I stood there mesmerized.

A little bell atop the door announced my entry, and I could see a large, well-dressed older lady who was being helped by a middle-aged male clerk. Taking time to look around, I speculated on the newest styles and became fascinated by the large number of hats that were worn, not straight on the head, but asymmetrically. They dipped slightly on the side of mannequin heads creating a rather risqué, flirtatious look. My favorite was a bright red one with a large bow, totally inappropriate for a grieving widow. I pulled myself away before I was tempted to try it on.

Continuing on to another counter where I found hats labeled "Greta Garbo Slouches." These seemed to be updated cloches with the addition of brims or little visors, ribbons, and accented top stitching. I knew that Garbo had worked as a milliner's assistant before she started acting and I thought about her gorgeous hats in *A Woman of Affairs*. As I scanned the display, a gray-green felt cloche caught my eye. It sported a three-inch brim with a dark green decorative frog in the shape of a fleur-de-lis, so tasteful and elegant. It had no price tag; I assumed it was expensive.

Glancing over at the other customer, I saw that she was deciding between two hats, both ordinary and quite boring. They were the new "mannish fedora styles," one was light gray and one dark gray, both made of felt. No decorations on either. I thought she had no clue that with her plump face and gray hair, either hat would have been equally unbecoming. This would be Sarah in twenty years.

I made my way to yet another counter featuring tams, berets, and turbans, so unusual and cute. Made of velvet, crepe, silk, and brocade, they were decorated with the prettiest pins, including flower, bird, and butterfly motifs. I realized that I should buy some hat pins if I continued to be serious about making and re-making hats. Small and simple, they added a delicate touch.

Moving on to another table, I studied the boaters, straw hats with colored bands. Definitely casual summer hats that resembled men's wear. The table offered bowlers, Panama hats, buckets, and swingers as well. I imagined how nice they would look paired with a flowered dress at a casual picnic. My mind was taking me to outings on parks, lakes and rivers where these hats would be perfect on a warm, summer day.

The clerk was still assisting the elderly lady. He was patient beyond belief, but didn't offer any suggestions to spruce up her choices. Had I been the sales clerk I would have shown her a gray hat trimmed with a bow or ribbon at the very least. Even one of the butterfly hat pins would have made her choices more appealing. Finally, she settled on the darker hat, made her purchase, and left with a red and black hatbox that was much prettier than the hat, all deposited into a large bag with the shop's name on it.

"May I help you?" The clerk turned to me. It was strange being waited on by a man in a ladies' hat shop; I hadn't expected that. I was a bit uncomfortable, but I had seen how patient he'd been with the previous customer.

"Yes, I hope so. I make hats and I wanted to find out if you would consider buying from me."

"Did you bring any samples?" He glanced at his pocket watch and then back at me.

"No, I had other business to attend to today."

"Well, that's probably for the better, business being so poor because of the Depression. I had to let my sales girl go a few weeks back and now I tend to the store myself."

"Do you sell supplies like ribbons, feathers, pins, and netting for veils?"

The clerk's eyes lit up.

"Normally we keep only enough to do repairs, but I've decided to go ahead and sell whatever I can. I'm sure you understand."

I nodded.

He led me over to a counter and began pulling out the most beautiful kinds of netting. Some pieces were different colors, and others had loose or tight weave, and some were filigree, with butterflies, flowers and abstract patterns. One had big green leaves that would need to be positioned somewhere other than over the eyes, perhaps over the forehead.

"Did you see Marlene Dietrich in *Shanghai Express*?" he asked me.

"Yes, I loved that movie."

"Well, these are the kinds of veils she wore, very fashionable." He pulled out two magazines with photos of Miss Dietrich wearing nose veils. Of course, I was hypnotized. I gazed at the magazine photos, and then back at the various veil supplies.

Then he pulled out ribbons, feathers, and a small parcel of hat pins. I was in heaven. All the supplies I'd need for five years, perhaps. Of course, I'd still need basic hats. But I might be able to get them from a wholesaler, maybe in New York or Paris.

"How much for all these supplies?" I asked.

He looked at me like I had asked to buy the store and then looked over all his goods. He glanced over everything again.

"Twenty dollars," he replied.

"I'll take it. But you'll need to wrap them so they're well-protected, in case it starts raining again."

I opened my wallet and drew out a twenty-dollar bill. It had come from a stash that Sam had left in a rusty coffee can on a window ledge in the large toolshed. The clerk looked at it, rubbing his finger across the edge, then went into a back room to put it in the safe. He was gone for a long time, perhaps ten minutes.

"Sorry, sometimes it takes a few tries to get the safe to work." He proceeded to wrap up each pile of netting, slowly adding some cotton fabric between each one.

I looked up at the clock above the door. It was two o'clock and my train was scheduled to leave in forty-five minutes. I knew that if I left within five minutes, I'd make it with time to spare since I already had purchased my return ticket. But I needed the clerk to speed up his packing efforts.

"Oh, how time has escaped me. I should be going in order to catch my train. I think you've done a good job. I need to leave."

The clerk started fidgeting with the layers, saying he needed to find a bag large enough for everything. He bent down behind the counter pulling out a variety of bags I instantly knew were too small for my purchases.

I made my voice more insistent. "I think a bag the size you used for your previous customer would do quite well."

Just then the door opened and two uniformed policemen came barging in.

"Is this her?"

The clerk nodded and handed one of the cops a twenty-dollar bill. The policeman held it up to the light and then ran his hand across it several times, rubbed it between his fingers and pulled out another twenty-dollar bill from his pocket and compared it. Then he asked me to show him what else was in my wallet.

"We have to take you down to the station. These bills are counterfeit."

⌇⌇⌇

Never had I been so humiliated in my life. If the ride to the police station wasn't painful enough, once we arrived, I had to surrender my hat, handbag, shoes and silver brooch for inspection. Not surprisingly there was a lot of interest in the two new savings account booklets in my bag. A large clock on the wall revealed it was 3:15; I'd missed my train. I started trembling and I couldn't focus my thoughts.

A pock-marked, oversized officer named Ray McGreevy, with slicked back greasy hair and an air of sadistic cruelty, sat across from me at a table in a tiny room. I really needed to use the bathroom, but I wasn't going to ask anything of this gruff, oily-haired, so-called public servant. He scowled, offered me no water or toilet break and pounded questions at me, one after another.

"Where did you get the money?"

"Where was it printed?

"What kind of printing press did you use?"

"How much do you have at home?"

"Where is the rest hidden?"

"Why did you come to Lansing today?"

"Did you deposit any cash?"

"Where were the checks from?"

"Why didn't you deposit your checks in Marshall?"

"Where did you get the fancy clothes you're wearing?"

"What kind of car do you drive?"

And on and on, relentlessly.

I tried to answer all the questions honestly. I really did. But my voice was quavering and my hands shaking. When I told him about finding the money in a baking powder can in the toolshed, Officer McGreevy laughed out loud.

"Found it in a baking powder can, did you?"

I nodded.

Disgust lined his face. "Well, missy, you're in a heap of trouble."

After the interrogation, he took me to a small holding cell guarded by a thin, young man, the "on-duty guard." The tiny cell contained only a cot and a bucket in the corner. There was nothing else, no pillow, no blanket. Presumably, Officer McGreevy was calling the Lansing banks to see if I actually had made the savings deposits with checks, not cash. In the meantime, I begged the on-duty guard to let me call my brother-in-law. He said he'd see what he could do. Once he slammed the door, I looked at the covered bucket and wondered how long I could hold my bladder. In about a half an hour, I was doubled over, unable to wait any longer. The bucket now looked like an oasis in the desert, and I found myself squatting over it in a most indelicate position.

I was in the middle of this process when I heard a quick knock on the door and the guard opened it and observed me, mid-stream. Try as I might, I couldn't stop. He frowned, shook his head, turned around, and slammed the door. Finally, after the longest pee of my life, I placed the lid on the bucket, adjusted my clothes, and lay down on the cot.

It took only a few seconds before tears began rolling down my cheeks. I cried unmercifully—the kind of tears people had expected at Sam's funeral. Now they were torrential, and I had no handkerchief, being reduced to wiping my face on my shirt tails. When they were too wet, I used my sleeves.

Even as I was crying, I got madder and madder at Sam for putting me in the middle of this mess. It didn't matter that Black Devil had killed him; I was being punished for his crimes. I cried and cried until I had no more tears inside me. Finally, I closed my eyes, although I wasn't expecting to fall asleep. It was then that the guard came in and told me I could make my telephone call. He took me to a dirty little booth with a phone and I had to call collect. Thank goodness, Wesley answered rather than Sarah. I'd already been shamed enough without enduring her criticism. Wesley seemed genuinely shocked at my situation and told me not to worry, that he would call Sheriff Conlin and ask him how to handle this. With that we hung up. I had no information on how long I'd be kept in the holding cell.

The on-duty guard took me back to the cell and said that at the very least I'd be kept overnight. He also indicated that someone would be bringing a plate of food for supper. I waited for about an hour for the food, but none arrived. So much for my chocolate ice cream sundae in the dining car. Giving up on supper, I lay back on the cot, fully dressed, and drifted in and out of sleep. All night long I ruminated about my life and how I could have prevented this day from occurring.

My thoughts ranged from accompanying Mother to Connecticut to leaving Sam after the first, second, or third time he hit me. Perhaps I could have lived with Wes and Sarah, if I'd bought them a new davenport. These thoughts were followed by what I'd do with my life if I got out of this mess, either with or without a jail sentence.

"Know thyself," one of my high school teachers had said at the beginning of a class, while all of us students snickered. Of course, we knew ourselves. The boys wanted to graduate and get jobs or become farmers. The girls wanted to get married. Simple. Or so it seemed back then. For me, money and marriage, in that order, Socrates be damned.

Now I knew differently. I looked back on my happiest days over the past year. Most were either spent with friends or family, creating beautiful hats, or riding Ginger down gravel roads and sleepy bridle trails. My best day with Sam had been the day he bought Ginger; the worst had been the day he pushed me off the wagon.

"Why me, why me?" became my mind's refrain. I was twenty-years-old, a widow and now Sam had put me in jail with counterfeit money. My head was spinning and my blood was well beyond boiling, perhaps at the hard-ball stage.

Then came the hours of should'ves and could'ves.

I should've figured out that Sam wasn't the guy for me back when we were courting. He never was willing to get together with any of my friends. Nor was he willing to go to any family picnics, nor did he ever have much to say to Mother. Those should've been warning signs. He justified all this by telling me that he "wanted to have special, private time with me."

Similarly, I should've taken note that Sam had no friends. Often, he'd have a little gift for me, and I would be so focused on opening it up, that I never questioned Sam's unusual behavior. A few little earrings and doodads displaced my suspicions about him. But there were clues: his endless bragging, his flaunting money, his superior attitude.

I should have known and part of me actually did. But Sam was so handsome and rich (I thought) that I didn't listen to that inner voice telling me to be wary. He wouldn't let me see the inside of his house before we were married. I should've guessed how dilapidated it was, every room needing repair of one kind or another. The old farmhouse had no amenities, no cute little wall cupboards for games, no fireplace for cold, winter evenings, no pretty little window seats for sunny days. It was dark, dank, and drafty, a house in total disrepair.

As the saying goes, "love is blind," but I doubt I ever was in love with Samuel. I was in love with being "well-to-do." With Mother's imminent departure . . .

With Mother's imminent departure for Connecticut, everything sped up so fast. Why didn't I just go with her? Then the test would have come. Sam would have been forced to come for visits. Then I would have known what kind of man he was. But now I knew. Unlike Wes, who made long trips to Marshall to court Sarah, I now knew that Sam would have never made any trips to Connecticut to see me.

There were incidents that I ignored. One day last summer, on our way home from church, Sam reined in Jasper to a stop. Right in the middle of the road was a long snake, perhaps the longest I'd ever seen, a blue racer, a handsome blue-gray color. Sam immediately jumped out of the buggy and pulled out his knife, cutting off the snake's head.

"Did you know that was a blue racer?" I queried him.

He nodded.

"Well, they're good snakes, not venomous and they stay away from people; there's absolutely no reason to kill them."

I saw Sam's face contort with rage. I was afraid that he'd hit me, right there in the buggy. He restrained himself, but that incident should have taught me Sam was not a person to confront.

Another incident had been even more revealing. One balmy evening last summer when we were courting, he had taken me to Adrian to the Crosswell Opera House to see a vaudeville act and I had laughed non-stop from beginning to end. Sam seemed to be fidgety, not laughing much, and frequently checked his pocket watch. When the show ended, we walked out to the buggy, and right in front of us was a little girl, perhaps six or seven, alone, crying. I went up to the girl and asked her if her parents were nearby. She shook her head and continued to cry. Then I asked her why she was crying, and she shook her head again.

"Come on, get in," Sam snapped at me. I reluctantly jumped in the buggy, and we drove away from that crying child, an action I still regretted. Why, oh why, didn't I acknowledge Sam's true character right then and there?

The night dragged on and on as I lay on that jailhouse cot. Mrs. Lutz, my English teacher, would have been proud at how I tried to get to know myself. By morning I had, perhaps, a tad more self-understanding, but I was still at the mercy of the judicial system. Whatever I wanted out of life might not matter if I was destined to spend the rest of my days behind bars.

Suddenly I jerked up to a sitting position. What was the worst that could happen? I wondered if using counterfeit money was a capital offense. However, they seemed to think I wasn't just using it, but making it as well.

I must have finally dozed off when a new guard walked into my cell. It took me a moment to realize where I was.

"This is your breakfast," he muttered, placing a plate on the floor by my head, turning and leaving.

I'd been too sleepy to ask him what was going to happen and how long I'd be there. I looked down at the food. Bread, butter, and some beans. Plus, a cup of water. My rumbling stomach told me to eat it, so I did. I ate mechanically, not tasting anything. Chewing, chewing, and swallowing. Thinking about all the mistakes I'd made and what I'd do differently if given a second chance.

Reverend Wesley Johnson

Thursday, June 7, 1934

Never in a million years would I have ever anticipated Polly's incarceration. I was reminded of the popular Bible verse Romans 3:23 that Paul wrote in a letter to the church in Rome. "For all have sinned and fallen short of the Glory of God." Reflecting on this reminded me that Paul was focusing on all mankind, not just Polly Wolcott Forrest or me. All of us were guilty of sin; none of us had lived up to God's perfect standard. Polly, like the rest of humanity, had fallen short. She deserved our kindness.

This all came about yesterday while I was trying to fix the cream separator in the back room. The phone was ringing relentlessly, and I was hoping someone else would answer it. Everyone who didn't have a phone said how lucky we were to have one. But it wasn't always a blessing. I waited, hoping that even Dorothy might answer it and end its persistent clamor. It turned out that Sarah was out in the garden picking strawberries with the children. Whoever was calling wouldn't give up. Finally, exasperated, I ran into the kitchen and answered it. Polly was in tears.

My heart fluttered. I couldn't stand to hear her weep and it took all my persuasive powers to get her calmed down. While I was reassuring her we'd get it straightened out, some bells went off in my head. I knew that the White House Police tracked counterfeiters as well as protected the President. Maybe Sam had been mixed up in a counterfeiting ring. After

186

telling Polly that I would do everything possible to get her out, I hung up and immediately called Sheriff Conlin.

"I can't tell you much right now, but I'll have Zeb call you later."

Both Sarah and I waited on pins and needles all afternoon, but the phone didn't ring. Sarah kept lifting up the phone to see if the line was clear. Twice she politely asked Mrs. Cross to get off the line since we were expecting an emergency call. We knew for a certainty that Viola Cross would be listening in on the call from Zeb. That evening around 9:30, when the kids were asleep, the phone finally rang.

I answered, waiting to hear the click from Mrs. Cross's phone. Sure enough, there was a single, discreet snap. Oh well, she'd hear about this soon enough anyway.

Zeb's voice was calm. "I've talked to the Lansing police and arranged to have Polly released in the morning so she can take a 10:30 train back to Marshall. Why don't you and I go down to pick her up at the train station at 2:00? I suspect she'll be upset."

Zeb picked me up in his old green Ford pickup truck, filling me in, while driving to the train station.

"Here's what I can tell you. The real Agents Stimson and Cavanaugh had been working on a counterfeiting case based in Wyoming. About a year ago, they had identified Mitchell Forrest's Wyoming ranch as the seat of the operation. In addition to Mitchell, there were two brothers involved, Ronald and Clovis Benson, who'd formerly run the printing presses at a couple of Wyoming newspapers. They're believed to be the printers."

"The imposters who killed Polly's dog?" I interrupted him.

"That's my hunch," Zeb responded. "But the barn on Mitchell's ranch burned up before the agents were able to find any evidence or make any arrests. They had no clues as to where they might have run." He paused. "Until now."

"Do you know if Sam was involved and do you know where Mitchell is?"

"No to both questions," Zeb answered. "But this situation isn't good."

We arrived at the train station a few minutes early and sat in silence until the train pulled in. Polly was a mess, stepping off the train, disheveled in her navy suit, her hat askew, a look of exhaustion on her face. She did produce a big smile when she saw Zeb and me waiting for her, as she attempted to fluff out her hair and wipe the wrinkles out of her skirt, to no avail.

"Thank you for coming. I'm so tired and dirty," she muttered, tears in her eyes.

After that, Polly said very little on the way home, nor did we. Anything that hadn't already been said was pure speculation.

Zeb dropped off Polly first, then me.

"Polly may be in more danger than she realizes, especially if the Benson brothers think she has a printing press, or engraved plates, or piles of money. Keep an eye on her."

I nodded in agreement and went into the house to answer Sarah's myriad of questions.

Sarah Wolcott Johnson

Tuesday, June 12, 1934

Dorothy was standing barefoot at the window, peering out, when she interrupted my reverie, shouting, "Mommy, Mommy. Aunt Polly coming. Aunt Polly coming."

I looked at Dorothy and couldn't believe her long legs. She'd grown three inches in a blink and no longer had that big, padded diaper bottom. Transformed from a baby into a little girl overnight, I wondered if once she started school she'd want to be called Dee or Dot. So many potential changes were looming on the horizon.

I walked to the window to join Dorothy. Polly and Zeb Bylowski were walking up the driveway, talking animatedly. It gave me pause. I hadn't seen Polly looking so happy since before her wedding. Dorothy ran outside to greet them and brought them into the kitchen.

"I have great news," Polly blurted out. "I'm no longer a suspect. The sheriff is no longer investigating anyone except the counterfeiters. I guess they knew I wouldn't be so stupid as to pass counterfeit bills."

"That's wonderful," I said, giving her a big hug. We all stood there in the kitchen. "What exactly did the sheriff say?"

"They found no evidence that I had acted in any way to bring about Sam's death. I imagine after the ordeal you and I went through with those two ruffians who killed Sailor Dog, the sheriff figured those two might have been involved in some way. Frankly, I can't help but think the same."

"We should celebrate." I thought for a moment. "Dorothy, go find your father and brothers. I'll make some pancakes, and we can have a big pancake dinner. Mr. Bylowski, can you join us?"

He nodded enthusiastically. "Please call me Zeb. It's my day off, but I wanted to give Polly the news myself, so yes, I'll definitely join you."

Hmm, I wondered. These two seemed awfully familiar. But for once, this was welcome. I'd observed this young man frequently over the past few months and he seemed to be of sound, moral character. Maybe it would be good having Polly take up with a man of the law. She didn't seem suited for a man of the cloth.

I busied myself making the pancakes and almost forgot the syrup, so Polly pitched in by melting some butter and adding brown sugar until it started boiling and became clear syrup. Today Polly seemed different. Previously she would have waited for me to make the syrup, but today she stepped right up. I was enjoying the new Practical Polly.

Our "celebration" was subdued because all of us were thinking about the two men who pretended to be White House Police, assumed to be Ronald and Clovis Benson. The shorter one who shot Sailor Dog was considered violent. Of course, we already knew that. Once we all had settled around the table eating pancakes, the boys took over the conversation asking Zeb about his gun and catching bad guys.

"Did you ever shoot anybody?" Junior asked.

"Fortunately, no, but I'm always ready in case I need to."

That was a response I was happy to hear. Relaxing in my chair, I smiled at Wes who was digging into the pancakes like there was no tomorrow. I'd made a double batch and all of us indulged; even Polly ate three or four. I knew that the flour I'd used would leave me short for Friday's bread baking, but so be it. Maybe Polly would have some extra flour I could borrow.

When the children had finished eating, they went outside to play, so the four of us sat around the table with full stomachs, a rare occasion these days. Polly cleared her throat. "Of course, the Sheriff's investigation had nothing to do with this White House business. The real Agents Stimson and Cavanaugh are coming next week to question me and look around the farm. Ever since Sailor Dog was killed, I've been looking for clues to a counterfeiting operation, but have found nothing."

We all knew that neighbors would be having a heyday with Polly's incarceration. Viola Cross had sharp hearing and was always the first with gossip. I'd deliberately not used the phone for a few days so I wouldn't have to pick up and hear Viola's voice. It was a certainty that Polly's ordeal was being broadcast across the township, if not the county.

I now wondered if the Bensons opened Black Devil's pen that fateful morning. I didn't see their flashy car anywhere, but they may have parked it out of sight behind the barn. Yet I wondered if they had opened the gate, why they didn't wait to find the engraved "plates" before turning Black Devil on Sam. And even if they had hidden the car, how did they get up and down the driveway without either Polly or me seeing them? And where was Mitchell? I contemplated all these unanswered questions.

Polly spoke up. "It's great that I'm no longer a murder suspect, but being held in Lansing for counterfeiting was tortuous. If Sam was involved, he never gave a hint. But it would explain why he spent every day in the barn, taking food out there and never allowing me to go up into the barn or other buildings."

Zeb didn't say a word. I wondered if he knew more about the case than he could officially tell us. The conversation took a new turn when Polly looked out the window checking on the kids. She came back smiling.

"I have something to ask, now that the children are outside and out of earshot. I've saved up some egg and milk money and I'd like to buy ponies for the kids." She looked at Wes and me. "Are you okay with that? I'd make sure to get good-natured ones and Dorothy's would be small, maybe one of those miniature Shetlands. Of course, I'd buy their feed and hay as well. I wouldn't want the church members thinking they were dropping nickels into the collection plate for the children's ponies."

The question came out of the blue; it stunned me. Once again, Polly was acting the rich girl, the aunt who bought ponies for her niece and nephews. From Practical Polly to Princess Polly in a few short minutes.

"No counterfeit money?" I asked. I couldn't tolerate more problems. I was also thinking that she might be using insurance money, leaving me with a bitter taste.

Wes interrupted. "Well, that's so very kind of you. Sarah and I'll discuss it, and let you know," he said in his most pastor-like, diplomatic voice. "And, Polly, why don't you get another dog? Even with a deadbolt lock and a telephone, we worry about you being alone in that farmhouse."

Zeb laughed. "I told her the same thing this morning."

Reverend Wesley Johnson

Tuesday, June 12, 1934

"I will *not* let my baby sister buy anything for our children with dirty money," Sarah exclaimed after Polly and Zeb headed for a pony farm on the other side of the county, *just to take a look.* I clenched my fists, wondering if Polly had hinted anything to Sarah about the day I fixed her cookstove. Sarah seemed upset and angry with Polly. I had prayed and prayed to be released from my attraction to Polly, and I believed that God had finally granted me this supplication.

To my relief Sarah seemed more focused on the ponies than anything else. I knew from conversations with Henry Fountain at the grist mill that ponies were going for a song. Anything not having to do with food and shelter could be bought at rock bottom prices and ponies definitely fit in the "recreational" group.

"She hasn't convinced me she wasn't involved in the counterfeiting herself," Sarah said.

"Do you really think she'd willingly use counterfeit money up in Lansing where she was jailed?" I countered.

"Well, knowing Polly, she might have gotten clean money mixed up with dirty money. She's always been careless, even sloppy. Her bedroom has clothes strewn all over and most days the kitchen sink is full of dirty dishes. The dust in the parlor is thick; she probably hasn't dusted since the funeral luncheon."

I had to admit that part of me was still questioning Polly's motives and wondering if Sarah was correct. It sounded like the counterfeiting operation might have been operating in Sam's barn whether or not Polly knew about it. The sheriff had told me in private that these kind of operations had popped up all over the country. They were plentiful before the Depression, but with the current hard times, the law simply couldn't keep up with all of the printing presses hidden in cellars, barns, and attics.

"I truly question whether Polly would buy ponies with hard-earned money rather than counterfeit," Sarah continued.

"She said egg and milk money," I answered. "She's probably got some money left from the sale of the cows and pigs, too."

"We need to do what's right."

Given Sarah's wariness, I knew I shouldn't oppose her, but I felt a compulsion to defend Polly.

"I know that Polly loves our children and she's extremely fond of Dorothy. Why not let her do something that allows her to spend more time with the children? However, if you're worried the boys would get too wild with the ponies or that Dorothy might fall off, that's another matter."

Sarah unfolded her arms and started fidgeting with the fringe on the lampshade.

"No, the issue isn't their safety. Living on a farm has its risks; we all know that. Ponies are simply another risk. My concern is whether we're encouraging Polly to spend money that she shouldn't use."

I thought about Sarah's point. "But Polly is turning all Sam's money over to the White House Police to find out if it was counterfeit." Sarah knew that Polly had dug up all the money jars that she'd buried around the farm. It was all locked in her back room awaiting the arrival of the federal agents.

If anything good had come out of this counterfeiting debacle, it was recognizing Polly as a vulnerable young woman. She needed our love and attention. She had been so bedraggled when Zeb and I picked her up from the train station. No longer Passionate Polly, but on that day, Pathetic Polly.

"And you keep inviting Polly to stay over here as if we have an extra bedroom," Sarah went on. "When she stayed over on the parlor davenport last week, I had extra cleaning and laundry. I don't want to look after her. It's like having another child. Mother roped me into taking care of her when I was fifteen. I've already had enough babysitting Polly. It would drive me insane if she started living here—or sleeping here."

I held my breath. Did Sarah know? She said nothing else.

"As long as she stays safe," I responded. "I hate thinking of that day the two thieves held the two of you at gunpoint, but I won't teach her to shoot since her motivation isn't hunting. I could never forgive myself if she were to injure someone with a weapon I'd taught her to use." I fidgeted for a moment, to see if Sarah would respond. She remained silent.

"Let's take some more time on the question of ponies," I finally offered.

Sarah nodded silently.

Polly Wolcott Forrest

Monday, June 18, 1934

The real Clem Cavanaugh and Jack Stimson showed up at my door at the appointed time. Common sense had informed them to come to the back door and they parked their old, battered Model T in an appropriate spot in front of the toolshed. Both men were wearing black suits, but looked very different from their imposters. Cavanaugh was tall, at least six feet, graying, about fifty. Stimson looked to be about thirty-five, thin, with a long face and mustache. They both showed me their gold badges and gave me business cards. I invited them into the parlor. Because I'd had so many interrogations since Sam died, I figured I could easily handle one more.

Cavanaugh started out the conversation. "So, you had visitors stating they were us."

"It was a terrifying situation resulting in one of them killing my dog. They had a gun drawn on my sister and me the whole time. I was worried they would shoot us for any crazy reason."

"We saw the sheriff's report. Can you give us a description of them again?"

I proceeded, giving them the same description I'd given the sheriff.

Stimson and Cavanaugh looked at each other and nodded.

Stimson handed me an old grainy photograph; the two men in the photo were unmistakable, earlier versions of the men I just described.

"Yes, it's them. And do you know about the counterfeit money I tried to use in Lansing?" They both nodded.

I reached into my pocket and handed them all the money I had dug up and taken out of the jars.

"This is all the money I found, hidden in different places in the outbuildings around the farm. It's possible it may all be counterfeit."

Cavanaugh took the money, counted it out and carefully wrote down the amount and put it in an envelope that he placed in his briefcase. Then he started speaking.

"Those men who shot your dog are Wyoming men who used to work at the Mitchell Forrest ranch in a counterfeiting ring. We think your brother-in-law Mitchell was the brains. These men are Ronald and Clovis Benson, two brothers who carried out the printing part of the operation. We were on the verge of closing in on them last summer when your brother-in-law's barn burned up. We found remains of a printing press in the rubble. Then we lost track of them until we got the call from Sheriff Conlin last week.

"It was stupid of them to impersonate us, but those two aren't reputed to be very bright and they probably thought that pretending to be us was a hilarious joke. They know how to operate printing presses but are otherwise unskilled." He hesitated for a moment. "Do you have a photo of your brother-in-law, Mitchell?"

"No. Actually, I never met him, so I can't even describe him."

"How about a photo of your late husband?"

I walked over to the cherry bureau and brought back our wedding picture.

"We'll need to keep this for a while. Do you have other photos of him or any boxes of family photos?"

I shook my head. "He didn't like to be photographed. I had to really push him to get this one."

"If the Bensons thought your late husband Sam was sheltering Mitchell, they undoubtedly were looking for drawings, engraved metal plates, and other equipment to continue the operation. These guys know how to print, but they're not artists or engravers, nor do they have much business sense. Mitchell disappeared last summer at the time of the barn fire. We're trying to find and question him."

I could hardly catch my breath. "Do you think Sam was involved?"

Neither responded. Instead Cavanaugh began questioning me again.

"Did your husband provide shelter for his brother at any time?"

"I've been here since we got married in early September." I hesitated. "Definitely not in the house, but I don't know about the barn."

"Why do you think he might have been in the barn?"

"Because my husband would spend every single day there, hours on end, and he forbade me from going in there. Most days Sam took food out there, too. At one point I thought perhaps Charlie Becker was sleeping out there. I supposed that was the reason he didn't want me going into the barn."

"Charlie Becker?"

I explained Charlie's situation, how Wes and John Newsom found him living in the church.

"Did you ever meet Mitchell Forrest?"

"No." I'd already told them that. I wondered if they were asking the same question to trip me up. Sheriff Conlin had often repeated himself.

They kept bombarding me with questions. My head began aching, then pounding. I didn't have time to think between each query. I wanted to turn tables and interrogate them, but I couldn't focus. I wished Mother were here or even nosey Sarah. I was having to endure this all by myself. Damn that Samuel.

Each time I thought they'd finished, there was yet another question. Each answer was "No" until they finally stopped and asked to search all the farm buildings and the house.

I agreed. But really, I didn't have a choice. Cavanaugh took the house, and Stimson the barn and outbuildings. I stayed right there in the parlor in the rocking chair feeling more and more out of sorts.

He saw that I wasn't moving. "I'll start in this room."

Cavanaugh looked around the room and began with the roll top desk. I giggled when he pulled out each drawer, checking for secret spaces, and then shaking each one. I tried to stop giggling, but it soon turned into laughter and as much as I wanted to stop, I laughed harder and harder. Cavanaugh stopped briefly and looked at me. That only redoubled my laughter so I bent over and put my hands on my head, trying to stop, but nothing worked. My guffaws were loud and I could feel tears coming to my eyes. I couldn't gain control sitting there with my head in my hands laughing for what seemed like an hour, but was probably only five or ten minutes. Finally, it subsided. I looked at the agent and apologized.

"I don't think this is funny at all," I explained, waving my hands to indicate the entire search. "I've never had that happen, the laughter." I folded my hands in my lap and recited the Lord's Prayer to myself in silence in order to sober up. The agent was patient and waited. After my noiseless Amen, I looked up at him.

"I'm sorry. This is so embarrassing."

He placed another drawer back in its place at the bottom of the desk. "What you're experiencing isn't uncommon and I've witnessed uncontrollable laughter before. We were told in training that it's a natural response to one's nerves." His voice was calm and even. I was thinking that he would make a good pastor. He seemed so reassuring. But was this deliberate? I told myself to remain vigilant.

Excusing myself to go out to the privy, I walked outside, noting the dahlias were beginning to bloom in their various shades of pink, magenta, and dark red. I needed the time to stretch my legs and regain my composure. Walking back to the house I couldn't help but notice the warm sunshine on my skin and looked up to see the cottony clouds in the early summer sky. I felt a calm that was both unexpected and unwarranted.

I was strangely detached. This beautiful June day was being wasted; all I really wanted was to get Dorothy and lie down on the grass and look at the shapes of clouds in the sky, finding lions, elephants, and perhaps even Sailor Dog. These past few months I'd become so close to Dorothy that I now realized that part of my fondness had to do with wanting to protect her from all the Sams of the world. No girl should have to suffer what I went through. This could have been a fine day to spend with my niece and observe animals in the snowy-white billows above.

When I got back to the house, Cavanaugh examined all the rooms on the ground floor, looking in nooks and crannies that I hadn't even realized existed. He went into the walk-in closet under the stairway and asked me to remove the clothing off the rack. I complied, but there wasn't much left since I'd been taking old clothes to church every Sunday for giveaways. I'd started with Sam's, then I took most of my older clothes, including dresses from my high school days.

Mr. Cavanaugh inspected the closet walls, ceiling, and floors. He took out a small hammer, knocking on each one; I guessed he was listening to see if any sounded different, was hollow, or loose. He found one loose floorboard but there was nothing under it.

Cavanaugh concluded the first floor with the kitchen, taking extra care to look through and inspect every shelf. His job would have been harder during good times, when there was lots more food to move around. I thought he might comment on the scarcity, but he kept quiet and resumed his job.

Next, we both went down to the cellar, he with a fancy flashlight and me with the kerosene lamp from the parlor. Farmhouse cellars were dark, dirty places, usually a refuge for mice. The furnace had been positioned conveniently near the coal bin. It was a large metal contraption with octopus arms that flowed up to different parts of the ceiling and ended at the floor registers above. One wall contained shelves for canned goods and a huge potato bin sat beside the coal bin, almost empty. About three weeks ago I had given Wes most of the remaining potatoes for seed.

Cavanaugh wasn't looking at the potato bin. He grunted as he checked the ceiling with his flashlight. Sam owned a flashlight, but I had no idea where it was; I hadn't seen it in the toolshed or old granary and wondered if it had been stolen by whoever had been moving things around in the various sheds.

Cavanaugh kept sweeping his flashlight along the ceiling. I knew there were lots of holes up in the ceiling rafters, but it was too dark to see them clearly. Myself, I always looked at the floor when I was down in the cellar, so as not to trip on anything and, more importantly, to avoid any mice scampering around.

Cavanaugh kept inspecting the holes in the cellar ceiling, checking with his flashlight and occasionally with his arm. He moved to the darker part of the cellar, and above one of the long arms of the furnace he reached up and pulled something out. In the dark I couldn't figure out what it was. Somehow it looked familiar but my brain wasn't keeping pace with the agent's hands. He had moved over close to me and used his light to illuminate the flat object he held. Then it struck me like a bolt of lightning. He was holding the sketch pad that I had left in the attic when I moved in. I couldn't figure out why it was in our dirty, dark cellar.

"Hold your lamp over here," Cavanaugh commanded. I did so, and was amazed as he flipped the pages filled with drawing after drawing of money, one to one-hundred dollar bills.

My heart sank. Did Sam sketch these? Did he leave the pad here to get me into trouble? Or did he leave it here only temporarily, anticipating that he would later want it?

Cavanaugh carefully took the pad up to the kitchen table and looked at it again while warm sunshine was streaming through the window. Once again my life had tipped upside down in a split second.

"Your name's on this pad," Cavanaugh remarked, looking straight at me.

"That was my sketch pad. I left it in the attic when I moved in last September. It was blank."

"Are these your sketches?" He flipped back to the front and I saw three sketches of Ginger that I had forgotten about. Very poor sketches, nothing like Sam's detailed drawings. I looked at them and nodded.

"I forgot about them. I thought the pad was blank."

"Let's go up to the attic next, and do the upstairs last."

Cavanaugh was acting like this revelation was normal. All in a day's work. But it implicated me in a counterfeiting ring. One that I had no knowledge of, but one that could land me in prison, perhaps for life. It was definitely my sketch pad with my drawings of Ginger, yet it contained pages and pages of incriminating sketches.

Cavanaugh returned to the cellar and found nothing more. We both moved up two flights to the attic. I hated the attic, mainly because my aversion to bats was worse than my fear of mice. Cavanaugh went ahead of me, looking at every box and bundle. Nothing went untouched. I hung back, noticing about a dozen bats hanging in the rafters, asleep. It took Cavanaugh three more hours of searching through everything in the house, but he uncovered nothing more.

Stimson returned from the barn and outbuildings with a box containing turpentine, linseed oil, muriatic acid, a dozen steel needles, and a magnifying glass. He was even dirtier than Cavanaugh, with dust and grime all over his black suit.

"Do you know what these are?" Stimson asked me, holding up the steel needles.

"I have no idea."

"Used in counterfeiting," he answered.

"But we found no paper, ink, or finished plates," remarked Cavanaugh.

Both agents examined my sketch pad at the kitchen table with grim faces. I wondered if this was evidence that could prove Sam had worked with his brother counterfeiting and whether Mitchell was as good at sketching as Sam. Perhaps Mitchell had made the drawings. I suspected he had already removed the engraved plates that the Bensons were trying to find in the old granary.

The peaceful calm that had enveloped me earlier in the day was long gone. After the agents left I noticed my hands were shaking and my breath was short. I was furious at Sam for putting me in the middle of this mess, but even more at myself for staying with him out of greed, not love. I should have left him after my first bruise. Now he was laughing from his grave. I was undoubtedly facing lifetime incarceration for his misdeeds. Knowing I was unable to tolerate one night in the holding cell at the Lansing Police Department, I wondered if I would die in prison.

This gave me pause. How could I have ever considered moving away with Sam? Before the wedding we'd talked about going to a large city like New York, Chicago, or my preference, San Francisco. Sam said he'd do something other than farming, perhaps run a bar once Prohibition was repealed, and I would start a hat shop. In December with much hoopla, Prohibition had been repealed, but by that time, I had no desire to go anywhere with Sam. He had beaten me so many times, I couldn't fathom being alone with him anywhere, particularly San Francisco where I didn't know a single soul.

As my broken bones and bruises began to add up, I realized that not only was I afraid of Samuel, but I found his cold, quiet demeanor untenable. Living on a solitary farm without friends was difficult, but not having a companion for conversation was unimaginable. I tried to compensate with my letters to Mother, portraying Sam not as he really was, but as the man I'd envisioned before we married. Then unbelievably, one day he died and my troubles were over. I had hit the jackpot. Or so I thought.

Today, my post-Samuel future was in jeopardy. As I contemplated a life behind bars, I grew morose. Even in death, Sam was delivering more punches. They escalated in their pain. Today's blows were more painful, more debilitating than broken ribs. As I considered all of this, I recognized the value of having Wes and Sarah next door. Despite Sarah's unending criticisms, they were family. Both were standing by me in this crisis. I pulled myself together and walked up to their house for solace.

Reverend Wesley Johnson

Tuesday, June 19, 1934

Polly came over to our house in late afternoon, a nervous mess. She wasn't crying, but was shaking and unable to speak coherently. Sarah finally convinced her to lie down on the davenport with her head on a soft pillow from Dorothy's bed. Polly lay immobile while Sarah warmed up milk for her.

After sipping the milk, Polly calmed down enough to tell us about Agent Cavanaugh finding her sketch pad drawings of the various bills, one to one-hundred dollars.

"He found it in the cellar above the furnace, placed on a rafter. Why would Sam hide it down there? It was like a magnet drawing the agent to it. Cavanaugh put his hand there and slid it along the rafter until he hit the sketchbook."

"You hadn't seen it since your wedding?" Sarah asked.

"I'd made a few sketches of Ginger, and that's all. I remember putting it in the attic. The cellar is a bad place to keep anything like that. The coal smoke would make it all dark and cloudy and the mice would chew it up."

"Well, I suppose Sam was hiding it," Sarah offered. "But why didn't he simply get rid of it, instead of putting it down there? It would have been easier to take it out to the burn barrel."

"I suspect he planned to give it to his brother or the Bensons," Polly responded. "Believe me, I've been pondering this. I also wonder if it wasn't Mitchell who sketched the currency."

She dabbed her eyes with her handkerchief. "Do you think he deliberately wanted to implicate me? They probably think I drew the sketches."

I looked her in the eye. "I think you'd be in their custody right now if they believed you were involved." Unfortunately, my words were firmer than my conviction. Sarah and I had both shared our concerns regarding Polly's involvement. We both understood her youthful obsession with money and wondered if she hadn't seen it as a venture to get rich quick.

My mind turned to my church community. I'd been neglecting my ministerial duties to attend to my family's problems. Mrs. Dykstra had been back in the hospital for a few days and I hadn't been there for a visit. John Newsom needed to find another home for Charlie Becker, and I'd promised to help him. More people had been getting splinters from the church pews that needed to be sanded and polished. Once again the water pump out in back of the church wasn't working. If that list wasn't enough, the Catholic church in Marshall had called a meeting of the clergy to discuss how to better serve our people during this Depression. They wanted me to coordinate the rural churches in a major county-wide effort.

In addition, last Sunday's sermon was the same one I delivered a couple of years ago. That didn't bother me as much as seeing Tom Riley nod off about halfway through. The family crisis was taking its toll. It was likely that Sam had been involved in a counterfeiting scheme that was shaking us all to the core. It never occurred to me that my quiet brother-in-law had been leading that kind of double life.

The knowledge that Polly could be implicated was even more unsettling. I looked at her closely, her face drained of color. She wasn't taking this in stride. No Perky Polly. No Pampered Polly. More like Poor Polly. Panicked Polly. Paralyzed Polly.

"What did they say when they left with your sketchbook?" Sarah asked.

"They said they needed an expert to examine it and they would get back to me."

"Any chance that the drawings might have been Mitchell's and not Sam's?" I asked.

"Yes, I suppose. Who knows? They could be anyone's. Anyone who could get their hands on my sketchbook and put it in the cellar without my knowing. The agents also took some linseed oil, turpentine and other stuff."

"Why?"

"They said it's used for engraving."

It occurred to me that they hadn't talked to Sarah, which was surprising since she could identify both of the Bensons. By a bizarre coincidence, right then the phone rang and Sarah took the call, a short one. She walked back into the parlor.

"They're coming to question me tomorrow morning at nine."

After the phone call, I retreated to my office and put together a to-do list. Simply getting it down on paper might make me sleep better. But that was not to be. I heard knocking at the back door, but I decided to let Sarah get it. A couple of minutes later, I could hear footsteps coming toward my office. I grimaced. The last thing I needed was an evening visitor.

Sarah opened the office door, let John Newsom in, and closed the door. I knew I was in for a heavy-hitting talk when he didn't start with "Whaddya know?" Instead he sat in the chair across from my desk and put his head in his hands, sighing.

I waited for him to collect himself. "Take your time."

John kept shaking his head and sniffing, his eyes wet with tears.

"When you're ready we'll talk. I can wait."

He fidgeted in the chair. "Mabel don't know I'm here."

"Is this about her?" I inquired.

"No, but I'm afraid she'll worry."

"How about I have Sarah telephone her and tell her you're here."

He nodded and tried to smile.

Sarah was in the kitchen and quickly agreed. I hardly had time to get seated before John started talking.

"We're gonna lose the farm. I have until the end of October, but with crop prices being what they are, I don't see how we can manage. I stayed up most of the night looking at the numbers in my ledger, but I jist don't see it. Even if we get rain at all the right times, and the crops are the best they've ever been, we're not gonna make it. I need to tell Mabel."

I tried to keep my voice calm. "Have you thought about what you'll do?"

"Constantly. I cain't get it off my mind. But I cain't come up with a plan. All of our parents are gone. My brother's in bad straits. He's been without work for a year, and they're losing their house in Grand Rapids. He asked if he could bring his family here to live with us. That's why I got started figuring out how many months we can continue. But I'm gonna tell him to come anyway. We should have enough in the garden to feed everyone over the summer and early fall, but come November we'll all have to move on. Don't know where."

"Does he have children?" I asked.

Finally, John smiled. "A boy who's seven and a girl who's five. Not quite old enough to do much work around the farm, but it sure will be nice having kids around. You know how Mabel and I have wanted kids. Last year we'd finally decided to adopt, but it didn't work out."

"I'm sure when you get back on your feet, God will show you a way to adopt."

"Trouble is, I need God to show me a way to get back on my feet."

We both sat in silence for several long minutes.

"Polly has three fields not being used."

"But it's too late for corn, wheat, oats—all the regular crops," John countered.

Another pause in the conversation.

"Hmm. What else could you plant there that would be of value?"

More silence.

Finally, John spoke. "I wonder about planting root vegetables that keep all winter: beets, rutabaga, turnips, parsnips, and maybe I could get in a potato crop. People are gonna need food in the dead of winter."

Then I had a thought. "There's also winter squash. My mother-in-law practically lives on squash up in Connecticut. They keep them in root cellars all winter long. Hard squash like Acorn, Hubbard, Butternut, Carnival and Turban. Not zucchini or yellow summer squash. They'd rot in a root cellar."

He nodded. "I'd need to get them planted right away, even this week."

"I'll check with Polly this evening to make sure she hasn't already offered the land to someone else."

"I'd be mighty thankful if you did," John said. "The vegetables might not make enough for the mortgage payments, but at least we'd have food for the winter."

"How long since those fields were last plowed?"

"Last year. Sam had corn in two fields and wheat in the third."

"If Polly's agreeable, I'll start plowing right away. Then I'll need to cultivate and get it leveled before planting."

"Do you have enough money to buy seeds?"

John nodded. "My brother and his wife should be able to help once they get here." He paused. "I still gotta find a place for Charlie."

I nodded, thinking that we might be able to use Charlie for our apple harvest in September and October, but I'd need to check with Sarah first.

John and I continued the conversation for a few minutes, but he was anxious to get home and talk to Mabel. I offered a short prayer before he left and wondered if we'd all be able to survive the Depression. So many people were asking for no more than a roof over their heads and food for their families. John Newsom deserved so much more.

210

Sarah Wolcott Johnson

Wednesday, June 20, 1934

"Mrs. Johnson, thank you for agreeing to meet with us this morning." Agents Stimson and Cavanaugh stepped into the kitchen and I led them into our well-worn, but quiet parlor. I was glad that I'd cleaned yesterday, carefully dusting all the furniture. Earlier in the morning Wes had taken Dorothy and the boys down to Polly's so we'd have no interruptions.

The men asked me the same questions they'd asked Polly, so I was prepared. But later Stimson asked, "Do you think your sister could have been involved in counterfeiting in any way?"

I cringed. "Absolutely not. She was unhappy with Sam because he spent every day in the barn and he wouldn't allow her to leave the house. I don't like to speak ill of the dead, but Sam didn't seem to care about Polly's well-being. She was lonely and he even refused to let her come up the hill to visit us. It seemed cruel at the time and still does." I realized I was portraying a different, more accurate picture of Sam than I had given the local authorities and wondered if this was a crime.

"Do you think Sam Forrest was involved in counterfeiting?"

"I have absolutely no idea. He was quiet. Kept to himself. I suppose he could have been involved, but, again, I saw no evidence."

"Did you ever see his brother Mitchell or other strangers wandering around the farm?"

"No. Well, once I saw Sam limping from the toolshed to the barn. I ran down the hill, yelling to ask if he was okay. But he didn't hear me. Or ignored me. It only occurred to me this week that it might have been Mitchell wearing Sam's clothes."

"Was Sam still limping the next time you saw him?"

"I can't say that he was. Frankly I'd forgotten all about it or I would have asked him."

The agents thanked me for my time and left. I doubted if they even noticed the dust-free parlor.

Wes came back with the children, instructing them to play in the yard. Then he came into the kitchen to see me. "Are you okay?"

"Yes, but this is all so unbelievable. Do you think Polly was involved in any part of a counterfeiting operation?" I asked, point blank.

He frowned. "I don't think so. She looked so beleaguered when Zeb and I picked her up at the train station."

We both looked at each other and shook our heads.

"She seems changed," Wes commented. "She told me she was happy to let John Newsom plant her fields, and if he wanted to use the barn or other buildings to store his supplies or equipment he could."

I nodded. I'd already noticed John going down Polly's driveway with his workhorse hitched up to a plow. We sat in silence.

Finally, Wes started speaking slowly. "I think the ponies are a good idea. We all need something lighthearted, a distraction from counterfeiting and Sam's death. Polly certainly needs to get her mind on something else, something wholesome. She might benefit as much as the children."

I agreed, wondering if I would later regret this decision.

Polly Wolcott Forrest

Saturday, June 23, 1934

For the first time in ages, I laughed my head off. Zeb and I had gone to the movie *It Happened One Night,* with Claudette Colbert and Clark Gable and it was so good to totally lose myself in the show. The screen star Claudette wore the cutest little knit cap tilted to the right side of her head, with a small tip at the top, perhaps two inches long. It looked so perky, so perfect for the petite lady. I was going to knit hats for Dorothy and me, exactly like hers. I'd ask Sarah if she wanted one too. The tricky part would be getting the tip right, so it stood up by itself. In the movie Claudette's cap was dark. Guess I'd make them either navy blue or black.

After the movie, I invited Zeb back for sugar cookies. Zeb was grateful for homemade food. He'd been on his own for five years and hadn't learned to cook anything other than boiled potatoes, fried meat, and eggs. Not a great diet and that made it easy for me because everything I made for him was a treat. Next time, I'd make Sarah's recipe for Poor Man's Cookies, an oatmeal cookie that required no eggs or milk. She got it from one of her favorite programs, *The Jake and Lena Radio Show,* and had shared it with just about everyone at church.

For the moment I had decided not to use any of the life insurance money; there were still too many unanswered questions about Sam and his secret life. I'd let Sarah believe she influenced me, but I was only being practical. If, God

213

forbid, I went to trial, I'd need a lot of money to pay a lawyer. For the moment, I was going to wait it out and see what happened once the White House Police caught Mitchell Forrest and the Benson brothers. If they actually caught them. Those thieves were slippery and seemed to have disappeared.

I'd already sorted through everything in the attic and basement. How liberating it was to get rid of so many things from my life with Sam. I took the clothing and household goods to the church, but even Sarah vetoed two old moth-eaten blankets filled with mildew and mold.

I kept looking for further clues that the agents may have missed. In the meantime, I was enjoying Zeb's company most Saturday nights. After spending time with Zeb, I now knew my infatuation with Wes was simply the remnants of a schoolgirl crush I'd hung onto for years. I would never let myself be swept away by Wes again, ever. I'd done some stupid things over the past year and that counted as the worst. Fortunately, I had the wherewithal to pull away from Wes. I never should have allowed it to happen in the first place. Finally, in the nick of time, God had allowed my mind to gain control and for that I was grateful. However, little else seemed to be bending in my favor.

I was too impulsive with Jacob Frond, as well. At that time any man seemed perfect compared to Sam. But I was learning to take more time; no more indiscretions for me. If I could get out of this counterfeiting mess, I would do my best to forge ahead in the straight and narrow.

After we finished the cookies, Zeb got up from the kitchen table to leave. I was hoping for a first kiss. I think he must have figured that out since I reached out to embrace him and suddenly his lips met mine.

To my surprise, I found my body stiffening. I wasn't ready.

"What's wrong?"

I realized we couldn't kiss until I was honest with him.

"I need to tell you some things. You deserve to know some of the pieces of this puzzle, even though I can't figure it all out."

Zeb looked alarmed, frowning. His eyes met mine, and I could tell he had no idea what was on my mind.

"Don't put yourself in jeopardy," he finally mumbled. "Remember that I'm a Deputy Sheriff. I care about you. Please don't say anything that would put you behind bars."

Ignoring his comments, I guided him to the parlor where I sat in the rocking chair and he rested several feet away in the faded, overstuffed chair that once matched the dark green sofa, a favorite color of Sam's first wife, Johanna.

"No, I've done nothing illegal, but this is hard for me. . . ." I stumbled over my words.

Zeb nodded and I went on.

"Of course, I didn't have anything to do with Sam's death. But truthfully, I was relieved when it happened."

Zeb narrowed his eyes.

"Honestly, I was afraid Sam would kill me. People were correct about my injuries, and there were so many more bruises on my arms and legs they never saw. Samuel was responsible for every single one. But he told me he was hurting me because I wasn't a good wife. He said my cooking was terrible and that I complained too much about the cold house. He'd torment me any time I asked for money. I think he was trying to kill me one day when he pushed me off a wagon and I fell into a ravine ending up with several broken ribs."

I began to stutter. "This is really hard for me to tell you. I'm so ashamed of my behavior, and that I let him hurt me so many times."

"I'm so sorry you had to endure those horrible things," Zeb assured me.

"But I haven't told anyone, not even Sarah or Wes, although Sarah questioned me repeatedly, particularly after my broken ribs. I've also kept it a secret from my mother."

"But why?"

"Because as a new bride I thought I was doing something wrong. I thought everything was my fault. Sam certainly told me it was. Over and over again. I felt so much shame. I couldn't tell my mother what a terrible wife I was. I just couldn't."

Zeb nodded, encouraging me to continue.

"Sam had forbidden me from going out to the barn so I thought maybe a hired hand like Charlie Becker was out there. I stayed away from the barn because I didn't want to scare or embarrass anyone. Now I wonder if his brother Mitchell was out there."

I paused. "Oh Zeb, you must despise me now. You must think I'm shallow and narrow-minded and dishonest."

"No," he answered quietly. "I don't."

"Maybe I could have prevented all this counterfeiting stuff if I had paid more attention to what was going on in the barn. Instead, I spent my time trying to keep Sam from hurting me. I quit complaining about the cold house and I really tried to improve my cooking."

"Why didn't you leave him?"

"He told me he would kill me if I ever left and I'm sure he meant it. The only reasonable place for me to go was next door with Wes and Sarah. He'd have found me there for sure. Same with my Mother's place in Connecticut. Every time he hurt me, he said if I behaved better he wouldn't hit me and for a while, I believed him. I kept thinking that he would start treating me better, like he did before we got married. But that never happened.

"In the fall he asked me to sign some papers, but, of course, I wouldn't sign without reading them and we had a horrible fight. It ended with him knocking me out, stone cold, on the floor. The next day I confronted him and he said the papers were life insurance policies in case anything ever happened to me. That's the exact moment that I knew my fate would be the same as Johanna's."

"Johanna was his first wife?"

I nodded.

"Did you see the life insurance policies?"

"No, I never did. Somehow I convinced him that I was on his side and that any life insurance policies should be in his name. He couldn't be collecting large amounts of money when he'd already received so much after Johanna's death. He should have known that husbands, not wives, take out life insurance policies. That incident was right before Thanksgiving. A couple of weeks later I found two insurance policies written for himself with me as the beneficiary. He had taped them to the underside of a drawer in his desk, like he was tempting me to find them.

"So, yes, I had a motive to open that bull's gate, but I didn't. I still don't understand why he bought those policies. He really didn't care about my well-being. In fact, in his cruel way, he seemed to enjoy hurting me. Perhaps he bought those life insurance policies to implicate me if he died. That would have been his last cruel joke."

Zeb kept shaking his head in disbelief. "But why didn't you tell us all this after Sam's death?"

I looked down at the floor. "Would you have believed it was an accident? Would you have thought for a moment that I wasn't responsible—even if I wasn't home the exact moment it happened? You would have assumed that I opened the gate and then ran up to Wes and Sarah's house and waited it out."

"I might not have believed you then, but I believe you now." Then he stopped and looked me directly in the eye. "Polly, what do you think actually happened?"

"Now that they found the sketchbook, I think perhaps Sam was hiding Mitchell in the barn. It would have been brutally cold out there, and I wonder how he could have managed sleeping in the haymow. Perhaps if Sailor Dog had slept with him he might have fared okay. Still, we had some savagely cold nights. Sarah or I would have seen him coming or going if he'd been boarding in Marshall or Battle Creek. But I think you should check out the old Dolliver place in case Mitchell was staying there. He could have walked back and forth to the barn without going down a road. The place has been empty for a few months now. It's a polio house, so be careful. Both Dolliver girls had polio before Mr. Dolliver was killed riding his tractor."

Zeb nodded in agreement. Then I remembered something else.

"Another thing—back in the fall I noticed an old feather bed was missing from our bedroom closet. Sam said he had burned it because it was infested with fleas, although we'd never had any problems with fleas, not even with Sailor Dog. Maybe he took it out to the haymow or to the Dolliver's. It never showed up anywhere. I've scoured the haymow looking for clues. In fact, Sarah jokes that I spend more time in the barn than the house these days."

Zeb hunched over and frowned. "Actually, Sheriff Conlin and I searched the Dolliver farm right after you and Sarah were held at gunpoint. We found some train riders and kicked them out. But nothing more. We've been checking that place from time to time, but the riders must have it on their maps as we've kicked out two more groups."

He looked at me so intently. "Polly, you could be in grave danger. Counterfeiters are a ruthless group and there are hundreds, maybe thousands, all over the country. It wouldn't surprise me if we have others here in Calhoun County. That's why the shop owner in Lansing was suspicious of your money. I bet he'd been stung before. I don't think there's a single store in Marshall or Battle Creek that accepts twenty-dollar bills."

I had no idea that counterfeiting was so widespread. Of course I knew it existed, but figured it was in far off places like Kentucky.

Zeb shook his head, frowning. "That Benson fellow killed Sailor Dog to demonstrate that they're capable of doing the same to you. It was a direct threat. Mobsters do that. You need to stay up at your sister's place or find a place in town. Ordinarily, I'd advise you to go to your Mother's in Connecticut, but with the White House Police investigation going on, you need to be around here for a while longer."

Zeb stood up and walked over to me.

Once again my body froze. "Wait, I have more to tell you."
He sat back down, again frowning.

"There was a letter from Sam that my mother, Sarah, and Wes read. In the letter Sam suggested that he might commit suicide. He told me that I should collect the life insurance anyway because he wanted to provide a good life for me."

Zeb looked at me with raised eyebrows. "That sounds like a caring, thoughtful man, not someone trying to kill his wife."

I nodded in agreement. "But Sam didn't write the letter."

"Who did?"

"Me."

Zeb looked at me like I was crazy.

"I wrote it, imitating Sam's handwriting. But no one knows. My family read it. Then I burned it."

"Why did you write it in the first place?"

"Same reason. I didn't want to admit to both Sarah and Mother that they were right about Sam. Sarah particularly. You know how she is. Always finding fault with me, pointing out how irresponsible I am and making me feel like a child."

"But still…" Zeb frowned at me. "Why defend a dead man who hurt you over and over again?"

"Pride, I guess, to make myself feel better. I faked the letter in order to feel justified that I married him. I didn't want to be wrong. It was a way to start my life anew without admitting my mistakes. Now I recognize how juvenile it was."

I looked Zeb straight in the eye. It hurt telling him how childish I'd been, but I wouldn't continue the lies.

"I wanted to think of Sam as the person I'd envisioned before we were married. The ideal husband. That's the person who would have written the letter. But that wasn't the real Sam. Writing the letter was a stupid thing to do and I regret it."

Zeb shook his head in disbelief.

"It turns out that Sam had money he never told me about; he'd hidden it from me. I've turned it all over to the White House Police. As you know, I deposited the life insurance money in those two Lansing banks, but I'm not going to use it.

I've decided to give it to the charity fund at church. I simply couldn't use it on myself and feel right about it. Sarah was correct about that."

Sighing, I tried to smile. "So that's the whole sad story. I've told you everything. The truth is that I have no idea if Sam was involved in counterfeiting and I don't have a clue where Mitchell is or those rotten Bensons, for that matter."

I looked in Zeb's eyes. "I only want this episode of my life to be over. In hindsight, of course, I shouldn't have married Sam. It was an immature, impulsive decision. Then I made several more mistakes along the way. My pride and greed took over. I have so much regret."

Zeb stood up. "So that's it? Is there more to tell me?'

"That's it. Isn't that enough? I've lied to my mother, sister, and brother-in-law. I've lied to you and Sheriff Conlin. I may have been harboring counterfeiters—totally unknowingly."

He caught me in his arms.

"I understand," he murmured as he drew me in.

Reverend Wesley Johnson

Sunday, June 24, 1934

After phoning Doris Dykstra yesterday to check on her health, I immediately left to visit her son Willard at the county jail. He had been caught stealing meat and eggs from Miller's Grocery. I used to think of stealing as an absolute sin, being immoral as well as illegal. Today I thought differently. Willard chose to steal because his children were hungry and he thought he had no other option. His mother Doris had been living with him and his wife and six children while she was recuperating from pneumonia until she was well enough to move back to her farm house adjacent to the church. Willard had lost his job at the cannery a few months back and they'd been living hand-to-mouth with his wife, the younger Mrs. Dykstra, tending all day to the six children as well as to the elder Mrs. Dykstra who was still bedridden.

"I'm a failure." Willard's eyes watered as he told me his story. "Darla had been telling me every day that we were running out of food and it finally happened. I'm even a failure as a thief. Moving isn't a possibility because Mother is so ill. Although where we'd go is beyond me."

I tried to console him, but these hard times produced no easy answers.

Since it was his first offense and the county simply didn't have the budget to keep people like Willard in jail he was released and I took him home in my buggy. But we stopped first at Miller's. I had a dollar bill that I kept in my wallet for emergencies, so I went in and purchased flour, sugar, rice, dried beans, oatmeal, and Spam. I was sure it was difficult for him waiting outside the store where he'd been caught stealing, but perhaps he'd be able to come back next time with money in his pocket.

Once I got back to the buggy where he was waiting, I asked him, "Do you have a garden in your backyard?"

"Yes, we've got green beans, peas, and chard coming on."

"All that will go fine with what I bought."

I hesitated. "Look, I don't have all the answers, but perhaps you could see if any farmers need help with crops, and ask if they can pay you with milk, eggs, and extra food from their gardens. It's only a temporary solution, but it might help until you can get a steady job."

Willard thanked me and asked if I knew any farmers that might be in that situation.

"Start with Tom Riley and Fred Torquini," I answered. I didn't mention John Newson, given all his problems. "Those farmers know your mother from church and they're good men with no sons to help out in the fields. They may not be able to give you work, but they're kind individuals and would turn you down politely. Go in person, so that they can see you're a big guy and can handle a pitch fork and throw hay bales."

After that incident, I returned home and wrote my sermon quoting Philippians 4:6.

"Be careful for nothing; but in everything by prayer and supplication with thanksgiving let your requests be made known unto God."

Written by the apostle Paul as a letter to the people of Philippi, it was advice to not have anxiety and to take your requests to God by prayer and petition—which, I admitted, was rather hard to do these days. But Paul was in prison, probably in Rome or Ephesus, when he penned these words, certainly a setting that would produce anxiety. I didn't have to look further than Willard Dykstra to comprehend his words.

I continued writing the sermon, ending with the verse that immediately followed, Philippians 4:7—words that were an inspiration to me.

"And the peace of God, which passeth all understanding, shall guard your hearts and minds through Christ Jesus."

This morning, finding myself at the pulpit I looked down at the congregation. No longer feeling rancor about our family's current situation, I told Willard's story veiled in anonymity, his mother being too ill to attend church, anyway. I mentioned the problems in my own family and the unknowns we were facing. Somewhere in the sermon I recited the list of sick members and the fact that right now almost all of us were facing challenges we'd never anticipated.

I remarked how we all wanted to be facing decisions about whether to electrify our houses and put in an indoor bathroom. Instead, we were facing decisions about how long we could hold on, and whether we'd lose our crops if rain didn't come, what we'd eat this winter if our gardens didn't produce and what we'd do if we lost our farms. I didn't think anyone expected me to be this specific about our collective worries.

"Lord, lift these worries from us. Lift them high above us. Lord, lift these worries from us."

Next I asked everyone to take a minute and count their blessings.

"Instead of focusing on what we don't have this morning, think about what we do have and be thankful. What are you happy about today?"

"I need an hour," my friend John Newson piped up. Everyone laughed.

By the time we started our last hymn, "Joyful, Joyful," there was a smile on every face, including mine.

Joyful, joyful, we adore Thee,
God of glory, Lord of Love;
Hearts unfold like flowers before Thee,
Opening to the sun above.
Melt the clouds of sin and sadness;
Drive the dark of doubt away;
Giver of immortal gladness,
Fill us with the light of day.
—Henry J. van Dyke 1907

One thing you find out when you enter the ministry is that every family has problems. Some are open about them; some not. But in the end you try to communicate the message of Christ's love. Then you pray that the congregation will be able to hear that message. Today, I believed that happened.

Sarah Wolcott Johnson

Tuesday, June 26, 1934

"Buttons, Buttons, I'm your new friend," Dorothy yelled out when Zeb and Polly delivered her new Shetland pony, a sweet brown and white charmer with a fluffy coat, small perky ears, and long mane. Polly led Buttons off the trailer and for everyone it was love at first sight. Wes had brought out a little step stool so Dorothy could brush her while we waited for Zeb and Polly to bring over the boys' ponies.

Perhaps Wes was right about allowing Polly to give ponies to the children. All my thoughts had been focused on Mitchell Forrest and whether he had been running a counterfeiting ring in Sam's barn. It was the talk of the town. We even had strangers drive by the house, pointing towards Polly's farm looking for the "counterfeiting barn." I had decided to hold my head high, despite this besmirching of my family.

To Junior and Zeke, it seemed an eternity for their ponies to arrive, but it was really only about ten minutes; the animals were already in Polly's barn.

"Boys, are you ready to meet your ponies?" Zeb yelled out as he and Polly led them over both driveways and up the hill to join Buttons.

One pony was a light brown, just a few shades darker than Polly's Ginger, with a flaxen mane and tail, and white boots on all four legs. The other was a bay, a medium brown with a black tail and muzzle. She had a dark marking on her forehead that looked like a star.

The boys couldn't wait to start riding. Of course, they thought they could ride down the lane, lickety-split, but I had insisted that the ponies not be pressed too hard. We settled on the compromise that each child would start atop the pony with an adult walking beside them around the yard. My plan worked only because Polly had brought over some freshly-baked molasses cookies, which she promised the children as a treat if all went well—no spills, no riding fast, always an adult with each pony.

Nevertheless, the boys were talking about mounting the ponies bareback.

"No, we have to saddle up first." Polly was carrying what looked like miniature saddles from the back of Zeb's old Ford pickup. "All the equipment is the same as for horses, only smaller," she said. "Junior, do you remember what we do first?"

"Brush her, put on the blanket, put on the saddle, and cinch her up," he answered by rote, like he was taking a school exam.

Zeb had lined up the ponies and stood them about ten feet apart. He'd already put on their bridles, so the boys started out brushing the ponies, with Zeb demonstrating which direction to brush.

"Always watch out for their back legs so they don't kick you," I warned.

"Yeah, yeah," they responded.

"Okay, we're gonna do it slowly so you see exactly how everything goes." Zeb patiently handed each boy a blanket, followed with a saddle with the stirrups thrown over the top. He supervised the whole process, calmly explaining to both boys the reasons for each step. While tightening the cinches, he showed Junior and Zeke how to adjust each one.

"So, what are you naming these beauties?" Zeb asked.

"Star," Junior immediately yelled out. Zeke took one look at his new pony and said, "Boots, because of the white around her feet."

I was relieved that they weren't fighting over the same pony, an event I'd anticipated and even spoken to the boys about at breakfast. They'd seemed to have worked that out the moment Zeb brought them up to our yard. I could see Junior and Zeke look at the ponies, then look at each other, and after a quick interchange, they ran up to the respective ponies to take ownership.

Polly had taken over harnessing Buttons, the Shetland, and had her ready to go with Dorothy in the saddle.

"Whee, look at me," yelled Dorothy, as Polly took the rope and led her down the driveway. Then she started waving at everyone.

"Keep both hands on the reins and saddle horn," Polly instructed her in an even voice. "You need to always have both hands down here holding tight." I was happy but not surprised that Polly was being so careful with Dorothy. It was the same as when she took Dorothy for a ride on Ginger.

Wes and Zeb led each of the boys down the driveway following Buttons. Once they got to the road, they turned around and Zeb urged Star to go a little faster, not quite running up the drive.

"Yippee, yippee," Junior yelled. He still continued to hold on tight and obeyed Zeb's commands.

Wes and Zeke sped up a bit, too. But Dorothy, under Polly's guidance, continued at a slow, steady pace. Once they had come back to me, I took Dorothy for another ride down the driveway and back.

In addition to the tack and gear for all three ponies, Zeb had brought over a large supply of feed in burlap bags. Wes had already instructed the boys about where the equipment and feed was to be stored and what their daily chores would be, including cleaning out the stalls.

Despite the children's effusiveness, Polly still seemed to be disheartened. After leading Dorothy around on Buttons, she simply sat on the grass and stared at the ground. I could tell Zeb was trying to cheer her up.

Zeb grinned and winked at her. "Polly, I think you need a ride on Ginger and a few of your own molasses cookies."

As I had gotten to know Zeb Bylowski, I liked him more and more. Just as Dorothy had an affinity for Polly, the boys got so excited when Zeb came by, even when he wasn't bringing ponies.

Polly responded to Zeb, "Sorry, I was thinking about those White House Police agents, and I'm so troubled about my sketch pad and all the implications." These were concerns Wes and I also shared. Polly seemed to be acting much more mature these days.

We had gathered in front of the barn and the kids were brushing the ponies once again. No one responded to Polly's musings. But my mood was certainly elevated by the new ponies. Indeed, the carnival-like atmosphere set my mind in motion regarding extending the warm feelings. I suggested that in a few weeks, after the ponies had become acclimated to the children and our farm, that we plan a Sunday afternoon event where our church friends could bring their small children and grandchildren over for pony rides. Wesley thought it was a splendid idea since we hadn't had a church event for a blue moon, and of course, all the parishioners were facing so many hardships. Polly suggested Sunday, August 19, her birthday. She had even agreed to make cakes, an extravagance most of us hadn't had in months.

The party would provide a few hours of escape for everyone. By then most of the farmers would have finished with hay season, and would be waiting for the wheat, oats, and corn to ripen. Apple season would still be ahead in the fall. In the meantime, all the women who would be putting up food from their family gardens would welcome a break. Both Polly and I continued talking about it, but no one mentioned the obvious. Surely, by then, Mitchell Forrest and the Bensons would be apprehended. If so, we'd have lots to celebrate.

Polly Wolcott Forrest

Wednesday, July 4, 1934

One more holiday uncelebrated: Decoration Day and now the Fourth of July. Zeb had suggested that Mitchell and the Bensons might be waiting for a holiday if the engraved plates were indeed still hidden somewhere on the farm. They'd need time to remove them when I was away celebrating, particularly if they were buried in several different places, a conclusion that I had come to long ago, after I had ransacked the house, barn, and all the outbuildings.

So today Zeb and I waited to see if Mitchell or the Bensons would show up to unearth the plates. We sat under the maple tree, playing rummy and drinking cold tea, making frequent visits to the old granary and hayloft to see if anyone was there or if anything had been disturbed. We walked down the lane a few times to see if anyone had walked over from Mrs. Cross's place or the Dolliver farm. Nothing.

The whereabouts of the engravings puzzled me because Sam's jars of money were so easy to find, placed on window sills and shelves, begging to be discovered. I'd scoured the farm for signs of land being disturbed. The only place was the sight of poor Sailor Dog's grave, which made me cry. I was missing my dear canine friend so much that I couldn't control myself—anywhere, be it at home, in town, or at church.

The phone rang once during the morning, the caller hanging up as soon as I answered. I wondered if I should have let it ring and the Bensons or whoever it was would fall into our trap. Another call came in the early afternoon. It was Sarah inviting the two of us for supper. We accepted and then Zeb and I went inside and I made scalloped potatoes, sliced tomatoes and cucumbers, and lima bean salad, the vegetables all being prolific in the garden.

"So I heard that you were the prettiest girl at Marshall High School," Zeb teased me, as he watched me cook. "You and Jacob Frond were King and Queen of the Senior Dance."

"Kid stuff," I responded. "But who told you that?"

"Clementine, last Saturday night when we were playing cards. I think you were in the kitchen fixing that amazing strawberry shortcake."

"So tell me about your high school days. I bet you were the good kid who never did anything wrong. Always the future sheriff's deputy."

He laughed. "One Halloween some of my friends and I hoisted a hay wagon up on top of Joe Morton's barn."

"Who was Joe Morton?"

"A cranky old guy who always yelled at us when we walked by his garden. He thought we'd been stealing stuff from it. I suspect it was really rabbits and coons doing the damage. Anyway, he had this old wagon that he kept out by his road where his wife sold garden produce in the summer time.

"So we waited until after midnight on Halloween and silently took the wagon. There were about six of us on the ground and six others on top of the barn, and we got that wagon right up at the top and left it there.

"A bunch of us wanted to watch him discover it in the morning, so we hid out in the bushes all night long, but the next morning nothing happened. We waited until way past sunrise, until it was time to go to school, so we all left."

"What finally happened?" I waited expectantly.

"He never took it down. It was up there for years. People called it the wagon barn. I'd even heard people give directions. 'Go down Verona Road, past the wagon barn, and turn left at the next road.'"

I laughed. "I remember the wagon barn. So that was the extent of your life of crime?"

"Well, that, and rushing Jackson Prison and releasing all the prisoners. Then joining up with John Dillinger for a few bank heists. Helping kidnap the Lindbergh baby, too. Those were merely the highlights."

"My gosh, you have a wicked imagination."

"All kidding aside, Polly, I've changed my mind about something serious. I'll teach you to shoot. I know Wes didn't want to, but he's a preacher and wants to save souls. I respect his opinion and I didn't want to counter him, but this search for the counterfeiting ring has gone on far too long. I thought we'd be done with this long ago. Let's take a look at Sam's guns, and I'll give you some basic instructions."

He walked to the gun case in the kitchen. There were two deer rifles and a shotgun.

"The boys have taught me how to use BB guns," I said.

"BB guns aren't serious and any crook knows that. You're not going to save your life with a BB gun."

I fell silent. Admonished. Both Sarah and Wes had already taught me that lesson.

Zeb took the shotgun and handed me a rifle. "We'll go back behind the barn and do some target practice before it's time for supper."

The area behind the barn was really quite beautiful. Someone had once had a garden back there and a few plants had self-seeded over the years. There were a few squash, peas, and some dill. I made a note to come back and pick everything for the church giveaway on Sunday. In back of the former garden were old grapevines and a few red raspberry bushes. Zeb and I walked over and ate the raspberries right off the vine. The quick pop of juice met my tongue with a sweet tang. Just when I thought we'd eaten them all, Zeb found a few more bushes on the other side of the grapevine.

"We'll get to the target practice once we finish off the raspberries." He grinned with bright red lips.

I wasn't feeling quite as playful, still worried that the counterfeiters might show up at any moment. How long, I wondered, would I have to wait before I could feel absolutely safe?

"You still haven't gotten another dog," Zeb commented.

"Tom Riley asked me if I wanted one of his pups. Cute little fluffy things, but I couldn't get old Sailor Dog out of my mind. His sweet collie face. He'd follow me around whenever I was outside. It wouldn't be fair to any new dog—my wanting the new puppy to turn into Sailor Dog." I'd been around dogs long enough to know they all had their own distinct personalities.

"Although Sam found Sailor Dog walking around town a year before we got married, once I moved in and started feeding and playing fetch with him, he became my dog. Even Sam knew that and hit me once because Sailor followed me to the garden instead of going with Sam to the barn."

I realized I needed to convey to Zeb how much I wanted to rid my life of Sam's ghosts.

"I'm so angry at Sam, if you can be mad at someone who's dead. Even now after his death, he's dictating how I live. I want to be done with him and his cronies once and for all. I want to be able to sleep peacefully."

"I'm going to ensure you're going to know how to use these guns. That should help."

Somehow I wasn't as confident about this as Zeb. He set up a paper target against a cherry tree at the far end of the field and walked me through some steps, paying particular attention to the recoil, which was pronounced with Sam's shotgun. He taught me how to line up the sights carefully, and how to press the trigger with a slow deliberate motion rather than a fast, panicked jerk.

I shot ten times and hit the target eight times, switching guns each time, to get the feel of the different weapons. Then Zeb moved the target to a few different places some closer and some farther away. He seemed pleased with my serious approach. I think the BB gun target practice with Junior and Zeke had helped me to breathe steadily and aim carefully.

As we walked back to the house, Zeb left one gun in the kitchen case, took one up and put it under my bed, and propped the third in the corner of the back room, close to the back door. I worried that I might have to use them. But our Fourth of July stake-out came to naught.

Sarah Wolcott Johnson

Thursday, July 19, 1934

"**M**other, is this one ripe?"

Zeke had pulled an ear of sweetcorn off the stalk. I walked over and looked at it in the early morning sunshine. Long luminescent rays were peeking through the tall rows of corn, dwarfing the boys. Any other day than today, I'd take a moment to appreciate God's beauty, but it was going to be a long hot day and I was anxious to get started.

"It's ripe enough, but don't pick any cobs with kernels smaller than this," I answered Zeke, after looking at the small whitish ear, not yet fully developed. "I'm going to try to get two bushels today, and then we'll wait a week or two and harvest the sweetcorn again. You boys pick all the ears you can reach, and I'll get the ones way up high."

I always dreaded corn-canning days. It was a long arduous process consisting of picking the corn, husking it, and pulling off all the stray silks. Next, the ears needed to be blanched in hot water, followed by a cold water bath. After that was the tricky task of slicing the kernels off the cobs. The jars and lids needed to be sterilized with hot water and kept hot. After that I filled the jars with corn, attached the lids, and put them in the pressure cooker for an hour.

Pumping and boiling the water was a chore in itself and I kept the boys busy running back and forth from the water pump to the kitchen with pails of water, along with wood from the pile to the stove. But it was Dorothy I was most worried about. She was too little to be of any real help, but she could easily get in harm's way.

Originally, Wes said he'd try to help, but both farm and church emergencies intervened. John Newsom called him last night and said that Sunday night's storm had sent a tree into a church window. He needed Wesley's help to first cut up the tree and second, replace the window. If that wasn't enough, Jasper had taken ill a few days ago, and despite all Wes's efforts, he wasn't improving. Wes called a veterinarian in Battle Creek to come out and look at him. Needless to say, we were both worried about the cost, and the fact that the vet might not be able to cure him. Then we'd be looking at a pretty penny for another horse, plus the vet's bill.

Wanting to get an early start because I knew the midday summertime heat would be brutal, I had enlisted Junior and Zeke to come with me to pick and husk the corn. Even so, I'd be sterilizing the jars over the hot cookstove when the temperature peaked.

Polly was supposed to come over and help too, but there'd been no sign of her. As soon as we'd finished picking the corn, and the kids started husking it, I called her.

After ten rings, Polly answered.

"Polly, did you forget that we're canning corn today?"

"Oh, sorry, Sarah. Do you absolutely need me?"

"Yes. Why? Are you sick?"

"No, I was thinking about taking Ginger out for a long ride before it gets too hot. It'll be a scorcher by noon."

I counted to ten. "Polly, have you ever canned corn?"

"No. Why?"

"Well, it's simply too much for one person and three kids. Particularly when one of the kids is only three and gets in the way. Wes has two emergencies to tend to and I'm not going to be able to get through the day without your help."

"Okay, okay. I'll be over in a half hour."

"Fifteen minutes would be better."

I heard her slam down the phone.

Polly arrived about an hour later. I was dipping the corn cobs into the boiling water, leaving them for three minutes, pulling them out, and plunging them into the cold water before putting them onto clean dish towels.

"Okay, put me to work," she sang out, as if she were right on time. I decided to ignore her tardiness and asked her to sit at the table and slice the kernels off the cobs. I gave her a big roasting pan so all of the stray corn would end up in it, not in her lap.

"Here are two different knives. See which one you prefer."

She tried the larger one first and quickly switched to the smaller one.

Zeke and Junior came into the kitchen carrying two pails of water. I wanted to hug and kiss my little boys who were more reliable than my twenty-year-old sister.

"What next?" Zeke asked.

He seemed to be enjoying the tasks whereas Junior was simply going through the motions.

"Bring more firewood in and stack it right there with the rest of the wood. You don't need to bring any kindling as we have a good fire going right now."

I continued to blanch the corn.

"What about me? I want a job," Dorothy piped up from her perch on the stool where she was watching me.

Polly looked at her in desperation.

"Why don't you go get Josephine, and we can teach her how to can corn," I answered.

I noticed that Polly was slicing the corn slowly; I imagined I could get six ears done in the time she took to do one. I didn't want her to cut her fingers, but we'd never get finished at her current pace.

"Polly, let's switch jobs," I suggested. To my surprise she agreed without complaint.

"Wow, how can you do that so fast?" she asked, watching me slice the corn. I stood each ear on end, and cut with fast downward motions.

"Lots of practice. But right now you need to add more water to your pot. Let it come to a boil before you put any more corn in, and then use the three-minute timer."

Dorothy was soon back with Josephine and began explaining the whole process to the doll in a loud voice. She definitely knew considerably more about canning corn than Polly.

After Zeke and Junior returned with the wood, I asked Polly to put more wood in the stove, and sent the boys out to the back room to carry the Ball jars to the kitchen table. The kitchen was getting hot and would be getting hotter. I wiped my forehead with my apron.

"This is so much work," Polly opined. "You have to run it like a military operation."

I nodded. "Next winter the corn will taste so good. But today, with all the smells and the steamy heat, I couldn't eat any if you paid me."

Junior interrupted, "We've finished the Ball jars. Can we go out and play now?"

"Yes, but come back in a half hour and replenish the water and wood." They moved quickly towards the kitchen door.

"Dorothy, why don't you take Josephine back to your bedroom. Otherwise she'll smell like corn for the rest of her life. Then you can come back and play with the potato masher."

Dorothy quickly jumped up with her doll and disappeared.

Polly wiped the sweat off her forehead with her hand. "I see why you wanted me to get up early. It didn't make sense when you called. But it's only going to get hotter and hotter. When we do this again, let's pick the corn the night before and we can get started right after morning chores."

"How I wish," I answered. "If you let the sweetcorn sit overnight it loses its sweetness. It would be edible, but wouldn't taste good."

"I just don't see how you can do all this," she remarked. "Raising three children in addition to keeping the house, and all the church chores."

I nodded. "It's a lot."

"I'm so glad you called me to help you. I had no idea."

"Thank you."

Polly came over to me, wiping her brow with her sleeve. She gave me a hug.

"I need to be a better sister and I need to tell you some stuff."

She sat down beside me and looked me in the eye. "First, I didn't open the bull's gate and second, I had nothing to do with any counterfeiting. And, yes, you were right about Sam. He gave me those bruises. I just didn't want to admit you were right about him. It's so hard admitting to you and Mother that I was wrong. As you suspected, I went into that hasty marriage just to avoid the move to Connecticut."

This was new behavior for Polly. "I wish you had come to us for help. Wes and I would have taken you in or made sure you were on the train to Connecticut before he even knew you were gone."

"It wasn't that easy. For a long time I believed him and thought I was doing something wrong, so I tried to improve things, like my cooking. Later I was scared to go anywhere. He threatened to kill me if I left."

I could sense tears forming in my eyes and I swallowed hard.

Just then Wes walked in. "Jasper's doing much better. The vet gave him raisins soaked with a potion of berries and whiskey." Wes grinned and shook his head. "Who'd thought all he needed was a good laxative. Next time I'll feed it to Jasper myself."

Suddenly the day looked rosier.

Reverend Wesley Johnson

Wednesday, August 8, 1934

Time dragged on. There was no progress in getting to the bottom of Sam's crimes. We'd all been uneasy with Polly alone in that house, but she said she was fine now that she had a phone and Zeb had taught her how to use the guns. I heard her practicing again this morning and I was secretly pleased with Zeb for doing this. I couldn't abide either Sarah or Polly being held at gunpoint ever again.

Later in the morning, when I was over removing silage, I saw her working in the garden and I stopped to say hello. I noticed she was picking string beans.

"Good morning," she called to me.

"I thought you didn't like string beans." I shot her a big grin.

"I really don't like them, but if I find myself starving next winter, I suppose I'll change my mind. Or I'll ask Sarah to trade some other vegetables for a few cans of these." She paused to change the subject. "How much silage is left out there?"

"It's down to about a quarter left. Do you need the remainder for anything?"

"No, Ginger eats hay and grain. I think she has a more delicate stomach than your cows. Take it all. When I sell the farm, I won't have any of that toxic stuff left in there."

"Anyone interested in buying?"

"No. Well, there may be interest, but no cash. For as bad shape as the house is in, the rest of the farm is fine and the soil is good. Since the farm borders the creek, there'd be potential for irrigation according to Paul Traxon. He's the only realtor I've talked to so far."

"Fancy stuff, irrigation," I commented.

"Paul said you could just dig a few channels from the creek to the fields. The Indians used to do that. But unless it has anything to do with hat-making I'm not terribly interested." She unleashed one of her million-dollar smiles.

Just then Zeb Bylowski pulled his truck up to the end of the driveway and joined us.

"There's been a couple of reports of seeing the Benson's fancy Plymouth Roadster in the western part of the county. Polly, perhaps you should go to Connecticut. Just notify Agent Cavanaugh and give him your mother's address and her neighbor's phone number."

"I have the whole garden coming on," she responded. "Maybe in the fall after the apple harvest. But until then, I need to put up lima beans, butter beans, peas, tomatoes, sweet corn." She threw up her hands in the air. "And everything else.

"Besides, I have the telephone, and I can call you if Mitchell or the Bensons show up."

She paused. "Yesterday I found one of Sam's sketches that may be a likeness of Mitchell. If so, he looks a lot like Sam. Different nose and lips and Mitchell seems to have a gap in his front teeth. I studied the drawing for hours last night. I think I'd be able to recognize him." She looked down at the bowl in her hands. "I'll go get it for you so you can take it to Sheriff Conlin." She ran into the house with her bowl of string beans.

"That girl is strong-willed and stubborn," I commented to Zeb. "I've had that same conversation urging her to go to her mother's place at least a half-dozen times. And Sarah, well, let's just say, she feels disrespected as the older sister when she offers any kind of advice to Polly. If you can figure out a way for Polly to go willingly to Connecticut, let me know."

Zeb shrugged. "She has a mind of her own, and she's not about to change it."

After supper, which consisted of watery bean soup sopped up with stale, dried bread, I told Sarah about my interactions with Polly and Zeb.

"Do you think the Lansing jail incident was an elaborate hoax to make us believe she wasn't involved in counterfeiting?" Sarah asked. "Why else would she risk her life staying in that house when she could go join Mother and Gramma Blessing?"

I thought a long time before I spoke. "I confess I've had the same questions myself. But it's been so long since those Bensons showed up, I'm inclined to believe that Polly no longer feels threatened. However, now that there's been sightings of that fancy green roadster, I'm worried."

Polly Wolcott Forrest

Sunday, August 19, 1934

I felt like a little kid in church this morning awaiting the afternoon's pony party, my birthday party. Mentally blocking out Wes's sermon, I went through a list of last-minute details. All seemed doable, and of course, Sarah would be there to help. Sarah had become such a stalwart in my life. I must have taken her for granted before now; I wouldn't in the future.

The party seemed to be on Wes's mind, too. His sermon was short and at the end he reminded everyone to come over to their house, whether or not they had children, to celebrate my birthday and enjoy the ponies I had given to their children. Junior, Zeke, and Dorothy all sported giant grins when he made the invitation.

After church, just about everyone came up to me and told me that they would be coming. While I was thrilled, I began to wonder if I had enough cake. I asked myself, giggling aloud, *Have I turned into Sarah, fretting about the details?* In the past I wouldn't have cared if we ran out of cake.

I hoped I was taking on Sarah's good characteristics. Or was this about coming to terms with myself, my failed marriage, and trying to start my life over? Admitting I'd been covering up my cruel husband's misdeeds was the first step, but I imagined it would take plenty of time to fully understand why I chose the deception.

Back to the details of the party: yesterday I'd made five cakes after borrowing pans from Sarah and Ruth Shaw, and using two that were already in my kitchen, Johanna's legacy. Almost all of my cooking pans and kitchen utensils had originally belonged to Sam's first wife. Sam had left the kitchen exactly as it was before her death, and I longed for the day when I could rid myself of Johanna's specter. I made a mental note to take her "legacy" items to the church giveaway, starting next week. The cake pans would be at the top of the heap.

It had been a couple of weeks and there'd been no more signs of the Bensons, Mitchell, or any news from the White House Police. I was hoping that the thieves were long gone, having moved back to Wyoming. But I was still getting phone calls from someone who'd hang up the moment I answered. At some point I realized I didn't care if Sam had a girlfriend. Good riddance to him and anything having to do with him.

I was beginning to enjoy the new farm routines. John Newsom had planted all three fields in the back forty, so I saw him every day, coming and going with his tractor along with his brother and Charlie Becker helping out. He'd planted two fields of winter vegetables and the third as soybeans, an experimental crop touted by Roosevelt's agricultural commission. Quite frankly I welcomed all the new farm activity. It felt safer now that I had a telephone. Also, John's labor meant I wasn't alone on the farm. Sometimes John would stop and say hi, but most of the time, he simply waved. I had the whole crew over for noontime dinner a couple of times, including Mabel, and his brother's wife Erma and their two kids. Also, I was continuing target practice, usually after supper around sunset.

After church, when I got in the buggy with Wes and Sarah, I noted that it would be a hot, sunny day. It was already warm at eleven in the morning. Zeb, who had finagled getting the entire day off, was bringing his friend Jim, and the two of them volunteered to organize the children's pony rides on Star and Boots. Wes would handle Buttons. Feeling grown-up, Junior and Zeke were in charge of parking—horses and buggies going on the east side of our long shaded driveway and cars on the exposed west side. We weren't expecting many cars. The boys' responsibilities included bringing pails of water for all the horses since it was going to be a scorcher.

Later, as I was walking up the hill to Wes and Sarah's place carrying a bouquet of zinnias for the cake table, Dorothy greeted me, with Wes beside her.

"Aunt Polly, Aunt Polly, look at me," she yelled out. She was wearing a yellow flour-sack dress that I'd made her and was carrying a large white fan, on which she and I had painted butterflies for today's occasion. Her job was to wave the flies away from the cakes, and she looked adorable.

"I love your fan," I said. "Wes, doesn't Dorothy look like she's the birthday girl, not me?"

He nodded. He seemed preoccupied, perhaps worrying about the safety of all the children coming today and he walked away. Fortunately, we had settled into a routine in-law relationship.

To get my attention, Dorothy whirled around, waving her fan as if she were a Southern belle. She was beaming, happy about having an actual job for the party. I was wearing my newest lavender flour-sack housedress with no adornments. This was an outdoor party, but I still wanted to look nice for Zeb. He'd seen the dress before, but it was the newest frock I owned. I also wore a big-brimmed straw hat with a large purple flower on the side. I wished I'd had a lavender one, but it was the Depression, and I was lucky to have purple.

I looked around. We were ready. Almost instantly, the first horse and buggy flew up the drive. It was Ruth and Tom Shaw. Their horse was young and spirited, and Ruth had told me how Tom let her go at her naturally fast pace.

"Park here, park here," Zeke yelled at them and Junior ran to the horse tank to bring their horse a pail of water. Tom had stopped at the stepping stone and Ruth gracefully stepped down from the buggy. Wes had moved the stone from the back forty for the ease of lady visitors. It made the descent from the buggy simple and modest, particularly for women in long dresses. When Mother had visited, she mentioned how much she appreciated the stone at the point she was getting older. I, myself, enjoy the elegance of descending from the buggy to a flat, dry surface.

I ran up to Ruth and greeted her. "I'm so glad you came. Don't let me forget to give you back your cake pan before you leave today. Right now, it's filled with apple cake."

Sarah had given me some Baldwin apples from their root cellar for the cake. They weren't the best baking apples for pies, but grated up in cake they were fine. I'd surprised myself that my cooking and baking talents had blossomed since Sam's death. I'd been so insecure about cooking for him, and now I was making cakes, cookies, and entire meals for my sister's family and the Newsoms.

Ruth was effusive in her greeting. "Happy Birthday, Polly. I'm so happy to come to a party; it's been so long since we've gone anywhere. It didn't take much convincing Tom, once he heard about the cakes."

I noticed that Tom was introducing their mare, Queenie, to Junior, who was offering water to the thirsty horse. Junior began talking to Tom like a little equestrian, asking Tom question after question about the horse while he responded to Junior in an adult tone.

"Tom will make a good father," I said to my friend. "Look at him with Junior."

"We're hoping to start a family, but we're not sure if this is the best time, when we're struggling to keep our farm. But at this point it's in God's hands," she whispered. We both smiled at each other, understanding the risks of having a baby in such uncertain times. This was a taboo subject for a party, but she was the first guest to arrive, and she'd become a bosom friend. We giggled and turned to await the arrival of more guests.

I'd begun to recognize over the past few weeks the importance of female friends and remembered how lonely I'd been after my wedding. Giggling with Ruth like school girls was so delightful. I was beginning to understand Viola Cross's obsession with calling everyone on the party line to relay gossip. It gave her a chance to connect to everyone in the neighborhood.

The Jordans were now pulling up beside the Shaw buggy and Zeke motioned where to stop. I could see smiles of bemusement on both of the adult faces. After they stepped out of their buggy, Junior took the half-full water pail over to their horse. The boys had become parking experts in the first few minutes.

Turning to Ruth, I said, "Let's talk more after the crowd gets settled. Can you help me with the cake?"

"Delighted," she answered, and we walked over to the table where Dorothy was dutifully fanning the cakes with Sarah's eyes on her, like a hawk. We cut the cakes and put pieces on Sarah's small dessert plates. She'd gotten her dishes from Grandma Blessing many years ago when Gram moved to Connecticut to take care of Great-Grandmother Tompkins. I loved those dishes with the light green backgrounds and pink flowers sprinkled in random patterns with gold edging around each plate; they were so much prettier than the heavy brown dishes I'd "inherited" from Johanna.

One after another, people arrived. There were about twelve buggies lining the driveway, and three cars on the other side. I noticed that Zeb, Jim, and Wes were heading to the barn. Soon they were back with the ponies, all saddled up, asking the children to get into two lines. Anyone five years or under got in line for Buttons. The rest of the kids made a single line for Star and Boots.

Soon the adults were lining up for cake. Charlie Becker was in the middle of the line, much at ease, laughing and talking. I noticed the fun he was having kidding around with the farmers; he was absolutely unrecognizable as the pathetic vagrant who had sat in the back of the church on Easter Sunday. I couldn't explain the joy I felt looking at him, transformed into a jolly neighbor.

As I looked at the crowd, noticing the smiles and friendly chatter, a blanket of peacefulness fell over me. This event with friends, children, ponies, and cake had created, perhaps, the happiest birthday ever. Exactly one year ago, Sam had taken me out for dinner at the Hitching Post and to a movie at the Bijou. It had been nice, but solitary. Today's event was one of happiness and sharing, a feeling that everything was right at this particular moment. I hadn't experienced such joy for a long, long time.

"Nice of you to share your birthday this way," John Newsom remarked. We'd become close neighbors after seeing him just about every day when he went up and down the drive to work in the back fields.

Mabel added, "You've been through so much with your husband's death and the aftermath. We're glad you can put it behind you and enjoy your birthday. Also, we appreciate your generosity. The fall crops John planted are looking healthy."

I nodded in agreement, but I had no idea that my sense of well-being would be short-lived.

"Polly, is that Ginger in your barnyard?" a voice shouted out. "Beautiful horse."

I'd checked on Ginger, who was secure in her pen before coming over, taking her some sugar, and reassuring her I'd be back to ride her in the early evening when it began to cool off. There was no way Ginger should or could be out. I quickly walked over to the top of the rise to peek over to the barnyard and sure enough, there was Ginger running around, somehow set free from her pen. My heart began to pound and my breath came so fast I couldn't talk.

"She wants in on the fun," someone else shouted, not understanding the enormity of the situation.

Wes and Zeb were suddenly at my side.

I stammered. "She was locked in her pen, both the gate and the door shut. Someone has deliberately let her out. I'd better call Sheriff Conlin and tell him what's happening." Wes and Zeb nodded in agreement.

Stunned, I ran into the house and called the sheriff's weekend phone number. It took a while before anyone picked up and I told the lady who answered that Ginger was out and that Zeb had gone over to check on her. The receptionist didn't seem to understand that the problem wasn't with Ginger being in the barnyard, but was with whoever had let her out. Nor did she seem to recognize Zeb's name.

"Probably the children let her out," the receptionist said. "I can hear children in the background. They seem to be having a lot of fun. I wouldn't worry about your horse."

"No, it's not about the horse, but whoever got into our barn and let her out," I explained.

"Well, you told me you have somebody going over there to check." She was talking to me as if I were a child and my pony was wandering around the barnyard. I couldn't get through to her.

"Please, please, call Sheriff Conlin," I begged. "He'll understand." The receptionist hung up without saying anything else. Did that mean she would call Sheriff Conlin? Uncertain, I called her right back.

"Are you going to call the sheriff?" I pleaded. "Someone has broken into the horse's stall. Tell him that it might be Mitchell or the Bensons."

"Okay, okay, calm down, Missy."

"Tell him Zeb is here," I insisted.

"Okay." She let out a long sigh, and once again hung up on me.

Reverend Wesley Johnson

Sunday August 19, 1934

When Zeb told me that he was going over to Polly's to see who had let out Ginger, I prayed silently for our safety, handed Buttons over to Tom Shaw and followed Zeb down the hill to Polly's place. I couldn't help but remember the day of Sam's death when I ran down to the horse tank. No one had yet determined who'd let out that deranged bull from his pen.

Considering this, I regretted not grabbing a shotgun from the gun closet, but it was too late now as Zeb and I arrived at the barnyard. Ginger was at the horse tank, the same place where I had discovered Sam's body and despite the hot August day, an icy chill ran down my back.

"You stay here at the horse tank," Zeb used a low, deliberate voice. "If there's any gunfire, just lie down here. These six inches of cement will protect you. I'm going to go through the milk house to the barn and toward Ginger's pen to see if anyone is in there." Zeb was also unarmed; Polly had asked him not to have his gun anywhere near the children. I prayed for his protection.

Hunched down in back of a six-by-six foot cement horse tank, I felt like a coward and hoped Sheriff Conlin and whoever else was on duty would arrive soon. I trusted Zeb but he was alone, unarmed. Torquing my back, I looked up at the party on top of the hill. Everything was still lively. Tom Shaw and John Newsom were now supervising the pony rides as if nothing unsavory was going on, exactly what I wanted. The noise level was still high, with lots of children yelling and rollicking around the yard when they weren't on the ponies. But I couldn't spot Sarah; consequently, I scanned the lawn for Junior, Zeke, and Dorothy. None of them were in my range of vision. However, I soon saw Sarah exit from the house with all three children trailing behind her, each with an empty tray to pick up dirty dishes.

I waited for minutes that seemed endless, and at several junctures, almost left the protection of the horse tank. The crowd up the hill in our yard seemed to have quieted down. I suspected word was getting around about the serious nature of Ginger's appearance in the barnyard. In the meantime, I wanted to offer more prayers for Zeb's safety, but I could no longer hide while he was putting his life at risk.

I couldn't wait a second more, my senses on full alert. Jumping up, I ran to the milk house, ducked inside and shut the door, passing by the floor-level cold water tank which fed water by underground pipe to the horse tank in the barnyard. Next was a cleaning room with a double sink for washing dairy equipment, filled with brushes and soaps. Continuing on I rushed by the milking stalls towards a sliding door that led to the interior of the barn. So far everything looked normal but Zeb was not in sight and I worried about what I'd find on the other side of the door.

I'd been in Sam's barn many times since his death, helping Polly with one thing or another, and, of course, I'd been removing silage every three or four days, so I knew my way around. A few weeks ago, Polly had moved Ginger from her small stall to Black Devil's old pen where it was much roomier, and she could saddle her up, right there in her pen. It also had the convenience of a small storage closet for hay and feed.

To slide the door from the milk house to the barn in silence seemed an impossible proposition. I grasped the door and pushed it sideways ever so slowly. It scratched and creaked a bit, but was quieter than I first thought possible. I peered into the barnyard. Nothing appeared out of the ordinary, but I wished I'd been wearing my boots as I made my way through the muck and manure toward Ginger's pen. As I got closer, I noted that the sliding door to the pen was open as usual. Sam never closed it. But today the gate also stood wide open.

As I approached, I could hear voices. I kept out of sight, pressed against the wall and tried to listen. But my attention turned as I saw Ginger approach from the barnyard. She sauntered up to the open door, looked in, and then looked back at me. Ginger knew me and chose to ignore my presence as she walked past me.

Zeb's voice rang out. "I got it to budge, but just barely. How many people did you have when you put it in here?"

"Don't matter," a gruff voice responded, "you're getting it out."

"Okay, okay," Zeb answered. "But if it falls over, it'll likely be damaged beyond all repair. You really need a second set of hands to move it."

I moved closer to the door and peered in. Ignoring me once again, Ginger nosed up alongside the gate and walked calmly up to her feed box. I stepped back out of sight, but jumped when I heard gunfire.

"Oh, why'd you have to do that?" Zeb groaned. "That lovely horse never hurt you. She was just coming into her pen for some food."

"Shut up," a voice growled again. I wasn't sure if it was the same one I'd heard before.

"Okay, okay, but you need to finish off the horse. See how she's suffering."

A second shot thundered out, followed by scuffling. I thought perhaps Zeb had made a move and I was worried.

I peeked in to see Zeb on top of one man, and another guy on the other side of the dead horse, trying to inch his way around her. I recognized them immediately—the Bensons.

Instinctively, I grabbed the weapon. "Zeb," I yelled. "I've got the gun."

Zeb backed off of the short man, yanked the gun from me, and stepped backwards toward the door. "Get out fast," he yelled to me.

He followed me out, shut the gate, slid the door across the opening and secured it with the large metal hook and eye.

"Stay here and don't let them out, no matter what they say. They'll say anything. They're dying, suffocating, drowning. Just don't open the door."

"They're the two Bensons who impersonated the White House Police. I saw them when they demanded to search Polly's house."

Zeb nodded. "I'm going to track down Mitchell Forrest. These guys were talking about someone who has the plates. I'll check the granary and haymow and other places around here. If Mitchell's here, he may have seen me coming and decided to hide."

I could hear the two brothers whispering inside Ginger's pen. They called out to me, probably checking to see if I was still there.

"Hey, the horse just stood up; it's a miracle," one of them yelled.

When I didn't respond, they started banging on the door. Afraid they might loosen some of the boards, which were unpainted and appeared to be pine, certainly not the strongest wood, I put my back against the door and leaned into it. It didn't take long for them to quit. Thank God they were neither athletic nor persistent.

Once again I prayed for Zeb. Mitchell Forrest would certainly be smarter than these two chubby yokels. Counterfeiters took lots of risk and were violent when cornered. Mitchell Forrest had already proven that he was not an easy prey.

My prayer was interrupted when Zeb's friend Jim peeked around the door to the milk house and then walked in. "We all heard the shots. I saw Zeb outside and he asked me to keep you company until the Sheriff arrives. There are several men outside willing to help. Zeb told them to stay put until the sheriff arrives."

"Who's there?" a voice called from inside the pen. "You know there ain't no air in here. We're suffocating. We don't have much more time."

I rolled my eyes and shook my head at Jim. "They're in the pen with Polly's dead horse. One of them pulled a gun and shot her for no reason at all. Polly's going to be devastated."

Jim and I waited for another twenty minutes, saying nothing to each other, stiffly guarding the door until Sheriff Conlin finally appeared. At that same moment, another sheriff's deputy arrived at the barnyard entrance and walked up to us.

"The two Benson brothers are shut in the horse's pen. I don't think they're armed. Zeb took a gun from one of them and left to look for Mitchell Forrest. There's a dead horse in there, too. It sounded like they were forcing Zeb to get something heavy out of storage, but I didn't see what it was."

The deputy nodded as he joined us. "Dan Harris," he introduced himself quickly.

"You two stand there by the door to the milk house," Conlin instructed Jim and me. "If anything goes wrong, find Zeb and tell him what happened."

Jim and I nodded.

"Okay boys, time to come out," Conlin shouted through the door. "If you come quietly, hands up, with no shenanigans, you'll have a nice Sunday dinner tonight. Otherwise it'll be dirty water. Get your hands up."

Then Conlin proceeded to unhook the lock and slowly opened the door and gate. Both men walked out, hands above their heads. The deputy was ready with handcuffs and ordered the men out of the barn. As Jim and I followed them outside, Zeb arrived shaking his head; he'd found no sign of Mitchell.

Sarah Wolcott Johnson

Sunday, August 19, 1934

Polly and I had tried to keep the party going so that all the children could have a pony ride, but once word got out that there were thieves in Polly's barn, most of the guests departed. When I heard the gunshots I jumped out of my skin. Polly looked at me, fear igniting her eyes.

"We need to stay here inside the house," I warned John and Mabel Newsom. "If they're the guys who killed Polly's dog, they're mean-spirited and violent."

"My poor Sailor Dog," Polly muttered. She proceeded to rip off her apron and charged out of the kitchen. From the window, I saw her rush down to the barn where the men had gathered by the milk house door.

"Come back to the house where it's safe," I yelled out the window, but Polly ignored me. "Come back," I persisted. The old Polly. She'd changed, but was still headstrong and impetuous.

Soon I saw Sheriff Conlin and Deputy Harris come out of the milk house with the two thugs who had held Polly and me at gunpoint. It took me back to that unnerving experience where they shot Sailor Dog. Infuriated, I tore out of the house and ran down to the sheriff's car. If Polly could go down there, so could I.

The sheriff herded the two handcuffed men towards his car and the crowd of men who remained uneasily silent.

"Where are my boys' BB guns?" I yelled at the thugs as they passed by.

"Where?" I screamed again.

"Don't answer," the shorter one snarled at his brother.

"In the back seat of our car," the taller one replied. "It's parked over at the Methodist Church."

"Why'd you tell 'em? Now they'll take the car."

"They'd find it anyway and those BB guns belong to her boys. I loved my BB gun when I was a kid."

The brothers' conversation ended when Sheriff Conlin spoke.

"Deputies Bylowski and Harris are going to take these fellows to the county jail. They'll be charged with breaking and entering and destroying property. I'll also be notifying the White House Police of their capture. Now I'm going back to the horse pen and find what was so important to these scoundrels."

"A printing press," the shorter one sneered. "Nothing illegal 'bout a printing press."

"Shut up, Clovis," his brother retorted.

Conlin ignored their comments and made his way back into the barn. Wes and Jim followed while Polly and I stayed outside and watched the deputies put the two thieves in the back seat of his car. Zeb jumped in the passenger seat, with a gun drawn at the Bensons.

The other men who had come down from our house quickly dispersed. Polly was shaking her head, looking exhausted. We both sat down on the grass, a sisterly silence between us.

There was a shuffling sound and men's voices and we both turned toward Polly's barn. Wes, Jim, and Sheriff Conlin emerged from the milk house carrying a large apparatus.

"First part of the printing press," Conlin said.

None of this made sense. Exactly where in the barn was the printing press and why hadn't Polly found it? Indeed, why hadn't the White House Police discovered it? And how could

Sam have gotten such a huge contraption in his barn? Surely Wes or I would've noticed.

I stood dumbfounded, trying to figure it out until it dawned on me. I remembered seeing Sam taking out his hay wagon, covered with a tarp, on a couple of rainy days. I had always thought Sam was careless, hauling hay around during wet weather. Perhaps it wasn't hay.

"Your telephone still working?" Sheriff Conlin asked me.

"Ooo-kay," he noted. "Mrs. Johnson, please call my office and ask them to arrange to transport this printing press from here to our evidence yard."

"Wait!" Polly exclaimed. "Where had they hidden it?"

"It was behind a false wall in that feed room in the horse's pen."

"False wall?"

"Yes, the little storage room where you had horse feed and bags. It's dark in there, and you couldn't see it, but they had put in a grimy wooden wall in the back, hiding the printing press."

Polly shook her head in amazement. "I was in there every day feeding Ginger. But never when Black Devil was in there."

Sheriff Conlin continued. "The deputies will be taking statements from the Bensons and hopefully they'll tell us where we can find Mitchell Forrest. I'm going over to the church to see if the Bensons' car is there. I'm not believing much of what they said."

The sheriff turned toward Polly. "And Mrs. Forrest, would you like us to dispose of the horse?"

"Horse?" Polly frowned.

"One of the men that we apprehended shot and killed your horse. Didn't you hear the shots?"

"Oh no!" Polly looked at me terrified.

"If these fellows have any good money, they'll be forced to make restitution," the sheriff said.

Polly's face turned red.

"I don't want restitution; I want them caught and punished—all of them." She tore off toward Ginger's pen.

When everyone had departed, Wes and I made our way up the hill to our house. I was in tears thinking of Polly's birthday ruined by the sudden turn of events. It simply didn't seem fair that now she had given up the façade of a blissful marriage, she continued to be affected by these heinous crimes.

Polly Wolcott Forrest

Sunday, August 19, 1934

Stunned and exhausted by the day's events, I sat alone under the oak tree near my back door. How could I go on without Ginger after also losing my precious Sailor Dog? I'd already learned my lesson about life not being fair, but both of my beloved animals? This was cruelty at a magnitude beyond broken ribs. My early morning rides on Ginger had kept me sane over these past months. I had nothing left.

Sam had tormented me all fall and winter. Now his Benson buddies, whoever they were, continued to plague me with their murderous crimes. I might as well have been a medieval peasant sent to a torture chamber, having to endure one impossible agony after another.

I thought about what I might do right then and there. I couldn't call Zeb since he and the other deputy were at the county jail interrogating the Bensons. Once again Sam had ruined my day—and my life. He was like the sound of chalk screeching over the blackboard, driving its harsh, piercing cry through my nervous system. It was as if Sam sensed that I was beginning to feel joy and peace, and he propelled his vile curse upon me once again, this time on my birthday.

I collapsed down on the grass, lying prone, despondent. I didn't know how long I laid there in utter silence, with the breeze drifting over me. I knew I should walk up to Sarah's, but fatigue glued me to the ground. A couple of ants were running down my legs, but I didn't have the energy to knock them off. My eyes closed and I felt my arms and legs begin to twitch. A fly was buzzing around my face. Still, I didn't open my eyes. Until I heard a voice, a sinister, ugly voice out of the past.

"Get up. Get in the house and make me some supper." Confused, I thought I was conjuring up an old nightmare. But I opened my eyes, and there stood Sam with his penetrating blue eyes and downturned lips. It had to be a hallucination. I shut my eyes, wanting to be rid of the hellish vision.

"Get up," the voice was louder and more insistent.

Opening my eyes, I saw him again. My mind couldn't comprehend what I was seeing. How could Sam be alive? Was this an apparition?

"Are you Mitchell?" I asked in confusion.

"You never could get things straight," he answered. That was one of Sam's favorite phrases. That and "Now, you deserved that, didn't you?"

Sam's face was contorted into a familiar look, one that had always ended with him hurting me. I needed to run up the hill to Sarah and Wes. Scrambling to my feet, I felt dizzy from moving too quickly. I steadied myself as Sam pointed a knife at me. But I pulled away and felt the knife slicing through my dress sleeve into my arm. He was alive and the knife was real. Blood was seeping through the fabric and dripping down onto the ground. This was no apparition, no hallucination.

"Into the house," he commanded. I obeyed, entering the back room. I glanced and saw the gun was gone from the corner.

"Yes, girlie, I got both rifles and the shotgun back at my hideout, so don't be thinking you can escape your Sammy boy." He chuckled. I'd forgotten how much I hated his chuckling. I grabbed a clean dish towel and wrapped it around my bleeding arm. The wound wasn't too bad, but I pressed the towel tight to staunch the flow.

"Use that new telephone to call your sister and tell her you're going to eat and sleep here tonight." He'd been in the house, removing the weapons and he knew there was a telephone. Could he have been the person calling me and then hanging up, waiting for me to be out of the house?

"Go on, call Sarah," he demanded.

I had no choice. How I wished I'd figured out some code with Sarah and Wes to indicate I was in danger. I mistakenly thought having a telephone would keep me safe. But no, it only worsened the situation. Without a phone, Sarah's curiosity would have gotten the best of her, and she'd have enlisted Wes to come look for me.

I picked up the phone and dialed.

"Sarah," I said. "I'm here, and I'm gonna eat here and sleep here, too."

She asked why.

"I need some time alone."

"It's not safe for you to be alone with Mitchell on the loose."

Sam was making motions with the knife for me to hang up.

"I'll be fine." Then I added one last thing. "Call Zeb and tell him not to come over for supper. I need to be alone."

Oh, how I hoped Sarah could read between the lines. *Call Zeb for help. Call Zeb for help.* I hung up before saying goodbye, which I never did. I expected Sam to ask who Zeb was, but he said nothing.

I was weary and my arm hurt, but I knew I'd need all my wits about me with Sam resurrected, standing in the kitchen. I gave myself a moment. If Sam had a weak spot, it was flattery.

I turned to him. "You outfoxed us. How did you carry off that so-called accident with Black Devil? It was so clever."

He sat down at the kitchen table and I followed suit, tightening the towel around my arm.

"Oh, that'd been planned for months, right after you thought you talked me out of buying life insurance policies covering you. Of course, I knew I'd never get away with that again, after Johanna. But if I were to die, and my pretty new wife redeemed my policies and turned the money over to me, then I'd be doing fine. I just hadn't figured out how. Gotta have the right opportunity."

Suddenly it dawned on me. He'd bought the life insurance policies not to help me, but to steal from me.

"So you're surprised to see me alive?" He exhibited the menacing grin I'd always despised.

Shrinking back into the kitchen chair, I nodded. "How did you do it? Everyone thought it was you out in the barnyard mutilated."

"My brother looked a lot like me."

"So, Black Devil killed Mitchell?"

"You stupid girl. He was already dead. I'd taken care of him." He held up the knife that still had my blood on it. "Black Devil did the cover up."

Sam killed his own brother. I was breathless. I told myself I had to stay calm and keep him talking.

"Amazing," I finally answered, trying my hardest to keep my voice even. "He was wearing your blue shirt and bib overalls and your boots. You fooled everyone. Were you involved in Mitchell's business all along?"

"Nah, they were amateurs. I knew he'd mess up sooner or later. But when they offered me fifty grand for the drawings and engravings, I bit. They needed everything new. The 1929 series had been in circulation for a while, and they needed to start over with the smaller bills; all their plates were outdated. Any new currency had to be the new series. The $50 Ulysses S. Grant; the $20 Andrew Jackson; the $10 Alexander Hamilton; the $5 Abraham Lincoln; and the $1 George Washington. A history lesson. I did them all and they're perfect. Both sides for each one, plus the seal."

He sported a wide grin. "Mitchell and those bumpkins weren't up to the task. But I was. I now have my life ahead of me. Fifty grand, plus I have the plates to set up my own operation wherever I choose."

He was chattering away, so proud of what he'd done. How could I have not realized any of it? Strange, but in a weird way it didn't surprise me.

"So, Mitchell was in our barn at night?" I asked.

"Well, there and the Dolliver house and barn. He had to be careful with vagrants who would come and go in that house. But, well, ... he got what he deserved. After Pa abandoned us, when I was eight and he was twelve, Mitchell left after a few months. I think he was surprised when he found me still alive at the old place five years later. I'd learned to take care of myself, whether it meant lying or stealing. Mitchell never apologized for leaving me there."

I felt no pity for Sam, but I needed to play his game. "Why didn't you tell me so I could help?"

He sneered. "Help? With the preacher and the preacher's wife and kids next door? The timing was off. When we met and married, I was ready to settle down and live the sweet life you wanted. But when someone throws serious money at you, it's a tough choice. Enough money to live off the rest of your life."

My mind was racing. Sam couldn't be telling me all this and expect me to be alive tomorrow. I also wondered if Mitchell had already paid him the fifty-thousand dollars. He must have paid or Sam wouldn't have murdered him. For the moment I needed to play his game. If he could kill his own brother, he certainly would have no compunction about killing me.

"We could still get out of here—go someplace else, and I'd have that hat shop I always talked about, and you could open a bar. Remember when we talked about leaving?"

"I do recollect."

"We could go to San Francisco. Wouldn't it be fun to live on the Pacific Ocean?"

He shook his head. "Ain't gonna happen. I got my life set up already and you won't be there."

I wondered again if he'd found another woman.

"But where's the insurance money? I need it," he growled.

I couldn't think of any diversion. Telling the truth might be the best bet.

"It's in two banks in Lansing. I didn't want anyone in Marshall or Battle Creek knowing about the money."

"Smart."

I jumped up and ran to his roll-top desk and brought him the two savings account booklets that I'd taped underneath one of the drawers. "Here they are. Not a cent withdrawn. It's all yours. But today's Sunday; the banks are closed."

I looked him in the eyes. "I don't want the money. I could withdraw it for you tomorrow, then I would leave for Connecticut right away. Mother sent me enough to pay for my ticket. You wouldn't need to give me a cent," I lied.

"Lansing, tomorrow? That won't work."

Once again I wondered if he had a new woman who he would send to the bank pretending to be me. I suspected the nosy officer at the first bank might remember me, but I doubted if the fellow at the second bank would remember a single detail.

I checked my arm and saw that the wound wasn't deep, but I grabbed another towel and wrapped it up again. It was my right arm; I wondered if in his anger, he'd purposely chosen my dominant side. Sam said nothing but contorted his face, the way he always did when angry.

"Fix me supper. I'm starved."

I thought a moment before responding to his request. "We've got some ground beef in the icebox, and I can pick some ripe tomatoes and sweetcorn from the garden."

"Sounds okay."

I turned to the cutlery rack and picked up a large knife, but he immediately grabbed it.

"No knife."

My heart sank, even though I clearly was no match against him. Even after his pronounced weight loss last autumn, Sam was still a big man at six feet.

He pushed me out the door to the garden, totally out of view from Sarah and Wesley's house. He grabbed a basket from the back room for the vegetables, and I picked six ears of sweet corn, pulling them off with my hands, trying to keep my right arm elevated. Then I plucked three tomatoes off the vine with my left hand. I stood at the end of the garden husking the corn, wishing someone would come up the driveway, turn, and follow it to the garden where they could see us. No such luck.

"I don't remember that dress," Sam said. "What do you call the color—light purple?"

"Lavender," I responded. I didn't want to tell him it was new. "It's a summer dress; you may not remember it." I looked at the new towel around my arm and saw some blood had appeared.

"I like it," he said. The compliment didn't sit well with me, so I didn't respond. The dress was clearly ruined with the slashed sleeves and blood stains.

As we walked back in the house, I threw my sun bonnet on a hook in the back room, and the phone started ringing.

"Don't answer it."

"But what if it's Sarah calling to borrow sugar or butter?"

"Okay, but get off fast."

"Hello."

It was Zeb. Sam must have heard his voice, because he grabbed me from behind with the knife at my back. I started trembling.

"What's this about supper?" Zeb asked.

I could feel the knife pressing into my back through my dress and camisole.

"I need some time alone, that's all." I was trying to keep my voice steady.

"Okay, and get some rest."

"Goodbye."

Perhaps this would be my last conversation with Zeb, ever. Once Sam finished eating, he'd be figuring out how to get rid of me. Literally. He might already have given up on the money in the Lansing banks since he'd have the fifty-thousand for the engraved plates. Having that much already, another thousand might not even matter to him. Still, he hung onto the savings account books.

After lighting the cookstove, I fried the meat and boiled the sweetcorn, while I attempted to concoct a plan. How could I escape? Running to the outhouse wouldn't get me anywhere, nor would trying to run to Sarah's. No matter how hard I tried to figure out a plan, nothing came to mind.

Flattery, I kept telling myself. The fact that I told him he was clever seemed to have loosened him up. I needed to keep doing that until I'd devise a scheme to get away.

I brought the meat, sweet corn, and tomatoes to the table, and set a plate and silverware at his regular place.

"Aren't you gonna eat?"

"No, I don't like my cooking. I've always been afraid I'd poison myself."

To my surprise he laughed.

After having set his plate in front of him, I remained standing. I edged over toward the counter and the knife rack.

"Sit here at your place," he ordered me. "For old times' sake."

I walked over and sat, trying to put on my prettiest smile.

"I found the letters to your mother in my desk. What an imagination you have. Which bedrooms we'd use for our children. Where to have a swimming hole. A rope swing. An ice skating pond. I was the kindest and most generous husband ever."

I thought for a moment I was going to vomit and grabbed my handkerchief and pretended to be blowing my nose while I swallowed to keep my stomach in check. Panicking, I realized I needed to respond to him, to keep him engaged in conversation. Sucking in a big breath, I started speaking.

"I don't understand how you did the . . . the counterfeit money thing. You made the drawings first and then engraved some metal plates? I'd never be smart enough to do that."

"Yes, that's the key to making money." He laughed at his own joke. "I labored over the details in the engravings. They're worth a fortune. All you gotta do is bleach out some one dollars to print up tens, twenties, and fifties. Voila." He snapped his fingers. "But these days, dollars are golden. People are scared to take the higher currency. Dollars are the road to riches."

I wondered if he knew the Bensons had been arrested this afternoon; I decided to say nothing.

"But where did you hide them? Those two brothers looked everywhere." I decided not to mention the real White House Police were here, too. He might not have been aware of that.

Sam sat back in his chair and grinned at me. It was that self-satisfied grin that I hated. "You'd never guess. What's the one building on this farm you've never been in?"

I had no trouble feigning a puzzled face. "I actually was in the corncrib last fall before corn picking. But that building has slats."

"No," he answered. "You might be able to bury the plates in the middle of the corn, but you'd scratch them up, and you'd have a hard time getting them out. You'd have to unload at least half the corn. Bad choice."

He picked up another ear of sweetcorn and buttered it.

It dawned on me that he was referring to the silo, which I'd never really considered a building, but more as an appendage to the barn. I'd deliberately stayed away from the silo because of the poisonous gas from the silage and my fear of heights. Even looking at the exterior ladder gave me goosebumps.

While Sam ate his sweetcorn, I contemplated the silo. The engraved metal plates must be hidden in there. I knew that it was now less than a third full of fermented alfalfa. Wes had been feeding it to the cows and pigs before I sold them and he'd been hauling it over to his barn to feed his own cattle. I wondered why Wes hadn't seen the engraved plates when he was working there. The only place Sam could have hidden them was high on the interior wall near the upper window since the silage was about up to fifty feet when he "died."

"Did you figure it out yet?" Sam asked me, pushing away his plate.

"No, can't say that I have."

"You wanna see?"

I didn't know how to respond. Was this a set-up to hurt me again? "Maybe," I answered. "I'm not anxious to go near Ginger's pen."

"Why not? You always liked that spirited gal."

"She died."

"Died?"

I nodded.

He grimaced, and moved around in his chair. Obviously he wasn't happy to hear about Ginger.

"You gave me money for Ginger—a wedding gift. I loved that horse. I'd moved her to Black Devil's old pen a few weeks ago. More room for her and her tack. It was easier to get her saddled up in there."

He looked surprised. I guessed he hadn't been hanging out in the barn much.

I wanted to ask him about how he got the printing press into Black Devil's pen, but I was afraid to let him know it was no longer there. Now that Sam's stomach was full, I didn't have much stalling time. I looked towards the window, then to my surprise, I heard Sam groaning. He bent over, pushing his hand into his belly.

"You poisoned me, you bitch, and then you joked about it. That's why you didn't eat."

I held my breath. I couldn't afford for Sam to suspect me of any wrongdoing.

"Sam, no. How could I poison corn and tomatoes that you saw me bring in fresh from the garden? And you saw me take the meat straight from the ice box to the frying pan. Besides, even if I had poison, which I don't, you'd taste it." Trying to remain calm, I stood my ground. "They put foul tasting stuff in rat poison so people won't eat it, especially children." I was fabricating this detail, but so what? It might be true.

"My stomach's been acting up a lot these days."

"Your family curse?"

He immediately turned his head and stared at me. "You know about the Forrest family curse?"

"You mentioned it when we were courting. One night after a movie at the Bijou Theater, you were bent over in pain and you said you were worried about the family curse."

"I'd forgotten about that. Your pretty face cured me of the symptoms for a while. But not long enough."

"Have you seen a doctor?"

He shook his head. "It's the Forrest cancer and there's no cure." He was shifting the knife from hand to hand, a nervous symptom I'd noticed in church when he'd passed the hymnal back and forth. Sam was probably right: cancer usually was a death sentence.

"There, it's subsided." He grinned again and I saw that one of his back teeth was missing.

"You're going to collect the engraved plates and leave?" I was hoping for a reprieve.

"Once it gets dark, I'll take them to my car. I was counting on Ginger to get me over there. Guess I'll take Jasper."

"He's up at Wes and Sarah's. Bessie died, and they're getting a new horse next week." I wasn't going to tell him that I'd given Jasper to them. Sam was never keen on Wes or Sarah, either one.

"Looks like I have to walk."

How could I get him to tell me where he'd hidden his car? Could he have left it at the church with the Benson's roadster? I figured it was most likely at the Dolliver place.

"I could help you carry them to your car. Is it far?"

He turned and looked at me.

"You're one stupid bitch. The Dolliver farm."

I'd already guessed it correctly. That farm backed up to Sam's, the boundary being a wire fence and a wooded field. I'd ridden Ginger down that path along the creek more than a dozen times to the Dolliver property line. It was a perfect place for Sam to hide out so he didn't have to drive down the road.

He could simply walk from the back lane up to our barn without ever being seen. Also, the fact that it was a polio house kept locals from snooping around.

Sam stepped up close to me waving the knife. "We're getting those engraved plates now." But suddenly he put his left hand on his stomach and winced again.

In a weird way, I felt sorry for him. It made no sense for me to feel this way; Sam would probably end up killing me tonight. Perhaps my empathy was a carryback from our early courting days when I believed he cared for me. Still I was curious about the engraved plates.

"Okay, I'll help you with the plates. Lead the way." I wondered if he could sense my false bravado.

Sam walked out, not towards the silo, but to the old granary. Once inside the granary, he picked up a crowbar, and we headed over to the silo. I remained silent. I wondered if he knew that the silage level was down more than two-thirds since "his death." Maybe he had already checked it out, but perhaps not.

When Sam headed not into the milk house that led to the barn entrance, but to the exterior ladder running up the outside of the silo, I had my answer. He expected the silage level to be near the top. It looked like he planned to use the crowbar to push open the hinged board covering the window at the top.

I figured out my plan. Once he got the window open, I would push him down to the warm, soft silage below and have enough time to run to Wes and Sarah's house to call the sheriff. Perhaps he'd try exiting the silo door to the barn, rather than immediately heading back up to the window. Then he would find that it was nailed tight from the outside, which would give me even more time.

"Climb up," Sam ordered. "Hurry up or I'll whack your ribs with this crowbar."

My plan to push him into the silo wasn't going to work.

"Hurry up."

"Okay, okay."

Having no choice, I started up the long, tall ladder that ran up the exterior of the silo to the small covered opening. I got up five or six rungs before my fear of heights kicked in. My body started shaking and I willed myself not to look down. I kept putting one foot above the other. The towel around my right arm had loosened. I let it fall to the ground, not wanting to let go with my other arm.

Every move required my mind telling my arms and legs to move. I was shaking so hard my hands could hardly grip the ladder. *You can do this,* I told myself. *You can. You can.*

"Keep going." His voice was piercing.

I willed my feet to move up the ladder. My body convulsed. I was about five rungs from the top when I stopped. Reason told me I needed to quit shaking and get my body under control or I would fall. Then it occurred to me. He wasn't going to push me into the soft silage. He was going to knock me off the top of the ladder down to the hard earth. I would be meeting the same horrific fate as Johanna.

My shaking worsened, but my feet remained frozen on the rung below. Right foot up, I told myself. But it didn't go up. Nor did my left. For the first time, I noticed I was panting and I seemed to be losing my grip on the upper rung.

"Come on, come on," Sam shouted in irritation. He was right behind me.

"I can't stop shaking and my feet won't move."

"Well, you climbed all this way; you can make it up a few more steps."

"I can't. Remember, I'm afraid of heights," I yelled back. "Besides, when I get to the top, I won't be able to get that board off the window."

"That's why I'm carrying the crowbar," he growled. "When you get to the top, I'll hand it to you. The board's hinged on top. You just need to pull out the U staples on the bottom."

"I want the crowbar now," I answered. I'd whack him with it and then drop it to the ground.

I could feel Sam pushing on me.

"Move over," he snarled, pushing me to the right so that only my left foot was on the rung below. Fear pulsed through my body. I dangled off the ladder as he climbed up beside me and hustled to the top. I panicked. I couldn't pull my body back. I willed my right leg to move back but it didn't budge. I couldn't get control of either arm or leg.

When Sam reached the top rung, he started pulling out the U staples with the crowbar. In that moment, by sheer will power, I pulled my whole torso back onto the ladder, gripping the next rung, shuddering. Sam was still yanking the staples from the window above.

I was only five steps from the top. I heard a creaking noise and looked up again. Sam had finished opening the window. He had climbed in the small opening and disappeared. It was too late to push him in and I was still five rungs below, shaking.

"Goddammit," he cried out. "Where's all the silage? Polly, get the hell up here and help me get these plates."

"It's too high," I yelled back. "I can't move."

"There's no time for that nonsense. I've got five double sets of plates to get outta here."

"Grab the first one and then hand it to me," I yelled back.

"No, I'm throwing them on to the silage."

I heard some clatter.

"One," he yelled in victory. "Two."

I had to do something. Either I would force myself to finish the five steps and hope that Sam would spare me or I could risk falling off the ladder while going down.

Silence.

I heard two blood-curdling cries from Sam, then more silence. I had no idea how I did it, but I pulled myself up the remaining five rungs and peered in. Everything was black inside. I flung my body through the window and clung on, finding purchase for my feet on an interior ladder.

"Fooled ya," Sam laughed. His laughter reverberated in a sinister echo through the abyss. "Fooled ya, fooled ya."

Finally, my eyes adjusted and I saw him below, standing on the silage holding a large package wrapped in black. Three more lay at his feet. "Did you recognize that cry from the day I died?"

I did, but I wasn't going to dignify him with an answer.

I was ready to start climbing back up through the window when he dropped the plates and bent over in pain. I could see one more set of plates hanging near the top on the other side of the silo. He clearly had hidden them well. They were dark and blended with the interior wall.

"Bloody hell, where did all the silage go?"

"I used it for the cows and pigs; they needed to eat. Why do you even care?"

"Because that last one's out of reach, and that's the one-dollar George Washington."

"You'll figure out how to engrave more plates. Your artistic skills plus. . . ." I didn't finish the sentence.

We both looked over at the last set of plates hanging high on the other side of the silo, thirty feet above the silage.

"I need that set." His voice was firm and clear. "We'll have to get a ladder in here."

Sam kept looking at the last set of engravings on the other wall. "We'll bring it in from the barn door. Just a matter of carrying it from the toolshed through the milk house to the barn."

Clearly Sam didn't know that Wes had nailed up the door from the barn side to keep the boys out. Neither Sam nor I would be able to exit via the barn. It was up and out for both of us.

"Okay, time to grab these and get out." He started gathering up the plates and heading toward the door that exited to the barn.

"I need fresh air. The fumes are giving me a headache," I lied as I climbed up to the open window. Sam turned and followed me to the base of the ladder.

At the top, I stuck my head out and pretended to gasp for fresh air. I turned to see if Sam was still at the bottom. He was, but he started trudging over to the other side of the silo to the sealed door. He was gasping and grunting and the echoes swirled inside my head.

This was my opportunity. I heaved my body through the window and flung my legs out, attempting to feel the first rung with my feet. I didn't know if Sam was following me. Putting one foot down and then the other I expected to feel a crowbar whack the side of my head at any instant.

I kept descending, neither looking up nor down, simply feeling each rung under my feet as fast as I could. I was shaking but my steps were firm as I flew down the ladder. When I reached the bottom, I looked up and saw no sign of Sam. He was probably trying to open the nailed-up door to the barn and apprehend me outside. I turned without looking back again and ran up to Wes and Sarah's house.

Wes met me at the door.

Gasping, I blurted out, "He's trapped in the silo. That's where he was hiding the engraved plates."

Reverend Wesley Johnson

Sunday, August 19, 1934

I could hardly comprehend Polly's words. Sarah was running to the telephone to once again call the sheriff's office. Was this the second or the third time today? Heart pounding, I looked down at my bare feet. I needed to put on my boots.

Sarah picked up the telephone receiver.

Polly turned to me. "I think he would have killed me, but he needed my help getting the engravings out of the silo. There are five sets of them and they look heavy."

Sarah cleared her throat and spoke into the phone. "Mrs. Cross, I need the line, please."

I sat down on the kitchen bench to put on my socks and work boots. Why was this taking so long? My nerves on fire, I dropped both socks on the floor, one landing in a small pool of water that Dorothy had spilled. I pulled the wet sock on anyway.

Where were the children? Were they outside playing? Were they in danger? I couldn't stay focused, but I heard Junior and Zeke fighting upstairs.

"Mrs. Cross, I need the phone line to make an emergency call. It's a matter of life and death." Sarah was shouting into the phone.

"Yes, we did have an emergency earlier today, but I need the line right now. Please!

I forced myself back to the matter at hand. "Do you know where he's been hiding?" I looked up at Polly.

"The old Dolliver place," she answered. "The riding trail goes down along the river. There's a path from the Dolliver house to the creek so he wouldn't have to go on any road. It'd be a slick short cut back and forth to here. He could hide his car in their toolshed or barn."

"I'll call you and answer your questions after I call the sheriff." Sarah was shouting into the phone. She, too, was panicked.

"Mommy, I need to go potty," Dorothy tugged at Sarah's skirt.

"Please hold on, Dorothy. As soon as I make this call."

"Thank you, Mrs. Cross. Yes, I'll let you know what happens." Sarah was panting, scowling into the phone. She dialed the familiar numbers to the sheriff's office and was silently waiting for an answer.

"Hurry, Mommy," shouted Dorothy.

"Hurry, Wes." Polly's voice cracked.

"I'll grab my shotgun," I said to her and rushed to the gun closet. I wasn't going to make the mistake I'd made earlier today by going unarmed. My hands were shaking as I grabbed some shot and loaded the gun. "Okay, let's go."

"No, don't go anywhere," Sarah shouted. "Stay here until Sheriff Conlin arrives. Just keep watch right here from the kitchen window."

I looked at Sarah, pleading with her. "He'll die if he stays in the silo with those noxious gasses. We can't allow one of God's children to be poisoned in that silo."

"Just wait until the sheriff comes."

"He'll take the plates and be long gone before the sheriff arrives," Polly's voice was high-pitched and tremulous. "Then we'll continue to live in fear."

I motioned for Polly to follow me out the door. When we got to the driveway, we both looked toward the road, hoping that the sheriff's car would be in sight. Most likely it would be thirty minutes to an hour before they arrived. I noticed that the sun was getting low—about another hour of daylight left. That would make Mitchell's apprehension harder. We rushed toward the silo but there was no sign of him.

"He has to come down the outside ladder," Polly insisted. "You nailed the interior door shut. We can wait right here for the sheriff."

"Hold the shotgun while I go up the ladder."

"No," Polly responded. "He'll kill you—he's got a crowbar in there. Just wait here for the sheriff."

"No, I can't let him die from silage gas. He's a fellow human being."

"And my husband," she responded.

"What?"

"We're still married."

I thought that Polly was suffering from some kind of memory issue, probably brought on by nerves.

"We've got him trapped. Let's wait until the sheriff comes. He's dangerous."

It was then that I noticed the gash on her right arm and the blood on her dress. That might explain Polly's lapse. I focused back on Mitchell in the silo.

"We can't let him die in there. I'll go open up the door from the barn and let some air in. He may already be unconscious from the gasses."

We both ran to the granary and I grabbed a large hammer to remove the U staples and proceeded to the interior of the barn as Polly followed. Next, an ungodly pain crossed the back of my head. Something pounded so hard I could no longer see. I blacked out for a while, but then I could hear faint voices. Remembering the situation, I realized I was on the barn floor and no longer held the shotgun or hammer.

I heard Polly gasping. "You broke out with the crow bar?"

There were some more scuffling sounds. "You're gonna be my beasts of burden." It had to be Mitchell. Same voice as Sam's. My vision was blurred to the point I kept my eyes shut, but I could still hear what was going on around me. "Polly, dear, carry these, and here are yours, Wes." Two large, heavy items were thrust into my gut.

I placed my arms around what I imagined to be two sets of metal engravings, wrapped in paper.

"Hurry up; your shotgun's ready to blow off your head," a loud voice pounded in my ears. "You ready to meet your maker, preacher? Get going and follow Polly."

It was Sam's laugh with a more sinister quality—it had to be Mitchell Forrest. I opened my eyes and tried to follow Polly's blurred lavender image. I was seeing double. Mitchell stayed behind me with my own shotgun forced into my back as he barked out orders to Polly.

We went out the sliding door at the back of the barn and walked past the old grape arbor, near Sailor Dog's grave. We were totally invisible to Sarah from here behind the barn. My vision was so blurred that I was grateful that Polly's dress was such a distinctive color so I could follow it. We arrived at what I knew was the beginning of the lane through the front fields and turned towards the back woods.

What would happen when we delivered the plates to Mitchell's car? Mitchell wouldn't need either of us.

I could feel Polly beside me, guiding me with her arm. She whispered to me to move slowly so she could figure out a plan. My head was throbbing and I was still seeing double. I wanted to reach out and wrap my arms around her but I was crippled by the weight of the engraved counterfeiting plates. Hopefully Polly would come up with a plan because my concentration was focused on a hundred hot knives pulsating through my skull.

Polly Wolcott Forrest

Sunday, August 19, 1934

Sam would surely kill both Wes and me once we reached the Dolliver farm and his escape; we both knew too much. If Sam could kill his brother and consequently urge Black Devil to eviscerate his body, shooting Wes and me would be easy. Knowing Sam, he'd take delight in it.

Wes was stumbling down the lane, a look of anguish on his face. He'd made it clear he could hardly see and there was little I could do but try to guide him. I kept my arm on his, but despite my aid, he'd trip over stones, tree roots, and ruts in the lane. He kept his head down close to my arm, and groaned whenever he tripped. Sam walked behind us, pointing the shotgun at our backs.

Every three or four minutes, I'd stop to rest and readjust the two packages in order to buy time for Wes to recuperate and me to think.

"Keep moving," Sam shouted each time I'd stop to rest.

"These are too heavy," I said. I was hoping that in exasperation he'd put down the shotgun and take one of the plates. In that moment, I'd grab the gun. But no such luck. I tried another tack.

"I need a long break. Do you have any water?"

Sam frowned. "Water, you want water? The creek's up ahead."

"Why didn't you put these into a wheelbarrow?" I was hot, thirsty and getting angry.

"I'd rather see you suffer. You deserve what you get," he retorted. Familiar phrases that I'd lived with during the long months of our marriage.

We kept trudging on towards the creek and woods. I knew that we were approaching the border of Viola Cross's farm on the other side of the stream, but I figured we'd be staying on this side of the water, following the bridle path until we reached the lane that led on to the Dolliver farm. Instinctively I knew that every extra minute I could get would be important to Wes's ability to run away. It would be suicide to attempt a getaway with his vision so seriously impaired.

I stopped for a break even though I didn't need it; once again I was hoping Sam would let down his guard so I could get to the shotgun. Pretending to be exhausted and dehydrated was easy for me and probably was accurate for Wes.

"Get up and get going," Sam ordered once more.

I got up slowly and picked up the two packages, stooped over in an effort to convince him I needed help. No luck. Sam didn't have a kind bone in his body. He'd always been oblivious to other people and their hardships. Wes dragged himself up as well and we shuffled farther down the lane toward the creek. By now I truly was parched and was focused only on getting to water. I knew that we could kneel down and drink just a few yards upstream where green grass met the water's edge. The stream was about six-feet across and I'd frequently stopped here and allowed Ginger to refresh herself.

Once we reached the stream, I threw down the packages and dipped my hands into the water, taking in large mouthfuls. Wes did the same. "My vision's coming back," he whispered. I slurped long and loud to cover up his voice, making no effort to move. Soon I felt the shotgun nudging my back and we reluctantly got up and continued plodding down the lane. Wes's breathing was labored and he continued to stumble. When I looked back at him, he winked; he was faking it.

"You can put down the gun," Wes said to Sam. "I'm not going to run away. I'm dizzy and can hardly see and what I do see is doubled." I looked back and to my surprise, Sam turned the gun from Wes's back to face the ground. Maybe I'd get my opportunity.

We weren't more than a quarter of a mile to the end of the lane where the narrow bridle trail continued along the creek. At that point the trail took a sharp right turn to the north. From this point on, briars and brush along the meandering creek hid the water from the path.

A shuffling sound and bird call across the water drew my attention, but I said nothing. It seemed as if Sam hadn't heard it or didn't think it was peculiar. I stopped to rest and listen. The brush across the brook hid everything on the other side, but I was convinced the bird call was human.

Sam was impatient. "Hurry up. Hurry up."

"These packages are heavy; I need to rest longer," I shouted, even though Sam was right behind me. If anyone was out there, I wanted them to hear.

Sam waited a couple of minutes longer as I lay prone on the ground and closed my eyes.

"No sleeping." Sam prodded me with the shotgun.

I got up, slowly, stretching my arms and legs, then helped Wes off the ground as we picked up the heavy packages. I heard the strange bird call again, and started walking ahead, quickening the pace, and gaining ten yards on Wes and Sam. When I approached the bend where the lane ended and the bridle path began, I looked around. To my surprise Zeb was crouched down behind a tall stand of prairie grass. He motioned me to get on the ground. I stopped walking and yelled backwards. "I can't go on. I need a rest." Then I dropped to the ground keeping my eyes pinned on Wes and Sam.

"Drop the gun," Zeb yelled out and jumped up to take aim at Sam. But Wes was still standing, immediately in front of Sam.

"Wes, get down," I yelled, and Wes went down.

I heard a gunshot and Zeb groaned in anguish. He was on the ground, and red blood stains appeared on his right thigh.

Looking back at Sam, I saw that he had fallen, too. Sam appeared to have no wounds. Perhaps the debilitating stomach cancer was flaring up.

I crawled to Zeb, pulled the gun he had dropped, and slithered past Wes towards Sam. More rustling sounds came from the bushes, and Sam quickly arose, picking up the shotgun, turning toward the brush. Apparently he hadn't seen me crawl up. I got to my knees and took aim. Perfect aim. The gun fired and I heard Sam's cry before he fell to the ground. I had shot him directly in the foot.

Sam continued to scream in pain, cradling his foot. I kicked the shotgun back to Wes, who grabbed it and ran back to help Zeb. More shuffling noises emerged from the bushes.

"I'm over here. Don't shoot me. Don't shoot me," a woman's voice squeaked out, as Viola Cross's head emerged from the undergrowth. She trudged out, flailing her arms as if swimming the breast stroke.

Still on the ground, Sam was moaning, holding his right foot as I stood frozen, still aiming Zeb's gun at him. Viola looked from Sam and me to Zeb and Wes, apprising the situation.

"Sheriff Conlin will be coming soon," Viola said rather calmly, given the situation. "He was with Officer Bylowski so he's right behind."

No sooner had she spoken than Sheriff Conlin appeared, panting and running up from the bridle trail. He looked at Zeb, then at me holding Zeb's gun, and ran to Sam, handcuffed him and ordered him to stay on the ground.

"Shot in the foot," Conlin muttered. "Smart move, Polly."

I handed Zeb's gun to Conlin and ran to Zeb's side. He needed help, a massive amount of blood covered the wound on his thigh. I pulled off the sash from my dress and tied it around his upper thigh to make a tourniquet. Viola, knelt down beside me and in one quick move, yanked off her white cotton petticoat and tied it around the wound. She pushed down on the injury with both hands. Zeb remained unconscious.

"We gotta get Zeb to a doctor," I screamed. "He's losing blood. Forget Sam. Right now."

In seconds, Wes and the sheriff were examining Zeb and arranging to carry him back with Viola holding his head.

"Keep the gun on Mitchell," the sheriff said to me. "He's gonna have to stumble his way back to my car. Mitchell here is going to need a doctor, too."

"Mitchell or Sam?" Wes asked.

"Sam," I answered. "He said he killed Mitchell and threw him into the barnyard with the bull. He wanted to collect on his life insurance policies before he killed me."

I was still shaking. "What's really bothering him is stomach cancer, his family curse. He has sharp pains that end with him doubling over."

We proceeded down the trail until the sheriff's car was in sight.

Once the wounded were in the Sheriff's car, Viola disappeared back down the lane as quickly as she had first appeared.

I stood by Zeb's side until he went into surgery.

Sam was treated and left in the sheriff's custody. Before driving off with Sam, Sheriff Conlin told me he'd call me with an update the next day. Wes and I stayed at the hospital until Zeb was out of surgery, explaining to his parents, now in the waiting room with us, all that had happened. Wes phoned Sarah twice explaining the Sam-Mitchell mix-up and giving her updates on Zeb.

Sometime in the middle of the night after the surgery was over and Zeb was declared stable, his parents drove Wes and me back home where Sarah was waiting up for us.

"How did Viola know about all this?" I asked Sarah.

She laughed. "Viola was listening in on my phone conversation with Sheriff Conlin. She called the sheriff, telling him she'd overheard you say that someone, hiding out at the Dolliver property, was trapped in the silo. When the sheriff realized Mitchell, actually Sam, was no longer in the silo, the Sheriff and Zeb, with Viola's help, set up an ambush at the creek where the lane meets the bridle path. Viola positioned herself upstream to create a diversion. It worked, except for Zeb getting shot.

Once again Sarah chuckled. "All because Viola listened in on the party line. God works in mysterious ways."

Sarah Wolcott Johnson

Monday, August 20, 1934

Viola Cross sat with us around the kitchen table, rehashing the prior day's events while the children asked questions. She was guarded in her response, clearly not wanting to talk poorly of the children's uncle. Nor did she want to make herself a hero.

"Who exactly was the bad guy?" Junior asked. Always leave it to kids to cut to the chase.

Viola looked at both Wes and me before answering.

"I believe it was a guy named Mitchell," she answered. "He twarn't from around here. He was the head of a counterfeiting ring."

"We're so happy you called the sheriff with the information about the Dolliver place," I told Viola, not for the first time. The sound of the back door opening drew attention to the kitchen door. Quick short steps clacked their way through the back room on their way to the kitchen.

"Yoo-hoo, yoo-hoo," Polly sang out as she entered and pulled up a chair joining all of us around the table.

"Hello, Mrs. Cross," Polly crowed cheerfully.

"Where were you, Aunt Polly?" Dorothy asked. "I call you two times." She held up two fingers.

Interesting, I thought. Dorothy was now keeping tabs on Polly; perhaps I wouldn't have to be so vigilant.

Polly looked down at Dorothy. "I went to the hospital to check on Zeb and he's in a lot of pain, so they won't be sending him home for a few days. Looks like he'll be going to his parents' place on Verona Road to recuperate. When I got there he could hardly stay awake, probably because of the morphine he received last night. He seemed glad to see me but kept dozing off. I left a small bowl of yellow roses and only stayed five minutes.

"Oh," Polly continued, jumping up out of the chair. "I almost forgot. I bought some coffee beans at Millers." She held up a small bag. "I'll grind them up." She ran out to our back room in search of the coffee grinder, acting like she owned the place. If this was a new Polly, I certainly liked it.

I got up and lit the cookstove, filling the coffee pot with water. All eyes were on the coffee pot as Polly came back and poured in the grounds.

"Mm, smells so good," I said, while reaching into the cupboard for cups and saucers.

"So how did you get to the hospital?" I asked Polly. I hated reminding her of Ginger, but I wondered if she had taken Jasper.

"Sheriff Conlin and Deputy Hill brought out Zeb's truck early this morning. The sheriff said that Zeb wasn't going to be using it for a while and wanted me to have it." She turned to Junior and Zeke. "Boys, I have your BB guns out in the bed of Zeb's truck." Hearing that, both boys raced outside to retrieve them.

"Sheriff Conlin said that the Bensons are in deep trouble with the White House Police so he didn't need the BB guns for evidence."

"I wonder what will happen to that Plymouth Roadster they were driving," I asked.

"They need to find out if it was stolen. If it wasn't and they're found guilty, the sheriff can sell it at the monthly auction," Polly answered. "I need a car, but not one quite so showy."

This was a first. Polly not wanting a showy car. Polly sharing coffee. Maybe this was a new start for my little sister. Plentiful Polly.

I started pouring the coffee and handing the first cup to our guest, Viola. Everyone looked down at the dark liquid with smiles. We couldn't have enjoyed a fine champagne any more than the steaming brew. Picking up on our high spirits, Wes lifted his cup. "Cheers. To better times."

"To better times," we all echoed.

Reverend Wesley Johnson

Monday, August 20, 1934

I woke up, thought about yesterday, and a warm flush of relief encompassed me. My muscles relaxed, the tension dropped out of my neck and shoulders, and I experienced a quiet calm. God was looking down on me, granting me grace and comfort, after a long slog through a muddy quagmire.

Sitting around the kitchen table enjoying the company of my family and my neighbor, I breathed more slowly, deliberately. When Polly jumped up to grind the coffee beans, Sarah looked at me and smiled. I felt such overwhelming love for Sarah. Overnight, life had become restful, almost peaceful.

Viola Cross was welcome to tell the story. It acquitted Polly, whom everyone had doubts about, including Sarah and me. Viola was sure to spread the word that Polly was not only innocent, but threatened by Sam and his brother's counterfeiting ring. Despite her earlier deceptions, Polly had chosen the straight and narrow, and for that, I gave her credit.

Sometime during this horrendous ordeal, I realized my attraction for Polly had metamorphosed into a sisterly love. I no longer looked at my sister-in-law with forbidden desire; instead I viewed her as a vulnerable human being. Polly was no longer that teenager who kissed me at her sister's front door, but an adult trying to navigate a difficult world filled with contradictions, misunderstandings, and crime. In the past few months Polly had emerged as brave, yet vulnerable and I, for one, appreciated her new demeanor.

Polly Wolcott Forrest

Tuesday, December 25, 1934

"Merry Christmas," Junior, Zeke, and Dorothy yelled out, bouncing up my front porch steps as I reached out to help Sarah and Wes, who were carrying a food basket and a bag of gifts. They started streaming into the living room, while my new little puppy, Wiggles, began jumping up and circling everyone.

"Wiggles, Wiggles, I love you, doggie," Dorothy effused as she stepped inside the front door and joined her family in taking off coats, scarves, mittens, and overshoes. Dorothy was wearing a tattered red and green plaid dress, a hand-me-down from someone at church. She was quickly on the floor playing with the fluffy yellow puppy, as the boys took sneaking glances at the gifts under the Christmas tree. They also were wearing their Christmas best, their Sunday pants, each knee carefully patched by Sarah, the pant legs riding high above the ankles.

Sarah and I proceeded into the kitchen where I had taken a tiny roast chicken out of the electric oven.

"I remember when Mother would roast two large chickens in this oven for Christmas dinner," I commented. Then wistfully, "But I guess we can be happy we all have a roof overhead and we aren't standing in a soup line."

Sarah nodded soberly. "The good ole days. When I was a kid I really got tired of the grown-ups talking about the past, as if it was so much better. But two large chickens sound pretty good today. I'm so hungry I could eat that whole bird!"

"Me too." I reached out to my sister as she, in turn, hugged me. "I remember having leftovers. There were definitely some good things from the good ole days."

Today we would make do. Sarah had brought a Ball jar of canned corn and a loaf of bread. With my boiled potatoes and mincemeat pie, it would be a feast. I'd been surviving on bean soup and boiled potatoes for a few months now, so anything else was welcomed.

Wes entered the kitchen. "Your first Christmas in the new house," Wes said, giving me a big bear hug.

"Well, first Christmas as the owner," I corrected him. In October I had purchased the Elm Street house, my childhood home, and at the same time, I'd sold Sam's farm to John Newson for the amount I needed to buy this house. Fortunately, he'd made some money on his experimental crop of soybeans, winter squash and root vegetables. That was a red-letter day. John and Mabel were delirious with joy, and I was happy for them. His brother's family had moved in with them, filling up the upstairs bedrooms. It was a financial stretch for me, but definitely worth the effort. I suspected that the Newsoms received some help from the church's charity fund. It had been replenished with the insurance money I'd donated.

After buying the Elm Street house, I became penniless, like everyone else. I'd been trying to find a job ever since I moved to town; the only one I could find was part-time at the library, which was helping, but didn't cover all my expenses. Sallin's Dry Goods had started carrying my hats, and every now and then I'd get a sale. A hand-to-mouth existence for sure, but for the first time in over a year, I was happy.

I'd done my best to decorate the Elm Street house for the holidays, with lots of pine boughs on the fireplace mantel and stair bannisters, and a Scotch pine Christmas tree that Zeb had cut down from his parents' back forty. Zeb and I had strung cranberries and popcorn for decoration, eating more popcorn than ended up on the tree. To add to the visual green-red contrast, I'd pinned red ribbon bows to the pine garlands. The house smelled like pine and roast chicken.

"Too bad Grandma Blessing is doing poorly; it would have been so nice to have Mother here today," Sarah said. She was unpacking food from her old wicker basket.

"Well, I was gonna wait until dinner to give you the news, but now that you bring up the subject . . ." I paused for dramatic effect. "You know I asked her and Grandma to come here and live with me. Well, this morning Mother called to wish me Merry Christmas and tell me that they're going to move back. What a Christmas present! She said they'll come in the spring. Won't it be nice? Grandma will have the little room on the main floor that I'm using now, and Mother and I will use the two upstairs bedrooms.

"I'll need to move my sewing and hat-making projects down here in the dining room. We'll be using every square inch, just like the old days. Mother may be interested in helping with the hats if I can drum up more business, and, of course, she'll try to get some sewing and tailoring jobs."

Wiggles was running around in circles, whining by the back door.

"Oh, Zeke and Junior, please let Wiggles out the backdoor to do her business." I needed to keep an eagle eye on the puppy at all times. I'd had far too many accidents to clean up and I wasn't excited about a Christmas "gift" from the puppy.

"Is Zeb coming over?" Sarah asked.

"Yes, but not until after dinner. He's going to his folks and will come over here later. He was so concerned that he'd miss giving his gifts to the children."

"No kittens or puppies, I hope," responded Sarah.

"No. I told him that toys are good, but not puppies. Wiggles has reminded me every day of the large amount of time needed to housebreak a pet."

"Well, at least all three of my kids are housebroken," Sarah joked, and then turned serious. "Are you expecting an engagement ring from Zeb today?"

"No. I've been clear with him that I must go slowly. I think because he saw everything unfold this year, he understands why I need to have some time to myself to figure things out." I hesitated, then continued. "I'm not over it. Sometimes I wake in the middle of the night with that dreadful feeling that Sam is about to kill me. Doc Grayson says to let some time pass; I hope he's right."

I could hear Wes reading a story to the children in the parlor so I continued on. "You and Mother were right about my marrying Sam too soon. I'm not willing to make the same mistake and Zeb says he's willing to wait. I sure hope so. That's a risk I have to take."

"You've changed a lot, Polly."

"Life has changed me," I answered her. The boys rushed back in with Wiggles and proceeded to the parlor.

"Funny thing, there were a few moments in that life that I loved. The times when Dorothy came over. Making cookies with her. Riding Ginger—but the trail is now clouded with dark memories. That's where Zeb was shot." I couldn't continue.

"Yes, of course," Sarah responded quietly.

"And where I shot Sam."

Neither of us said anything.

"I've been waiting to tell you this in person. Yesterday, I got a call from Sheriff Conlin. Sam died at the prison hospital in Kalamazoo on Sunday. He tried breaking out, but he didn't get much beyond the fence before he passed out. The guards didn't even wound him. He was that sick."

"Well, it's probably for the best," Sarah said. "Now there'll be no more worries he'll be coming back after you, or any of us."

Wes poked his head in the door. "Need any help?"

"Yes, you can cut up the chicken, then we'll be ready."

When we sat down at the dinner table, I told everyone how happy I was that they were here at the house that was both my old and new home. Wes then offered the blessing.

"Heavenly Father, we thank you for the food set before us and for our health and well-being. We thank you for getting us through all the difficult times and trials this year and we thank you for sparing our dear friend, Zeb, and for healing his leg, and for keeping our dear sister and aunt safe and well. This Christmas, as we continue to face hard times, please allow each of us to remember the birth of Your Son Jesus and celebrate all the joy and wisdom of His message. In Jesus' name we pray. Amen."

Zeb arrived just as I was cutting the mincemeat pie. Wiggles ran circles around Zeb and jumped up on him as he took off his coat and gloves. The children, too, gathered around him. "Merry Christmas to all, and where's the Christmas pie?"

"Your timing is perfect," Wes announced.

Zeb had brought a small flour-sack bag of gifts that the kids were eyeing.

"Hey, can you give me the flour sack? I could make Dorothy a blouse out of it," Sarah asked. "I love that pink print."

"It's yours," Zeb shot back. "Actually, I was planning to give it to you anyway. What would I do with a pink bag?" He shot a look at me and grinned.

This year I had made gifts for everyone. Hats for Sarah and Dorothy, and knit scarves for Zeb, Wes, and the boys. I couldn't wait to give Sarah her new present, a gray wool cloche that would match her winter coat. The hat had no feathers, but was trimmed with a black satin ribbon and the tiniest forehead veil.

I went all out on Dorothy's hat, a hand-knit pullover tam with flowers of all colors all over the top, reinforced at the ears with ties to be extra warm. She'd be able to pull it on by herself, and I'd teach her how to tie it up under her chin.

The kids ate hardly any pie, wanting to get on with opening the gifts. After we all settled into the living room, Zeb handed packages to Sarah and Wes, but there was nothing in the bag for the kids or me. All three children had long, forlorn faces.

"Oh, would you kids like gifts, too?" Zeb was grinning with a twinkle in his eyes.

All three nodded.

"Go outside and look on Aunt Polly's front porch."

The children tore out of the room, not bothering with coats, hats, or mittens. The rest of us followed. There, sitting along the porch, were three sleds ready to be taken out at the next snowfall. All three kids screamed with glee, including Dorothy, who had run up to the smallest one, guessing it was for her.

"What do these do?" Dorothy finally asked. She knew that her brothers were ecstatic, so she had feigned it. But she was perplexed looking at the contraption.

"You slide it on the snow," Zeke yelled out.

"Oh boy," added Junior. "Thank you, Mr. B," which was followed by two more echoes of thank you.

"You're probably wondering why you didn't get a gift from me," Zeb said, settling back into my flowered davenport after Sarah, Wes, and their family had departed.

"Seeing the kids with those sleds made me so happy. That was the best gift ever. Watching their faces light up like that. Even Dorothy, and she didn't have a clue what a sled was. That was more than generous."

"Well, I do have a gift for you," Zeb went on.

He took my hand. "But we need to be alone."

I thought I had made it clear to him. "Zeb, you know I care for you. But it's too soon. I'm sorry if I've misled you. I need more time to make my own life here in town and distance myself from everything that has happened over the past year. Besides, I have to convince myself that I'm no longer that greedy, immature child you met last year."

"Yes, I know, Polly. I'm willing to wait. But . . . ." He caressed my hand again. "I have a gift for you out at my parents' place."

I raised my eyebrows.

"In the stable to be exact. In the pen right next to Jackson. Do you want to take a drive out and see? I think you'll like her, a bit spirited like Ginger, but an entirely different horse altogether. A beautiful black filly who's got pinto spots on her face, sides, and legs. She'll be great riding alongside Jackson."

At that moment, I knew I could make a fresh start with Zeb. Even so, I cautioned myself. Was I being taken in by a gift once again? On the one hand, Zeb was such a different person than Sam. But was this a repeat of my life with Sam? After all, he had given me Ginger as a wedding gift. Was I falling down that familiar rabbit hole? A voice inside my head told me I needed to be cautious. The new Polly would be Patient Polly, unlike the old Impetuous Polly.

It would soon be a new year and time for more reflection. I recognized that my future, while skewed by an ill-fated marriage, was not irrevocably doomed. I'd decided to take my time determining the next steps. In the meantime, I decided I would train my puppy, make hats, and, perhaps, just perhaps, listen in on the party line.

Polly Wolcott Forrest

Tuesday, January 1, 1935

One of my passions was making hats with veils. Netting actually. Tulle made out of cotton, silk or other fibers, it came in many varieties and colors. Pretty, but vision-impairing. Life with Sam was veiled. On many occasions, I pretended not to see, until I couldn't. If that weren't enough, I imperiled others in the layered haze.

My good fortune was to be surrounded by people who loved and supported me, despite my failings. People who put up with my deceptions and were willing to forgive me, just as I, now, viewed them with appreciation and love. I had come to recognize there was room on this beautiful earth for people who were different from me, people who would risk everything to help a relative, friend or neighbor. People who were judgmental. People who were busybodies. People, who despite their outward demeanor, had love in their hearts.

I had made this journey slowly. Veils blocking my way at every juncture. Cloudy vision, an astigmatism I didn't comprehend. Then, one day, wanting to see more clearly, I was granted a blessing. I had the opportunity to lift the veil.

Acknowledgments

Book writing may seem like a solitary undertaking but it takes a village. I am grateful to so many friends and family who have encouraged me throughout the process and whose support was undeniably necessary. Their names are not listed here, but they know who they are. Keen editors, beta readers, and book developers kept me focused and on track through several revisions. In particular, I'm grateful to Ana Howard, Jan Shubitowski, Mark Nielsen, Kathy Finch, Richard Kussman, Diane Escalante, Megan Goodwin, Ann Videan, Barbara Zaret, Nancy Stupsker, and Helene Stupsker who each made very specific and necessary contributions. Also, gratitude to publicist Stephanie Barko who kept me on track at the end of the journey. Finally, special thanks to my husband Bill who read various drafts and whose sense of humor kept me sane through the entire process.

Discussion Questions

1. Why do you think the author titled the book *The Unveiling of Polly Forrest*? How is the concept of veils represented in the book? What veils become lifted during the course of the story? Does the reader actually see Polly Forrest unveiled at the book's conclusion?

2. The book is set in 1934 during the throes of the Great Depression. How much do "hard times" impact the characters and their actions? When many farmers are faced with the threat of losing their farms, what behaviors are altered by economic circumstances?

3. While set less than a century ago, much is different from contemporary life. Discuss the differences and their impact on the story.

4. Which characters, if any, do you identify with? Is Polly a victim of circumstances or a flawed personality? What about character flaws in Sarah and Wes?

5. Discuss the pacing and the suspenseful moments. What scenes were the most memorable? How does Polly's fear of heights set the tone during the silo scene?

6. What makes for a good villain? Discuss the role of the villains in the story.

7. Discuss sibling rivalry and how it manifests in the story. Is the eleven-year gap in ages between Sarah and Polly a barrier between them?

8. Polly's letters to her mother at the beginning of the book may
   not be entirely truthful. What is your reaction? Do you prefer
   reliable or unreliable narrators?

9. Discuss the attraction between Polly and Wes. Does the
   forbidden nature contribute to the attraction?

10. Discuss the role that particular animals play in the story.
    What impact do Ginger, Sailor Dog, and Bessie have on the
    main characters? On the reader?

11. Much of the setting is on two adjacent farms. How is the plot
    intertwined with the rural setting?

12. Thematic elements include secrecy and deception, agency,
    family, and community. Discuss how they play out in the
    story. How do minor characters such as Viola Cross and
    John Newsom have a role in developing these themes?

About the Author

Charlotte Whitney grew up on a Michigan farm and often heard stories about the difficult years during the Great Depression. She is the author of two nonfiction books and a romance novel, *I Dream in White*. Her much acclaimed, debut historical novel *Threads: A Depression Era Tale* solidified her love of writing historical fiction. The author resides in Arizona with her husband and two Labrador retrievers.

Learn more about the author's upcoming books and subscribe to her free newsletter at:

www.charlottewhitney.com